GODS

OF

MANHATTAN

CAST OF CHARACTERS

Rory Hennessy—*A thirteen-year-old boy; the last Light in New York City*

Bridget Hennessy—*Younger sister to Rory Hennessy*

Hex—*A mysterious magician*

Toy—*A papier-mâché boy*

· THE RATTLE WATCH ·

Nicholas Stuyvesant—*Son of Peter Stuyvesant*

Alexa van der Donck—*Daughter of Adriaen van der Donck*

Lincoln Douglass—*Son of Frederick Douglass*

Simon Astor—*Son of John Jacob Astor*

Albert Fish—*Son of Hamilton Fish*

· THE M'GAROTH CLAN ·

Fritz M'Garoth—*Lieutenant-Captain and Rat Rider of M'Garoth Clan*

Liv M'Garoth—*Captain and Rat Rider of M'Garoth Clan; wife of Fritz*

· COUNCIL OF TWELVE ·

MAYOR ALEXANDER HAMILTON—*God of Finance; Mayor of the Gods of Manhattan*

Adriaen van der Donck—*God of Justice for Those Who Get None*

T. R. Tobias—*God of Banking*

Walt Whitman—*God of Optimism*

Hamilton Fish—*God of Connections*

John Jacob Astor—*God of Excess*

Babe Ruth—*God of Heroes*

Boss Tweed—*God of Rabble Politics*

Zelda Fitzgerald—*Goddess of Trends*

Dorothy Parker—*Goddess of Wit*

James Bennett—*Co-God of Newspapermen*

Horace Greeley—*Co-God of Newspapermen*

Caesar Prince—*God of Under the Streets*

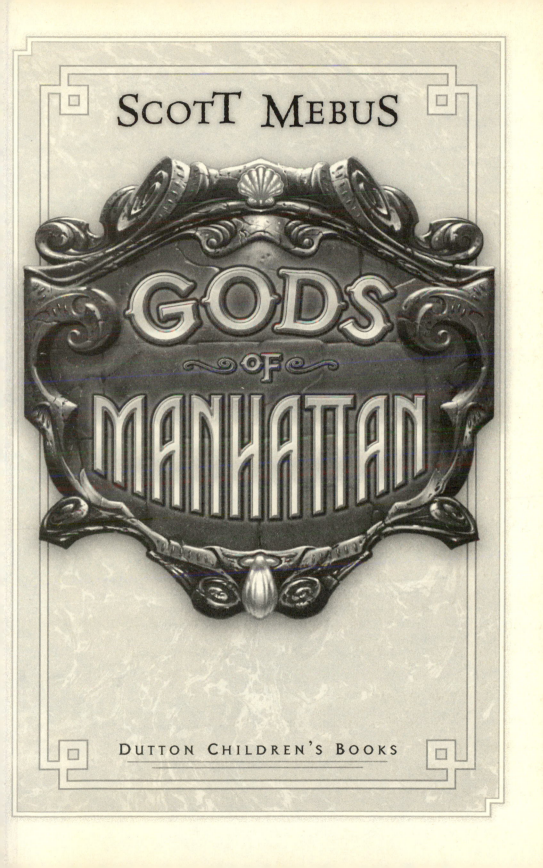

SCOTT MEBUS

GODS OF MANHATTAN

DUTTON CHILDREN'S BOOKS

DUTTON CHILDREN'S BOOKS
A division of Penguin Young Readers Group

═══ PUBLISHED BY THE PENGUIN GROUP ═══

Penguin Group (USA) Inc., 375 Hudson Street, New York, New York 10014, U.S.A. • Penguin Group (Canada), 10 Alcorn Avenue, Toronto, Ontario, Canada M4V 3B2 (a division of Pearson Penguin Canada Inc.) • Penguin Books Ltd, 80 Strand, London WC2R 0RL, England • Penguin Ireland, 25 St Stephen's Green, Dublin 2, Ireland (a division of Penguin Books Ltd) • Penguin Group (Australia), 250 Camberwell Road, Camberwell, Victoria 3124, Australia (a division of Pearson Australia Group Pty Ltd) • Penguin Books India Pvt Ltd, 11 Community Centre, Panchsheel Park, New Delhi - 110 017, India • Penguin Group (NZ), 67 Apollo Drive, Rosedale, North Shore 0632, New Zealand (a division of Pearson New Zealand Ltd) • Penguin Books (South Africa) (Pty) Ltd, 24 Sturdee Avenue, Rosebank, Johannesburg 2196, South Africa • Penguin Books Ltd, Registered Offices: 80 Strand, London WC2R 0RL, England

Text copyright © 2008 by Scott Mebus
Map illustration copyright © 2008 by Brandon Dorman

Library of Congress Cataloging-in-Publication Data
Mebus, Scott.
The hidden light/by Scott Mebus.—1st ed.
p. cm.—(Gods of Manhattan; bk. 1)
Summary: Twelve-year-old Rory discovers a spirit world that thrives alongside his contemporary New York City, filled with fantastical creatures and people from the city's colorful past who have become gods and goddesses and who have chosen Rory to perform a dangerous mission.
ISBN-13: 978-0-525-47955-0 (hardcover: alk. paper) [1. Fantasy. 2. Space and time—Fiction. 3. Gods—Fiction. 4. Goddesses—Fiction. 5. Spirits—Fiction. 6. Adventure and adventurers—Fiction. 7. New York (N.Y.)—Fiction. 8. New York (N.Y.)—History—Fiction.] I. Title.
PZ7.M512675Hi 2008
[Fic]—dc22   2007018113

Published in the United States by Dutton Children's Books, a division of Penguin Young Readers Group
345 Hudson Street, New York, New York 10014 • www.penguin.com/youngreaders

Interior and map design by Jason Henry
Printed in USA • First Edition
1 3 5 7 9 10 2 6 4 2

To Derek, for sharing this
crazy wavelength with me

~ ACKNOWLEDGMENTS ~

IT WOULD TAKE A LARGE TOME to list all the books and websites concerning New York history that I combed through to research this novel. So I will be merciful and mention only the vital ones: namely *The Island at the Center of the World* by Russell Shorto, which gave me great insight into Dutch Manhattan and introduced me to Adriaen van der Donck, Peter Stuyvesant, and Willem Kieft; *Unearthing Gotham* by Anne-Marie Cantwell and Diana diZerega Wall, which used archaeology to paint an intriguing picture of pre-European and early colonial New York; and www.forgotten-ny.com, a truly fascinating website detailing many of the secrets of New York's past hiding in the shadows of the present (with photos!). Ric Burns's documentary *New York* also served to set me on the path by capturing my imagination when I marathoned my way through all seven tapes during a lazy vacation week a few years back.

On a personal note, this book would have gone nowhere without the unswerving belief and never-say-die attitude of my agent, David Dunton. He is the agent all authors dream of having. Julie Strauss-Gabel did a fantastic job editing, as well as keeping me afloat with her enthusiasm. Much thanks to the whole staff at Penguin for their hard work and willingness to take me out to lunch, which cannot be overestimated. And lastly, thanks to my family and friends, especially my brother, Derek, and sister, Alison, Mom and Dad, the indefatigable Izzy, and, of course, that foxiest of relationship pundits, my lovely wife, Kristina.

·CONTENTS·

GODS OF MANHATTAN

THE MAGICIAN

Adriaen van der Donck raced over the Henry Hudson Bridge at the northern tip of Manhattan, urging his steaming horse to go faster as he made a break for the Bronx. Maybe he'd be lucky. Maybe his enemy had neglected to pick an assassin with the right kind of blood. He heard the sound of a horn in the distance. Was that the Trumpeter? He hadn't known the old fool was still haunting the river where he'd met his death centuries before. Oh well, no one had heard the man then and no one hears his ghost now. Just like nobody heard Adriaen. And now it might be too late.

His horse weaved around the cars whizzing across the bridge. None of the drivers even glanced in his direction. Adriaen had known his rival was planning something, but he'd never imagined anything like this. He needed to reach his farm, where he could get some sort of message to his daughter, warning her and the rest of his allies of their enemy's new, impossible weapon. If only the river would buy him some time—

Glancing over his shoulder, his spirits sank. The assassin smoothly galloped across the bridge without pausing, meaning he must have Bronx blood. Adriaen's enemy had planned for everything. Urging his horse onward, he flew down the side streets, the assassin hot on his trail. Now he could only hope to gain enough time to send a message off. But his horse was tired while the horse behind him was fresh. He'd only just crossed the boundary of his own farm when the assassin reached him.

A hard push knocked Adriaen off his horse. He landed heavily among the rows of towering cornstalks. Pushing himself to his feet, Adriaen turned to face the assassin, who had dismounted and was approaching him warily, knife in hand. *That knife.* How had his enemy made that knife? Killing Adriaen, or any god, was supposed to be impossible.

But everything was different now.

No time to warn his compatriots, not anymore. The only message he could send would be back to this killer's master. He gave a silent prayer for his daughter and the rest of the Rattle Watch. *Look after my city*, he whispered, *and keep watch over the hidden Light. All will be for naught if he is taken.* The assassin shifted his grip, getting ready to strike. Adriaen braced himself as he readied one last, desperate ploy. Maybe he'd save his city, though he couldn't save himself. The assassin sprang, and Adriaen van der Donck stepped forward to meet him, his final trick ready to be played.

"I think this is yours!" the magician exclaimed as he held up the undamaged dollar bill he had cut into shreds just two minutes before.

The girl sighed in wonder and took the bill back as the small crowd of children sitting in the Hennessy living room clapped loudly. Every eye was on the short magician in the long blue robe as he bowed at the applause and began his next trick. He pulled out a dove and called upon a boy to place the bird in a box. The children held their breath as the magician pulled out a match and waved it through the air.

Rory Hennessy, thirteen years old and never fooled, leaned in closer to watch the magician at work. There had never been a magic trick, or a sleight-of-hand maneuver, or any other so-called illusion, that had not been picked apart, seen through, or laid bare by the eagle eyes of the elder Hennessy. He could always spy the magician slipping the twenty-dollar bill into the volunteer's pocket. He unerringly knew where the five of spades was hidden. He would point to the shell with the marble under it every time. He couldn't really explain how he knew. He just did. Rory would look a magician in the eye and suddenly the performer would no longer be a mystical practitioner of wonder, he'd be a sad little man with a weird hat. He'd start to stammer, his rabbit would fall out of his sleeve, and he'd press the wrong button and pour water all over his pants. Rory didn't do it on purpose. It was just his gift.

Therefore, Rory had long ago decided to give magic shows a miss. He'd only agreed to attend this particular performance because it was his sister Bridget's ninth birthday party. She had begged and begged for a magician, and since Mrs. Hennessy could never resist her daughter's pouting, a magician was hired and a brother was warned to keep his big mouth shut. Rory promised, and so far so good. He should have just hung out in his room, but instead he found himself leaning against the wall and watching intently. He couldn't help himself; he had to *see*. And up until now, he'd been less than impressed, as usual. Bridget's *ooh*s and *ah*s got on his nerves, but he said nothing. Sometimes it seemed like she wanted to be fooled. She couldn't wait to be fooled. But not him. He saw the world the way it was. Somebody had to.

Sure enough, he picked out the moment when the magician—Hex was his name—slipped the dove into his sleeve, just before setting the box on fire. Rory shook his head in disgust as Bridget whistled in awe when the bird reappeared, magically unharmed. Bridget's cardboard sword lay in her lap, the word BUTTKICKER written on the side in Magic Marker. She never went anywhere without the stupid thing. She liked to say their father left it behind for her when he disappeared, but Rory knew that wasn't true. She'd only been a baby when their father left, walking out on the three of them and leaving then four-year-old Rory as the man of the family. Bridget loved to make up intricate stories starring their father as the magical knight doomed to wander, or as the wretched prisoner of the evil dragon, always fighting to come home to his beloved children. But Rory didn't buy it. It was just another fantasy, a trick to see through, and he saw through all the tricks.

"I need another volunteer. How about you?"

Hex pointed past the sea of raised hands right at him.

"Pick my sister," Rory said, nodding at Bridget, whose arm was waving crazily like she'd stuck her tongue in a socket. Hex smiled slyly, winking at Rory as if they were the only two in the room.

"You're the one with the storm-cloud face. I think you need a little magic."

Rory didn't like the way Hex was smiling, as if he knew something Rory didn't. Rory glanced over toward the kitchen, where his mother stood with arms crossed. Her face silently begged him to play along. He sighed.

"Fine."

He stepped forward as Hex held a deck of cards in front of him.

"Pick a card."

Rory grabbed a card, making a face. Hex made a big show of turning his head.

"Show everyone your card. Let them see it!"

Rory turned the card toward the kids and let them see that it was the eight of clubs. Hex pointed to his table.

"If you'll look down at my special table, you'll see a Magic Marker, black in color. This is an ordinary Magic Marker, much like you'd find at any stationery store. Please pick it up, Rory, if you would be so kind."

Rory picked up the Magic Marker. He looked it over closely but could see nothing strange about it. Hex kept his head turned away.

"Now, Rory, I want you to write something on the card with this ordinary Magic Marker. Make it very personal, something only you would think to write. All right? Are you done?"

Rory finished writing on the card and nodded.

"Good," Hex said. "Now place the card back in the deck."

Rory did this, sighing to himself. Hex wasn't even going

to stick it in a little envelope and burn it up. This really was amateur hour. At last Hex turned to look at Rory.

"Now shuffle the cards. Go on, don't be shy. Shuffle away, young man."

Rory carelessly shuffled the cards, rolling his eyes the entire time. Hex reached out and took the deck from him.

"And now the magic begins!"

Hex waved his hand above the deck, making a big show of casting his magic spell. Then he turned to Rory, asking a question that caught him off guard.

"Rory, did you get your sister a present?"

Unsure where this was going, Rory nodded.

"Could you bring it here?" Hex asked.

Rory paused, glancing over at his mother, not sure what to do. Mrs. Hennessy soundlessly pleaded with him, asking him not to ruin things. Shrugging, he headed over to his bedroom, returning a moment later with a small wrapped package in his hand. Hex pointed to Bridget.

"Why don't you give it to the birthday girl?"

Even more confused, Rory handed over his gift. Bridget dug into it, tearing the paper to shreds. She suddenly stopped, gasping. The entire audience fell into an awed hush. Even Mrs. Hennessy couldn't believe what she was seeing. But nobody was more shocked than Rory. He found himself fighting for breath as Bridget reached down and peeled the playing card off of the small book of scientific facts it was taped to, the one he had so carefully wrapped himself. He hadn't put that card there. He was sure of it. Hex smiled triumphantly. "Which card is it, Bridget?"

Bridget's voice came out small and filled with awe.

"The eight of clubs."

"And what does it say?"

She wordlessly lifted the card into the air. There, written on it in black Magic Marker, were the words HEX IS FULL OF CRAP! She looked up at Rory.

"Did you write that?"

Rory couldn't speak. He could only nod as the kids broke out into huge applause. Hex gave him a special smile, a satisfied smile, before moving on to the next trick. But Rory couldn't move on. Because for the first time in his life, he was lost. That trick was impossible. No matter how carefully he went over each piece of it in his mind, he couldn't figure it out. It wasn't possible. Unless it wasn't sleight of hand at all . . .

Rory's world tilted, the blood roaring in his ears like he'd stepped into a waterfall. A face flashed in his head, a face he'd seen in his dreams, and he thought he heard a brief snippet of low chanting in a foreign language. No one seemed to notice his distress; Hex had moved on, taking Bridget and everyone else with him. But Rory stayed behind, that impossible feat of magic smacking him off his nice, predictable path into an unknown world he knew did not exist. It couldn't exist. He wouldn't let it. *Breathe,* he told himself. *Just breathe.* His head cleared as he regained his composure. He'd missed the moment when Hex had made his move, that's all. That didn't change the fact that it was just a stupid card trick. Convinced that he was convinced, Rory went back to looking for the holes in Hex's magic, which he once again found easily. But the thrill was gone. All because of one stupid, impossible trick.

After the show, Hex packed up quickly as the kids moved on to a piñata on the other side of the room. Rory kept his distance, watching him from the corner. As Hex turned to leave, he glanced back at Rory and spoke softly, too softly to slip through the noise of the party. Yet somehow Rory heard him as if the magician stood right by his ear.

"What do you dream about, Rory?"

Rory jumped, too startled to reply. Hex couldn't know about his dreams, about the strange man, the mumbled foreign words, and the white circle. That was impossible.

"Does it frighten you?" Hex continued. "You need to see me at my shop. You have my card. We have a lot to talk about."

He tried to say more, but by that point Rory had placed his hands over his ears and was humming loudly. Hex forced his way through with his urgent voice.

"You could be in danger. Don't be a fool."

Rory hummed louder, pressing hard against his earlobes. Hex stopped talking and stood there staring, his eyes deep and unreadable. Then Mrs. Hennessy tapped him on the shoulder to give him his check, and his wizard's smile reappeared like magic. He gathered his pay and left without a backward glance. Rory tried to calm his pounding heart. The crash of the piñata bursting open made him jump a mile. He quickly headed for the door and the street below.

When Rory stepped out onto his stoop, his head was still reeling. His family lived on the second floor of a two-family house on 218th Street, way up on the northernmost tip of Manhattan in the small section of New York City called Inwood. His mom had grown up in Inwood, as had her father and grandfather and great-grandfather before her, and Rory could trust the familiar neighborhood to calm him down. If he didn't know Inwood, he didn't know anything.

The street was quiet except for the sounds of kids playing hoops down at the playground. He looked across at Columbia stadium, where the college students came to play football in the fall. It stood empty now, since summer had just started. Though lately, it always felt like summer. Rory used to sled down the hill to the river, but they hadn't had enough snow in years. This past winter, Bridget had even worn shorts in February! The whole world is going mad, his mother would say, and right now Rory believed it. He sat down, breathing in the scent of water coming off the river, trying to calm himself. He'd dreamed it. Maybe the guy snuck in while he was sleeping. But those words, in his handwriting . . . his vision blurred. When it cleared, he blinked once, slowly, then froze. At the foot of the stairs leading up to his front door, staring back at him without moving, stood a rat. And on the rat's back, holding reins in its hands like it was riding a pony, sat a cockroach. It cocked its head as if it was regarding him, watching him. It lifted one insect arm and waved.

Rory didn't know what to do. He was cracking up, obviously. That magician had broken his mind. But he refused to give in to the hallucination. He was in control here, and he knew what could be real. So without changing expression, he slowly looked away. He kept his eyes frozen on the apartment building next door, the one with the gargoyles on the roof. They stared out into nothingness, never moving, never changing. He could rely on them.

After a few moments, he couldn't stand it. He glanced back at the base of his stoop. The sidewalk was empty. The cockroach that couldn't be was gone.

Afraid the impossible thing would come back, Rory returned his attention to the roof of the old apartment building, trying to force the cockroach from his mind. He could make out a small pigeon hopping along the roof's edge. It was just a normal city pigeon. There wasn't a gerbil in a Robin Hood hat on its back or anything. It inched along the edge of the roof near one of the gargoyles, a lion's head with its stone mouth open in a growl. The pigeon stopped just short of the gargoyle, looking away at something on the roof. Then, in a flash, the gargoyle head turned and gobbled the pigeon up in one huge bite. Feathers burst out of its mouth and floated softly down toward Rory's astonished face. He would have thought he'd imagined this, too, if the gargoyle wasn't still chewing. Finally, with a swallow, the gargoyle went back to stillness. If not for the falling feathers, nothing would have been different.

Rory let out a strangled cry. This was just too much. Something was happening to him. He was definitely cracking, going crazy, losing his grip. A feather floated down into his open hand. He stared at it, running his fingers over the soft down. It was real. He twirled around to see if anyone had witnessed his mental breakdown, but the street remained empty. Except . . . down the road, past the stadium and toward the river, where the old trees of Inwood Hill Park pushed right up to the sidewalk, he thought he saw something in the shadows. Someone staring at him from beneath the ancient branches. He took a step toward the woods, almost against his will. He could barely make the figure out. Then the wind blew, shifting the leaves and letting the sunlight fall on the dark form. Rory froze at the sight of that figure under the trees, shocked by what he was seeing. Finally, a loud horn sounded, startling him into action. Rory staggered back, tripping over his stoop in fright. He dropped the feather to the sidewalk and ran up the steps, diving back into the safety of his apartment, his room, his bed, his world—where everything was just as it was supposed to be.

He didn't dare look out his bedroom window. Who knew what else he might see? Instead, he put his head under his pillow and stayed there the rest of the day and night. He heard his mother call him in to dinner, but he ignored it, just as he ignored the faint horn he could still hear blowing in the distance. He pretended to be asleep when she peeked in to check on him. But the thought of that figure kept him awake long into the night. He replayed the moment in his head of when the light fell and revealed the tall, bare-chested Indian warrior standing beneath the trees, watching him. He could still see the feathers bound up in the Indian's hair, the bow slung over his shoulder, and the copper spear in his hand. But most of all, he remembered the feeling that came over him when the Indian was revealed. The warrior's face was . . . *familiar*. It was the face from Rory's dreams. But he couldn't be real. That was just a dream. This all must be one big dream. It had to be.

INDIANS AND
SQUIRRELS

At the top of one of the tallest buildings in the city there was a room. A floor higher than any staircase or elevator reached; not even the architect knew it existed, nor would he believe it if he were told. The room was dark, though the shades could be pulled aside to reveal windows everywhere, looking out over the city below. But the man sitting behind the desk liked the dark best, so the shades remained drawn. A small fire gave the room its only light, the wavering yellow barely reaching the man's face. Only his eyes shone from shadows, black and deep. They burned into Dutch Schultz as he stood ready to make his report.

"Is it done?" the black-eyed man asked softly.

"You bet," Dutch Schultz said, trying not to shiver. He'd been shaking almost nonstop ever since he had sunk that crazy knife into Van der Donck. The old loon hadn't stopped whispering to himself even as he fell to the ground with a mortal wound. When Dutch had leaned in to figure out what he was saying, Van der Donck suddenly grabbed his forehead, scaring the bejesus out of him. It must have taken everything he had to commit that last hopeless act of defiance, because the old god fell dead the next moment. Dutch shivered again. Why couldn't he stop?

"I am pleased, Mr. Schultz," the black-eyed man said. "May I have my knife back?"

Those black eyes seemed to bore into his soul. Dutch couldn't help himself, he shivered again. He'd been a famous gangster back in his mortal days during the Roarin' Twenties, and he'd killed heaps of men. He prided himself on not being afraid of nobody. He'd fallen in with the black-eyed man years ago, a lesser spirit attaching himself to a god, and he'd been sittin' pretty ever since. This filly was the right one to back, he'd tell himself. This knife, this crazy knife that could do the impossible, it proved it. Dutch would kill a thousand dried-up old gods if that's what it took to gain power. So why couldn't he stop shaking?

"Mr. Schultz, I'm waiting." The black-eyed man was not pleased at the delay.

The assassin was shocked to find himself hesitating. Dutch Schultz, noted murderer and gang leader, was scared. A voice spoke up inside his head, almost as if it came from outside. *I have the knife, do I not? I am the powerful one now. If I strike quickly, I could take the power for myself and stop the shivering.* As the words rang in his head, an odd calm came over him. He suddenly knew exactly what he had to do. Without stopping to wonder where the voice came from, Dutch leaped toward the black-eyed man, knife aimed at his heart.

The black-eyed man did not even flinch. He reached out and grabbed Dutch by the throat, pushing him to the side. Dutch thrust wildly, sinking the knife into the other man's shoulder. The hand around his neck tightened, and the last thought on Dutch's mind as the blackness overtook him was, *Did I just try to bump off the big guy? What was I thinking . . . ?*

Holding his bleeding shoulder, the black-eyed man calmly regarded the dead body of his assassin. He knelt down to take back the knife, wiping it off on the assassin's jacket. He then reached into the dead man's pockets, searching.

"You underestimated me as always, Adriaen," he muttered to himself. "You may have turned Mr. Schultz against me, but all it cost me was an assassin. And I have more, Adriaen. I have more—*Ah!*"

He pulled out a small gold locket. Smiling cruelly to himself, he regarded the locket and the knife, his black eyes glinting in the firelight.

Rory awoke to a thump on the small of his back.

"Get up!"

Rory sleepily waved behind him in a useless attempt to get the intruder off of him. He was still half in his dream, something about a bright white belt. Bridget's voice whispered in his ear:

"Get your butt out of bed, mister, or I'll knock you silly with my great sword, Buttkicker! Your tender butt wouldn't be able to take it! It would sting and turn red and you'd cry out, 'It hurts! Oh, great knight Bridget, your mighty sword stings my poor butt!' But I'd keep whacking you, because sleepyheads deserve no mercy!"

"Fine. I'll get up. Just please stop talking!"

Rory pushed himself up onto his knees. Bridget remained attached to his back, so Rory reached around to tickle her. She squealed.

"No! I will not fall for your evil tickling! I am too great a knight to giggle!"

But that just wasn't true as Rory reached right in with a wiggling finger and tickled her to tears.

"See, Bridget, that's why knights wear armor. Otherwise the dragons would tickle them to death."

"Let your sister up, Rory. Her squealing's gonna wake up the neighbors."

Mrs. Hennessy stood in the doorway in her work clothes, a no-nonsense white blouse and brown suit pants, looking down at them with a half smile. Rory stopped as asked, feeling a little sheepish, and Bridget immediately sprang up out of reach. She raised a fist in the air.

"You just caught me off guard, that's all. The next time you try that, Rory, I'll be waiting to whack you!"

Rory fell back in bed. Mrs. Hennessy reached down and pulled the covers off of him.

"No you don't. Breakfast is ready. I want to see you eating before I head out."

Mrs. Hennessy worked down on Wall Street as a legal secretary for a large law firm. Every morning during the week (and often on the weekend) she left at seven A.M. to walk down to the A train and ride it the length of the island to Wall Street. It was the longest subway ride in Manhattan. She never came home at night before eight-thirty, and sometimes ten or even eleven. By then, she'd poke her head in to see Bridget asleep and then make her way to Rory's room to ask how the evening went. Rory's reports were always glowing; every night with him in charge was a successful one. She'd kiss his forehead and then wearily make her way to her room. One day he'd make lots of money, so she could stay home whenever she wanted. Then maybe she wouldn't look so tired.

This summer was especially difficult. There wasn't money to send Bridget to camp, so Rory had to look after her. He made a big show of hating the idea of dragging his little sister everywhere he went, but truth was he liked it. It wasn't like he had a big crew of buddies waiting for him at the corner to go play ball. He didn't mix well with the guys at his all-boys Catholic school; all they cared about were sports and hitting each other on the arm really hard. They never seemed to realize how tough the world could be outside of their hundred-dollar sneakers and their video games and their fathers coming home at night for dinner. He used to have one sort-of friend, Alfred, but they parted ways after Rory let slip about his dad's disappearance in a moment of confidence and his supposed friend blabbed about it to everyone at school. Overnight, Rory became the Kid Whose Father Walked Out, which just proved to him that it was a bad idea to trust anyone who wasn't a Hennessy. He didn't really want friends, anyway, he told himself. He had his mother, and he had Bridget. That was all he would ever need.

This morning, as Bridget ate her Lucky Charms and Rory munched on his English muffin, Mrs. Hennessy explained her plan for the day.

"The Central Park Zoo has a brand-new exhibit on squirrels. Why don't you take your sister?"

"Come on, Mom," Bridget said, groaning. "Why can't we go to the Bronx Zoo?"

"I don't like the idea of you two wandering around the Bronx. The Central Park Zoo is a perfectly fine zoo."

Bridget poked her cereal with her spoon, splashing milk all over her side of the table. "They have parrots and goats and donkeys and things. All their animals eat grass. The whole fun of the zoo is hoping a gate is left open and the animals break out and eat each other."

Mrs. Hennessy reached down and stopped Bridget's spoon. "Is that so? That happens all the time at the Bronx Zoo, does it?"

"Like every day! Just the other day, an antelope got out and mauled a giraffe. Just bit off its face like it was nothing!"

Rory snorted. "You don't even know what an antelope is, do you?"

"It's not a stupid grass-eating squirrel."

Rory let out a big sigh. "I'd better take you to the zoo, or you'll go through life thinking squirrels eat grass."

Bridget stuck her tongue out at him and went back to splashing her cereal. Rory took a sip of orange juice and marveled at how distant the events of yesterday felt. Like he'd dreamed the whole day. He finished his glass and set it down, feeling pretty good about the world. Bridget tossed something at him.

"By the way, you left this on my present."

It was a playing card. His Magic Marker writing was scrawled across the little black clubs, taunting him.

A large rat raced through the tunnels that crisscrossed below the streets of Manhattan, a small cockroach clinging to its back. Fritz M'Garoth held on tightly to the reins as his rat steed, Clarence, bore him south toward City Hall. His heart beat fast as he considered the implications of what had happened.

He'd become so used to watching the boy unseen, that at first he hadn't realized something had changed. He'd waited for Rory's eyes to defocus as they passed right over him; after all, they always did. But this time, Rory tossed the script, starting in surprise and staring openly at the cockroach atop a rat watching him from the sidewalk. Thrown, Fritz had panicked and waved. *Waved*. He was such an idiot. The minute Rory looked away, Fritz got out of there before he could do any more damage.

Fritz had gone to his clan's village under the Dyckman Street Playground to warn his elders, but they'd waved him off. Ever since coming north to escape the Mayor's wrath when they resigned from his service a hundred years before, the M'Garoth clan had pulled away from the world. Only Fritz and his wife, Liv, as the clan Rat Riders, dared lead patrols outside the village. And only Fritz seemed to care what happened out there. Sometimes he felt like he was the only one to remember what it truly meant to be a battle roach, defending the peace against those who would break it. In the old days, M'Garoths had led the charge against criminals of all stripes.

But now, only Fritz carried on their legacy. He alone among his clan remembered that a battle roach was born to fight.

Since he couldn't shake his clan from their self-protective stupor, he'd decided to ride down to Adriaen van der Donck and warn him of this new development. Adriaen had understood the importance of keeping an eye on Rory, of keeping him *alive*, and now that the boy had somehow woken up, Adriaen would know what to do. *Rory is lucky to have such a wise benefactor*, he thought. The world was dangerous for a Light. Unprotected, Rory wouldn't last a day. . . .

Rory tried to keep his mind off his growing insanity, letting Bridget chatter as they walked through Central Park toward the zoo.

"It's such a pretty day. We should head down to the Statue of Liberty or something. We don't need to see some stupid squirrels in a cage. We could go to the top of the Empire State Building. Or play basketball in the park. Or go down to Coney Island and ride the Cyclone! Why don't we do that?"

Rory kept right on walking, not answering her. Bridget bounced around him like a tetherball. She pointed to all sorts of things as they walked along the tree-lined pathways.

"Look, a mime! Let's go throw stuff at him! I bet you I could make him say 'Ouch!' Wait, let's go over there! They paint your picture while you wait! Can I get my picture painted, Rory? I'm one of the world's great beauties, after all."

Rory kept walking. Bridget didn't seem to need any response

to her yammering. The park was alive that day with people and sound, for which Rory was thankful. He didn't want to hear himself think. If he just ignored all of this, everything would go back to normal. A couple rollerbladed by, splitting him from Bridget for a second. Once they passed, she stepped in front of him.

"What's going on, Rory?"

Rory stopped. Bridget's face was uncharacteristically serious. She had her hands on her hips and everything. Rory forced a laugh.

"Nothing. Just enjoying the day."

He tried to brush past her, but she wouldn't move.

"You've been weird all day. You were weird all day yesterday, too. Not all day, actually. Just after that magician. You know, if you hate magicians so much, why did you help him with his trick?"

Rory avoided her eyes.

"I didn't help him."

Bridget hopped excitedly.

"I knew it! I could tell you were surprised. He's a real magician, isn't he!"

"Of course not. You know that's all a bunch . . . of . . ."

Rory trailed off. Bridget cocked her head to the side. He was looking past her, toward a large elm by a small footbridge.

"What? What are you looking at?" she asked.

Rory didn't answer her. He knew she couldn't see what he was seeing. Because he was going crazy and that's not really a team sport.

Across the path was the strangest thing he had ever seen.

It beat everything up to that point, including the gargoyle. For under the elm, in broad daylight, a squirrel and a rat were fighting kung fu.

They seemed pretty evenly matched to him. The rat was smaller but more agile. Its kicks came quicker, and the squirrel had to throw its paws up with lightning speed to bat them aside. The squirrel, on the other hand, packed a stronger punch. Though it only landed one shot for every four from the rat, its punches sent the rat reeling. One particularly hard chop to the neck knocked its foe to the ground. The rat lay there while the squirrel circled, gesturing with its paw to come get some more. The rat cleared its head with a quick shake and leaped up to its feet. It performed an intricate dance, swishing its paws through the air. Then it sprang at the squirrel, beginning the fight anew.

Rory stood there watching, knowing that he was officially crazy. Bridget stood next to him staring intently at the elm. Rory felt bad for her, having to see her responsible big brother, her rock, break down right in front of her. She nudged him.

"Is that a rat?"

Rory froze, slowly turning his head to look down at his sister.

"You can see that?"

"I see a rat and a squirrel. What are they doing? I can't tell."

Rory looked back at the elm, where the two rodents were flying at each other, trading punches in midair. *Why not?*

"They're fighting."

He heard Bridget gasp.

"Oh my God. They're fighting like in those old kung fu movies, but with fur."

Rory stepped back and stared at his sister in shock. She had her eyes locked on the battle by the elm. Was she making fun of him? She flinched.

"Oh, you shouldn't kick someone there. Even if he is a rat."

"You can see it?"

Bridget looked up at her brother, her face wide with excited wonder.

"You bet I can. This is the coolest thing ever! I bet the squirrels at the stupid zoo don't have black belts."

"It's really there?"

"Of course it is. I didn't really know what I was looking at until you told me, but then I could see them clear as day. It's amazing."

Rory wondered if she was fooling herself, pretending to see what he was seeing because she wanted to see it. He turned back to the battle. The rat had climbed halfway up the squirrel's back and was head-butting it from behind.

"Okay. So what are they doing now?"

Bridget flinched.

"The squirrel just ran backward into the tree with the rat on its back. It's trying to shake it! Ouch, man. Rodent fights are dirty."

And sure enough, the squirrel kept barreling backward into the elm, attempting to shake off the rat. Bridget could barely contain her excitement.

"This is amazing. Do you see stuff like this all the time?"

"No. Only since that magic trick yesterday."

"What have you seen? Give me all the gory details!"

The rat flipped around, head-butting the squirrel. Rory rubbed his forehead in sympathy.

"I saw a gargoyle eat a pigeon, and I saw a cockroach riding a rat."

"Like that rat?"

"It was a bigger rat. Less . . . martial artsy. I also saw an Indian, I think."

"Like Gandhi?"

"No, the American kind. He had feathers and stuff. That kind of Indian."

Bridget hit him.

"They're *called* Native Americans, stupid."

"Fine, sorry," Rory said wryly, rubbing his side where Bridget had smacked him.

"This is awesome!" she said. "What does it mean?"

"I have no idea."

Bridget grabbed his arm as the rat and squirrel rolled around in the dust, each vying for an advantage.

"We gotta find out!"

"There's nothing to find out. If we just ignore it, maybe it'll go away."

"That is just plain stupid, and you know it. Ignore it . . . there's a whole world we've never seen before! This is the best thing ever!"

Rory pulled his arm away.

"You don't know what you're talking about. A little kung fu fight and a hungry gargoyle don't mean there's some hidden world. There's probably a good explanation for it."

"Like what?"

"Nuclear testing."

"In Central Park?"

"Genetically engineered animals."

"Who would engineer a cockroach? No one likes cockroaches. Not even Carl from my class, and he eats worms."

"Look, it's probably something."

The rat kicked off the squirrel, knocking it back into the tree, where it slumped to the ground. The rat advanced to finish the job, rearing up with one paw ready to swipe, when it shuddered. Out of nowhere, a long stick with feathers on the end had sprouted from its back. The rat fell forward, facedown in the dirt. Rory and Bridget stopped their argument, looking on in astonishment.

"Is that an arrow?" Bridget whispered.

"I think so."

"Where did it come from?"

In answer to her question, a shadowy figure loped out of the trees, silently gliding toward the dead rat. A ray of sunlight hit the dark form, giving them a good look at the archer. Rory felt his breath catch as Bridget looked up at him with big, round eyes.

"Is that him? Is that the Indian you saw?"

Rory shook his head no, too taken aback to point out his sister's use of the word *Indian*. Tall with long, flowing dark hair twisted up around various brightly colored feathers, this new Indian kneeled down by the rat. His chest was bare, with scars running down his shoulders and around his back. A small quiver of arrows slung easy over one shoulder, while the bow sat ready in his hand. He pulled the arrow from the rat's back with a quick tug and turned to tend to the squirrel. The small animal began to twitch as it regained consciousness, shaking its head before running up the Indian's arm to rest on his shoulder. The Indian glanced up to the sky, forcing a gasp from Bridget's lips.

"Look at his face!"

"Don't stare, Bridget."

But she couldn't look away. Each of the Indian's cheeks bore a tattoo of a barking dog, teeth bared and ready to bite. The dogs seemed ready to spring from his face and attack. Bridget's eyes bulged as she took it in.

"That is the coolest thing I've ever seen!"

A new voice whispered from beside them, "You should start running now."

Almost jumping out of his skin at this new voice, Rory spun around to see a young Indian girl leaning against a tree. She wore a simple leather shirt and wraparound skirt and her feet were bare. She smoothed her long braid of hair as she smiled at them.

"He will see you soon if you don't," she said matter-of-factly.

Bridget stepped toward her.

"Are you a squaw?" she asked, wonder filling her voice.

The girl gave her a disgusted look.

"Please do not insult me. I'm trying to give you a head start."

"What are you talking about?" Rory asked as Bridget fell back, stung.

"He is hotheaded and does stupid things. I am levelheaded," the Indian girl said, her eyes twinkling. "That is why I will be a great leader one day and lead my people back to the land. He likes to run around and shoot for sport. He does not care for thought. It hurts his head. Shooting is so much simpler. I think life would be easier if I followed his path. Which path do you follow?"

Her pretty smile made Rory feel like a clumsy idiot.

"I'm . . . I'm levelheaded, too, I guess," he stammered.

She laughed.

"Everyone thinks they are. You have a nice nose. But you really should think about running."

Uncertain what was going on, Rory glanced back at the tattooed Indian, who was checking the body of the squirrel for injury. Suddenly, the warrior swiveled his head to stare right at them. His eyes lit up in an unpleasant way as he quickly stood up.

"Rory," Bridget whispered, "I think we should go."

"Who is he?" Rory asked the Indian girl.

"He is my brother, of course," she answered. "I really would start running now."

The tattooed Indian reached behind him toward his quiver and that was all the Hennessy children needed. They spun and took off as the girl's voice followed them.

"Good luck! Maybe he will only wound you!"

They had no breath to reply as they burned down the path toward 59th Street. It had never seemed so far away. Bridget turned quickly to look behind them.

"He's gaining, Rory! He's pulled out an arrow! Do you really think he'll shoot?"

"Do we really want to find out? Faster, Bridget! Come on!"

They raced around the people strolling under the trees enjoying the beautiful day. More than one couple found their hands torn apart by the fleeing children. Various angry yells followed them in their wake as they almost knocked over half the people they sped past, but still the exit stayed just out of sight. Bridget sneaked another look.

"He's got the arrow in his bow! How can he run and do that, too? I can't even watch TV and eat at the same time without getting it all over my shirt!"

"We're almost there!"

Finally, the exit popped into view from behind a tree. They weaved around the path as a whistle sung past their ears. The tree ahead of them suddenly sprouted an arrow. Rory redoubled his efforts, dragging his sister along behind him. With a final burst of speed, they shot through the gap in the wall out onto the sidewalk. Bridget tripped, pulling them both to the ground. They spun around just in time to see another arrow flying their way from the other side of the exit. Rory prepared to shield his sister's body from the missile, but the second the shaft reached the exit, it burned away into nothing, the ashes blowing back into the park. The tattooed Indian stood framed by the gap in the wall for a moment, as if daring them to come back in, before turning to disappear into the trees.

A small crowd had gathered around the two children lying on the sidewalk. An elderly woman leaned over.

"Are you two all right?"

Bridget hopped up, her eyes glowing from excitement and fear.

"We're A-okay! You're kind to care!"

The crowd dispersed, satisfied that no one was hurt. Bridget stared down at her brother, hands on her hips.

"What's your explanation for that?"

EYES IN THE
SHADOWS

The five members of the Rattle Watch were pretty pleased with themselves. Nicholas and his friends were standing defiantly in front of the door of the main council room at City Hall, facing the full wrath of the Council of Twelve seated around the large table before them. Not only were most of the council members who ruled over the Gods of Manhattan—including Albert's and Simon's fathers—there to berate them, but they'd even dragged in an uncomfortable Frederick Douglass, Lincoln's dad, who didn't even sit on the council. Of course Nicholas's father, Peter Stuyvesant, was absent as always. But as long as Adriaen arrived soon to enjoy the circus, Nicholas's satisfaction would be complete.

All in all, it had not been a bad day's work for the Rattle Watch.

"We can no longer turn a blind eye to your acts of vandalism!" the Mayor said, his handsome face burning with disapproval as the other council members looked on with solemn faces. "The list of your actions against certain members of this council is long and shameful. The incident with the garbage monkey and the jar of honey at the Patroon Day Parade was particularly odious. Mrs. Astor had to be scrubbed down with a horse brush. But today's stunt at the bank went too far."

Too far? Could they ever go too far against those who'd aid and abet the enemy? Nicholas didn't think so. Adriaen van der Donck had come to Nicholas and his friends to form the Rattle Watch and to keep people in the know, to expose the enemies in their midst. But he had never said *how.* So, the five eternal teenagers had taken it upon themselves to embarrass, harass, and generally drive their enemies to distraction.

And it was good to have a purpose. As children of gods, Nicholas and his friends would never mature, never advance past puberty . . . never do much of *anything*, really. Blessed—or cursed—with their famous parents' immortality, most children of gods coasted through their unending lives, going to party after party and leading lives of meaningless privilege with no responsibility. After all, what was the point in caring about anything? They'd never be gods like their parents: one had to have been mortal to be elevated to godhood, and none of them had ever been mortal.

Nicholas was different. He may have appeared to be no older than sixteen, but he'd already seen three centuries go by, and he was tired of watching and doing nothing.

At Nicholas's side, Adriaen's daughter, Alexa, was frowning as she scanned the room for her father, who still hadn't arrived. With her big hazel eyes and lustrous amber hair, Alexa could have easily made herself into a beauty queen and lorded over the world of lavish luxury that consumed their peers. Instead she pulled her beautiful locks into a no-nonsense bun and plunged headlong into the fight. She was her father's right hand. Nicholas had always envied her close relationship with Adriaen, who served as a second father to all of the Rattle Watchers, whose own fathers so frequently let them down.

He glanced at the rest of his friends. The excitable Lincoln Douglass bounced in place, ready to fight the world all at once if need be. His father, Frederick Douglass, God of Freedom, looked on with exasperation, probably wondering how he'd ever given life to such a spastic son. Next to Lincoln, Simon Astor, looking a little ridiculous in a loud, wrinkled shirt (the one he wore especially for being brought before the council), lazily stuck his tongue out at his dad, John Jacob Astor, God of Excess. Unlike Frederick Douglass, John Jacob Astor appeared downright angry as he scowled at his son. Though the laid-back, somewhat hapless Simon didn't seem to care, Nicholas always worried about what his father would do after one of their pranks. The God of Excess was not a nice man. . . .

Lastly, to Nicholas's right, the dashing Albert Fish was smirking openly. His father, the image-conscious Hamilton Fish, God of Connections, didn't seem to like it one bit. Fun-loving with a devilish streak a mile wide, Albert had been the one to hatch the plan to let the gigantic sandhog loose outside the bank, and it had worked to perfection.

Nicholas smiled, too, thinking of the huge pig they had relocated from the East Side, where it had been at work eating out a tunnel for the new Second Avenue subway line. Bred to excavate, sandhogs had long been regarded by the Manhattan mortals as simply a colorful name for the men working deep underground. *A guy with a shovel would have been easier to catch, that's for sure,* thought Nicholas.

Once they'd set it free in front of the bank, the elephant-size pig had immediately burrowed into the ground, digging a large ditch up to, and partially through, the side of the building. It hadn't gotten too far, of course, before the Brokers of Tobias had corralled it. But to stick it to that tightwad T. R. Tobias had been more than worth the punishment they'd be receiving. The rotund God of Banking pretended to run his First City Bank for the good of the city, but the Rattle Watch knew he worked only for himself. *And,* thought Nicholas, *for the First Adviser, Tobias's lord and master.*

"If I may," Nicholas said, bowing low and adding a sweep of his arm, which caused Albert to repress a chuckle and Alexa to roll her eyes, "it was not our intention to hurt anyone. We merely wanted to make a point. The bank represents the safe world we pretend we live in while the sandhog represents the tunnel of truth that needs to be dug through the thick walls of self-denial that this council, nay, all of Mannahatta has encased itself in!"

The Rattle Watchers each gave him an incredulous look. Alexa mouthed *Tunnel of truth?!* her eyes twinkling. Nicholas shrugged. Okay, fine, maybe they just did it to make Tobias cry. The Council of Twelve didn't have to know that. There was always room for a little bit of revisionist history.

"What is this nonsense?" Tobias snorted, sounding half annoyed and half bored. "They were probably trying to break into my vault. A futile enterprise, as many would-be thieves before them have discovered to their everlasting chagrin. Now, Mayor, I have money to count. Could you please—"

Before he could go any further, a commotion was heard outside the council room. The doors flung open and Stephanus van Cortlandt, God of Noble Politics, burst in.

"Murder!" he declared. "Van der Donck has been murdered!"

Nicholas felt like he'd been kicked in his stomach. He turned to Alexa, whose face had gone ashen.

"It can't be," he said, and his denial was echoed in the faces of his friends.

The council burst into frightened chatter. The Mayor pointed to the Rattle Watch.

"Get them out of here."

Nicholas and his friends were rushed from the room. As the doors closed behind him, he could see the almighty Council of Twelve shouting back and forth, devolving into a big mess.

It couldn't be true. Who would save them all now?

Rory sat on the sidewalk in Times Square, thinking. He figured that the busiest intersection in the world would be a good place to hide from Indians and squirrels while he figured stuff out. Bridget, unable to sit still, amused herself with her favorite game: hailing cabs and then pretending to be surprised and confused when they stopped for her. Eventually, she grew tired of the angry honks and plopped down next to her brother, who was turning the eight of clubs over and over in his hand.

"I guess we better find Hex," he said. "He might have some answers to all this."

Bridget grabbed the playing card.

"You have really bad handwriting. I think that Native American girl was flirting with you."

Rory snorted.

"Yeah, right. The imaginary Indian girl was trying to get my number."

"She said you had a nice nose."

"And then her brother tried to shoot it off!"

"Maybe she'll be your first girlfriend!" Bridget smiled innocently, as if daring Rory to poke her. Though he didn't want it to, the Indian girl's face popped up in his head. She did seem to smile at him an awful lot. He shook his head. This was so stupid. He had to concentrate.

"We can't lose focus, Bridget! Hex said something to me about a card. Did he leave a business card?"

"Not that I know of. Mom might know."

Rory froze. Out of the corner of his eye, he caught sight of something strange. A dark shadow at the opening of a small alley between two buildings behind him seemed to shift as people walked in front of it, slipping to the left and right as it popped in and out of view. He looked up to see what cast the shadow, thinking it might be a construction crane in front of the sun or something, but there was nothing there. He looked back, his hair standing on end as he noticed how the shadow had grown. Two small specks flickered within. They could be reflected light from a car parked on the street. Or they could be eyes. He felt a shudder run violently through him as the glowing specks began to grow, darting left and right, *looking* for something. . . .

"Rory! Mr. Focus! I said, should we call Mom?" Bridget asked.

Her voice snapped him out of it, and he looked back to see Bridget staring at him, waiting for an answer. When he glanced behind him again, the shadow had shrunk. No glowing eyes peered out from the alley. He must still be freaked out from the park. He turned his attention back to Bridget.

"We don't want to get her involved. She has enough to worry about. Maybe the phone book."

Bridget turned the card over.

"Or we can look on Raisin Street."

Rory glanced at her.

"What's on Raisin Street?"

Bridget pointed to the card.

"The home office of Hex Magic, Ltd. It's on the back of the card."

Rory snatched the card back, where sure enough, a small address was written on the bottom: HEX MAGIC, LTD. 234 RAISIN STREET. He pushed himself to his feet.

"Let's go, then. This shouldn't be too hard to find."

A few hours later, Rory was ready to admit he might have spoken too soon. According to the map, there was no such road as Raisin Street. Bridget asked everyone she could with no success, until one old coot sitting in a lawn chair outside an

ancient butcher shop mentioned he might have heard of a Raisin Street down in the Village, off of an old road called King's
Way, so off they raced downtown.

Unfortunately, the Village was the hardest place to find
anything in the whole city. While most of Manhattan was
made up of orderly streets laid out in nice, neat rectangles,
Greenwich Village refused to play along. Here in this small,
tucked-away corner of the city, the streets were a maze. Small
roads with long names lasted a block, then vanished forever.
Mothers warned their children never to wander off down these
side streets. People had been known to get lost for days before
emerging, impossibly, all the way across the island (a story
Rory always thought ridiculous, until now). You never knew
where you were while you walked or where you were going; you
just packed a lunch and hoped you made it out all right.

The streets were narrow. The old brick town houses leaned
over them as they wandered underneath, searching in vain. Looking up at the next street sign, Bridget threw up her hands.

"Bedford Street again! Maybe we passed it!"

The street corner opened up to a small park filled with
tall, leafy trees breathing cool air down onto them as they
walked underneath. The sounds of the cars whizzing along the
city streets seemed far away, easily overpowered by the chirping of birds above. Rory sat down on a bench, scattering the
pigeons.

"This is stupid. It's a made-up street."

"No it isn't! It's got to be here!"

Bridget stood on the bench, looking around. Rory found
himself staring at the pigeons. He wondered if they'd do some

kind of choreographed musical number for him or something. A dance remix of "Tuppence a Bag" maybe. Bridget took out the map again and studied it intently.

"I know it's here. Maybe that's it!"

She ran over to check a street sign they'd already checked five times. Rory watched the pigeons, wondering if he should just give up. Suddenly, a chill ran down his spine, prompting him to glance toward the corner of the park. A clump of trees cast a patch of shade over two park benches below. As he watched, the dark splotch began to grow, spreading out from the benches and spilling onto the ground. Two bright spots rose up from within, flicking around, searching. *Searching for him.* Rory's skin crawled as he watched the twin lights get brighter and brighter. They were coming for him, coming to get him. He knew it in his gut. But he couldn't move. The feel of something touching his arm made him cry out.

"Relax! Geez," Bridget said.

Completely unaware of the shadows, Bridget pointed to a side street they hadn't noticed before.

"Let's try that way. We have to at least find this King's Way. Find that and we find Raisin Street. What do you think?"

Rory glanced back to the bench. The shadows were gone. He needed to keep moving, he knew that much.

"Let's go."

They dove back into the Village. With each turn, the streets grew thinner and the brownstones came closer together. Everything felt older somehow, like these stately structures had been around for centuries. Maybe they had. Even a house or two popped up between the taller buildings, complete with small yards in front. No cars drove through, and the sidewalk stayed clear of people. The sounds of the city faded completely, leaving only the breeze and the odd chirping of a lonely bird. Rory looked up at the windows of the brownstones, wondering if anyone even lived in them. Bridget grabbed his hand.

"Let's walk faster. It's a little creepy here."

They sped up, trying to outrun the silent, empty streets. Rory glanced behind him frequently, but to his relief the shadows stayed shadows. He kept his eye out for either Raisin Street or King's Way, but he found only more quiet town houses with peeling paint and closed windows. Bridget skipped out into the center of the road, peering off around the corner.

"I don't see anything. Just more twists and turns. Maybe it is just a made-up street."

Out of nowhere a loud crack split the silence. Rory and Bridget both jumped, twisting around to see where the sound had come from. Another small explosion crackled through the air. Where was it coming from? After the third bang, Rory started to get a bead on it. He walked carefully toward the sound, which seemed to be coming from beside a small converted carriage house complete with a stable door. Rory and Bridget warily approached the side of the house, where a small space a few inches wider than Rory's shoulders separated it from the next building. Bridget pointed.

"Look at the wall!"

Gazing up at the side wall of the town house across the small alley, Rory could just make out some faded gold letters, which were barely readable.

KING'S WAY

Bridget peered down the tiny passage between the buildings, which faded into darkness after a few feet.

"This gets a name? It's tiny. That's like naming the hallway
to our bathroom Bridget's Way."

Rory stepped into the dark.

"Let's get this over with."

They made their way down the dark, narrow passage. After
a bit, the alley brightened as it widened into a larger corridor.
The air felt murky and heavy as they stepped around several
large puddles at their feet. Rory tried to think back to the last
time it rained.

"A week ago, at least."

Bridget glanced up at him.

"What?"

"Nothing. Stay close."

A small object fell in front of them, making them both
jump back a step. It looked like a miniature cigarette, still lit.
Before Rory could approach it, it exploded with a loud bang.
He cursed under his breath.

"Firecracker."

"Good one, boyo. You've got quite the eye on ya."

A teenage kid leaned against the wall to the side, a handful
of firecrackers sitting in his palm. His clothes were way out
of date, like something out of the 1800s. Everything from his
strange cylindrical hat down to his worn, broken boots looked
old, from another time. Rory pushed Bridget behind him and
stepped forward.

"Who are you?"

The boy tossed another firecracker, sending a resounding echo through the alley.

"I'm Sly Jimmy. I'm one of the B'wry Boys. Who you with?"

Rory exchanged a confused look with Bridget before answering. "Um, no one."

Sly Jimmy didn't like that answer. His next firecracker landed at Rory's feet, sending him hopping back.

Bang!

"You gotta have a gang. Somebody's gotta get your back. If you got nobody, you're all alone."

Bridget's head shot around Rory's elbow.

"Yeah, well we're part of the Hennessy Gang. We're stronger than your stupid B'wry Boys!"

Rory shot her a warning look. She shrugged, as if to say she refused to take his crap. The kid pushed his hat back.

"Is that so?"

A small blade appeared, as if by magic, in Sly Jimmy's hand. Rory backed away with Bridget held firmly behind him.

"Look, Jimmy. You don't have to go playing with knives. I'm sure your gang is stronger than our gang. You don't have to prove it."

Sly Jimmy took a step forward, spinning the knife in his hand.

"But I likes proving it."

He started to advance. Rory knew if he tried to run, Jimmy would catch up with them easily in the tight passage. He had to stand his ground, but what then? He had just about run out of ideas when the temperature dropped suddenly. A familiar chill ran up Rory's spine as the shadows behind Sly Jimmy began to move, pulsing like radio waves. Sly Jimmy seemed to feel it, too, and he dropped his evil grin to look around in confusion.

"What's going on?"

Twin specks of light rose up out of the shadows like fireworks about to explode. Bridget whispered up to Rory, her voice tense with fear.

"What's happening, Rory?"

"I don't know. Don't worry, I'll protect you."

"How?"

Rory didn't answer as Sly Jimmy backed away from the shifting darkness. He turned to look fearfully at the younger boy.

"It's a Stranger!"

The darkness pulled in on itself as the specks of light rose up into the air. The black began to spin, calling up a wind that whipped their faces with dirt and dust. Bridget's arms tightened around Rory's waist as she finally found something that frightened her. Rory didn't know what to do. He couldn't move. He knew the shadow was there for him. Sly Jimmy's eyes locked in on his; the older boy knew it, too.

"Sorry, friend. It's a rough way to go. Glad it ain't me!"

With that, Sly Jimmy turned tail and ran back down the alley, disappearing into the dark. Rory wanted to follow him, but he couldn't move. He whispered down to Bridget.

"Run. It's not here for you. Get out of here."

Bridget's grip tightened even further.

"No. I'm not leaving."

"Go! You have to!"

"No!"

Suddenly, the dark spun away, leaving something behind. Something completely unexpected. Rory blinked in confusion.

"What's going on?"

A small boy, who looked no older than six, stood before them. He wore a little polo shirt and dirty brown slacks, and a pair of Keds on his feet. His brown hair hung in a bowl cut across his forehead. He looked lost, as if he'd wandered off by mistake and just wanted to get home to his mother. Rory couldn't help himself; he stepped forward.

"What are you?"

The child stared back at him, not answering. He seemed completely helpless, looking out at him from under long lashes. He reached out an arm and then he spoke in a small, pathetic voice.

"*Come.*"

Completely thrown, Rory shook his head.

"I can't. Sorry."

Bridget peered around his chest.

"He's just a kid. What is he doing here?"

The little boy tilted his head and stamped his foot in frustration.

"*Come! You come now!*"

Rory relaxed at the petulant sound in the boy's voice, an odd calm coming over him.

"I can't. What's your name?"

The boy stamped his foot again and beckoned, but Rory didn't move.

"*Come!*"

The boy opened his eyes wide. Suddenly, the searing bright lights were there, filling his eye sockets, burning out at Rory. Before he could react, the boy raced toward him unnaturally quickly. Alarmed, Rory lifted his arm to ward him off, but the boy opened his little mouth to reveal razor-sharp teeth. Rory screamed, falling back in terror as the little boy sank his teeth into his forearm, biting down hard. Rory fell to the ground, vaguely aware that Bridget was shouting.

His sight grew dim as his efforts to shake the boy from his arm weakened. Everything felt heavy. Finally, he gave in to the feeling. The last image he had was of those sharp teeth clamped tight in his skin. Then everything fell away into darkness.

MANNAHATTA

Lincoln paced anxiously outside the council room, prompting Albert to flash him an irritated look.

"You're going to drive me crazy if you don't stop that, Linky. Alexa, tell him to sit down. Just watching him is making me dizzy."

Alexa was distracted, searching the portraits on the wall for the only one that mattered to her. But she knew that Albert was trying to get her to smile, so she did. It came out tired and sad. Everything felt tired and sad since she'd heard the news about her father. She could only hope to feel better once the council caught the murderer and brought him to justice.

"I'll sit down when I know what the council is going to do," Lincoln said, not slowing down. "And stop calling me Linky! I didn't like it a hundred years ago, and guess what, I don't like it now!"

"Touchy." Simon smirked from his spot against the wall. "I think Linky needs a nap."

Alexa sighed. She exchanged a long suffering glance with Nicholas, who stood apart, lost in thought. She turned her attention back to the portraits on the wall. The entire room was filled with portraits, thousands of them hanging in every direction. Directly outside the council room, the Portrait Room was bigger than one would think possible. Easily the largest room in City Hall, and probably the whole city, it stretched onward and upward and out in every direction, far into the distance. The ceiling could be seen way above, barely, a glass roof letting in the fading sunlight of late afternoon. The opposite wall seemed days away, a long line shimmering in the distance. The wooden floor stretched out like a flat, brown desert; it could take weeks to cross. On the walls hung paintings, evenly spaced, each about the size of an apartment window, covering the off-white plaster in all directions as far as the eye could see.

Every god to ever watch over Manhattan hung on the walls of the Portrait Room, and there were thousands of them. The clothing of the gods differed wildly. Some wore jackets and hose from days long past, while others looked no different than the people on the streets of present-day Manhattan. But their eyes were all the same. Eyes that stared out like a trick, much more real than the paintings themselves, as if someone stood behind the wall and peered through holes cut in the canvas. Eyes that showed the subject was still alive, still remembered. When memory faded, the eyes faded. When the god died, the eyes died. Then only a dead portrait remained, a lesson in fear—and obsolescence—to the gods still standing.

Alexa's father had always been proud of the fact that there were so many gods in his city. He liked the care for small things as well as big things these gods represented. And since they lived in a democracy, every god had a chance to be Mayor or sit on the Council of Twelve. Of course, they've had the same Mayor for two hundred years and the council often seemed to be made up of his flunkies, so things didn't work perfectly. But there was always hope. At least there had been—

Her breath caught. She had finally found it, halfway up the wall. Alexa felt Nicholas come up behind her to look at the portrait she was viewing.

"I didn't really believe it," he said sadly. "Not until now."

She tried not to feel anything as they all took in the portrait of Adriaen van der Donck. The frame was old and weathered; the portrait itself had been one of the first ones hung. The kind face, the dark Dutch clothing, the firm jaw, everything looked the same. Except for the eyes. The eyes had become lifeless, painted on and dim. It was true. He was dead.

The door opened to discharge two councilmen taking a break from the meeting. Albert leaped to his feet, but when he saw who it was, his face soured. The shorter of the two men sighed.

"Albert, please go home. You know you shouldn't be here."

"And yet, here I am," Albert said, smiling innocently. His father, Hamilton Fish, suppressed a scowl and turned to speak to Nicholas.

"The council is taking a break until tomorrow," he said. "They're sending Councilman Babe Ruth up to investigate, since he's the only one with Bronx blood on the council."

"Let me go with him!" Alexa cried. "I have Bronx blood! I can cross the river!"

"I know you can, but it's too dangerous," Hamilton Fish

said. "We will take care of this, children. I know you're hurting, but this is not your concern."

Walt Whitman, a tall gentleman with a dark beard, nodded. The laugh lines around his eyes spoke of a cheerful nature, but his face was grim.

"Some might not trust the Babe to do anything but hit a ball and eat hot dogs, but I have no qualms letting him head this up!" he said. As the God of Optimism, he had a habit of ending his sentences with an exclamation mark. "I'm sure we'll get to the bottom of this in no time!"

"Please let me go!" Alexa pleaded again. "I want to know who did this."

"We already know who did it," said Nicholas darkly. "It was that black-eyed, black-hearted First Adviser. This is why Adriaen has been warning you about him!" Lincoln and Albert nodded at his side.

"Don't go spreading slanderous rumors, young man," Fish said sternly. "Especially you, Albert. I will not have you embarrassing me. The First Adviser is a valued member of our society. He has never given reason to be suspected of any foul play. Only the patroons ever had bad words to say about him, and I chalk that up to bad blood from their mortal days. Anyway, we've already established that a god couldn't have been the murderer. We will find the killer, but you and your little band of troublemakers here are to stay away from this case. This is a matter for the council."

"How do you know a god couldn't have done it?" Alexa asked. "I've never heard of a god being murdered before, and I've been around a lot longer than you."

Hamilton Fish bristled at Alexa's brash tone, but Whitman smoothly stepped in.

"It's true that as far as we know, this is the first murder of a god in the history of Mannahatta," Whitman said, much more kindly than his fellow. "Gods pass on when they are forgotten or when that which they are god of is no longer valued. Never are they killed. Spirits can be killed, yes, but never gods. And there is a reason for this. There are rules gods must follow. We have no choice but to adhere to them; they come with the job. And one of those rules forbids us from killing another god, or even to be a part of his or her death. It is not for us to decide which gods survive; that is only for mortals. So no matter what you may think of the First Adviser, he is a god, so he is above suspicion. He couldn't have even ordered Adriaen's death. Which is good news!"

Nicholas stepped forward.

"But maybe he got around it! Maybe he figured out a way!"

"We appreciate the enthusiasm, lad!" Whitman cut him off, his eyes sympathetic. "But this is not for you or your friends. This Rattle Watch that Adriaen assembled could get you all in a serious amount of trouble. I know you mean well, but you're stirring things up, which might do more harm than good. We will handle this incident. Everything will be fine! Better than fine! There will be justice, Alexa. I promise."

The two gods said good-bye and headed off into the distance, talking softly to each other.

"I can't believe he's going to get away with it," Nicholas muttered.

"We don't need anybody else," Lincoln said boldly. "We can take him. It's five against one."

"No," Simon said dejectedly. "It's everyone else against five. Five kids who aren't even gods."

This thought deflated them all.

"So what do we do?" Albert asked. Nicholas looked around at the uncertain faces of his friends.

"I don't know," he said. He had never felt so helpless.

Rory woke up out of the dark to an aching head. He forced his eyes open to let in the light, revealing a strange ceiling above him. He became aware of a throbbing in his arm, but he ignored it as he let his head fall to the side. A small couch came into view. Behind the couch, the wall was covered with hand-drawn pictures, but his eyes were still too blurry to make them out. Nestled in the center of the couch was Bridget, who had just noticed that her big brother's eyes were open. Her face lit up as she hopped off the couch to rush to his side.

"Rory! You're awake! I'm so sorry! I couldn't do anything! It was so scary! I didn't know what to do! It was just a kid and then it opened its mouth and bit you and you fell. I was so scared. I'll never let that happen again, I promise. Next time, I'll know what to do, I swear! But you're okay. Right? Are you okay?"

Rory shook his head to clear some of the fog and discovered that, somehow, he actually *was* okay. His right arm ached a little, but nothing like what he would have expected. He pushed himself up to sit, looking around. He had been laid out on a small cot in the corner of what seemed to be an office. The windows looked out at some brownstones across the street, bathed in the golden light of afternoon. The pictures he'd first glimpsed covered all four walls, drawn in everything from a child's hand to the crisp lines of a talented artist. The subjects of the drawings ranged from large green monsters to an all-too-familiar cockroach astride a rat. One picture in particular tugged at his memory. It showed a simple white-beaded circle, which, somehow, he knew to be a belt. He'd seen something like that before, but he couldn't quite place it. He returned to his sister's worried face.

"I'm okay. Where are we? How did we get away?"

Relieved, Bridget stepped back and pointed over his shoulder.

"He showed up."

Rory turned to behold a strange sight. A kid, around ten years old, stood there holding a glass of water out to him. He was a strange-looking child. His short brown hair didn't move, as if it were frozen in place. His face was waxy and delicate, and his skin reflected the light in a weird way. His features seemed thrown on, almost painted. Only his eyes, bright and hard, had any real life. Rory took the water, trying to understand what he was looking at.

"Thank you. What's your name?" Rory asked.

The boy stared back at him, mute. Bridget whispered loud enough to make a drill sergeant jump.

"I don't think he can talk."

"Do you know his name?"

A new voice interjected.

"It's Toy."

Hex stepped into the room, quietly closing the door to the rooms within. Instead of the robes and hat he'd worn to the party the day before, he had on a simple shirt and jeans. The magician held out his hand, which contained two small white pills nestled in his craggy palm.

"Take these. They'll help."

Rory put them in his own palm, though he was wary.

"What is it?"

Hex lifted Rory's injured arm slightly, forcing a gasp of pain out of Rory's mouth.

"Some of the poison is still in you. The pills will counteract it. Otherwise I would have saved you now only to watch you melt away in a week or so."

Bridget peered at the pills.

"We're not supposed to take stuff from strangers."

Hex chuckled ruefully.

"You've already met the Stranger and you survived. You've got nothing to fear from me."

Though Rory didn't entirely trust this medicine, the ache in his arm hurt too much. He downed the two pills and quickly chased them with the water. Almost immediately, his arm felt better. Hex smiled.

"See? You are a lucky boy, Rory. Bridget told me all about your little adventure. Sly Jimmy saved your life. He's always setting off those firecrackers out in the alley. I was marching over to send him on his way when I heard your sister's scream. I sent Toy ahead, and he was the one who knocked the Stranger off you."

Bridget cut in, her eyes wide.

"Toy came out of nowhere. He just flattened that Stranger thing. And the thing kept trying to bite him, but it couldn't get him. Finally there was this bright light and I couldn't see anything but little black spots like the ones you get when you stare at a lamp too long. When the spots finally went away, that thing was gone!"

Hex lifted Rory's arm again, checking it for abrasions. To Rory's amazement, the skin where the little beast's teeth had sunk into him now appeared smooth and unbroken. Hex noticed Rory's expression.

"Creatures like the Strangers don't leave marks where everyone can see them. That's what makes them so dangerous. You don't think to treat what you can't see. The real worry comes when one of the Stranger's teeth chips off and gets lodged in your skin. You'd have no idea it was there if you didn't know to look for it."

Rory poked at his arm with his other finger, marveling at his close call.

"What would happen then?"

"You'd change. I've never seen it myself, so I'm not sure what happens exactly, though I've heard tales. But you'd change, all right. Don't worry, you're fine. I did know what to look for and I didn't find a thing. In an hour or so you'll be right as rain. I promise. To finish the tale, I came on Toy's heels and sent the Stranger on his way. Rory, the Stranger will come back. It may take a little while to heal, but then it will come looking for you again."

Rory pulled his arm away, his frustration breaking through.

"Why? What did I do? What is a Stranger anyway? And who are you, *really*? I don't understand what's going on!"

Hex took Rory's ranting calmly. He leaned back against a small desk.

"Those are good questions, and there are no simple answers to any of them. I'll pick the easiest first. The Strangers live in the shadows, feeding off children like wolves, calling them into the dark where no one can see and devouring them. When your parents tell you to stay away from strangers, these predators are who they are unwittingly warning you about."

Bridget pulled herself up on the little cot beside Rory.

"But it looked like a little kid!"

"That was adaptation at work. They take on the shape of children, small and innocent. No one feels threatened by a child, not until the child's teeth bite into their neck."

Rory shuddered, remembering those sharp teeth.

"Bridget told me that you have been jumping at shadows all day," Hex continued.

Rory nodded. "I kept seeing eyes watching me."

"That is what makes this unusual," Hex said. "Strangers are scavengers, not hunters. They prefer to pick off the weak, not track their prey halfway across the island. And once it did corner the two of you, it never should have gone for the larger, stronger male. Which can only mean one thing: this particular Stranger was after you, Rory."

Rory shuddered again.

"Why does it want *me*? What did I do?"

Instead of answering, Hex gestured toward Toy.

"What do you see when you look at Toy, Bridget?"

Bridget looked closely at the small boy, narrowing her eyes until she could barely see through the slits.

"Um, a kid."

Hex turned to Rory.

"And you, Rory? What do you see?"

Rory glanced over at the boy, noticing how the light bounced off his face.

"I don't know. There's something wrong."

"What do you think is wrong with him?"

"He's too shiny. There's something weird about his skin."

Hex allowed himself a slight smile.

"And what do you think is wrong with his skin?"

Rory took a closer look. That frail, thin, almost papery skin . . . *paper*.

"It's paper. His skin is made of paper."

Hex nodded slowly, pleased.

"Yes. Yes indeed. His skin is made out of paper."

Bridget's mouth opened. She peered closer at Toy, almost falling off the cot. Toy stared back at her blankly. Her eyes widened.

"You're right! Why didn't I see it before?"

Hex grabbed a chair, sitting down with creaking knees. He rubbed them absently as he spoke.

"Because you don't have the gift. Now that Rory's shown you the world behind your world, you'll be seeing more and more of it on your own. And it's actually quite impressive how quickly you're seeing what he's showing you. But that's nothing compared to what your brother can do. Rory is the real prize. The big bear at the fair."

"What are you talking about?" Rory retorted. "I'm nobody's bear."

"Of course you're not. I'm talking metaphorically. I do that from time to time; I'm trying to quit. Rory, you have a special gift. You can see what's there."

"Wow," Rory said sarcastically. "Where do I pick up my cape?"

"Don't scoff. Most people walk through the world blindly, never noticing what's right under their noses. You, on the other hand, can see it all. You see what's there. You see the truth."

Rory shot a glance over at Toy, who was still staring at Bridget.

"So he's really made out of paper?"

"Yes he is. Papier-mâché."

"Like a piñata!" Bridget exclaimed.

Toy flinched. Hex reached over and patted his hand, an affectionate look on his face.

"It's all right, Toy. He's a little sensitive. And I don't blame him. It's hard going through life made out of papier-mâché in a world filled with sticks. But I try to protect him as best I can."

For the first time, Toy's eyes softened and Rory caught a glimpse of affection on his face.

Bridget hopped down from the cot and walked over to him. "I'm sorry, Toy. I didn't know. I would never make fun of you. You're no piñata."

Toy stared at Bridget, his eyes unreadable. She turned to Hex.

"Why can't he talk?"

Hex patted Toy's hand again.

"Unfortunately, he has no tongue."

"That's horrible." Bridget reached out and took Toy's hand. "I don't care if you are paper. You still saved my brother's life and that makes you cool in my book."

Toy's face didn't change. He just stood there, letting his arm be moved up and down, staring at Bridget. Hex placed his hand softly on the back of Toy's neck, like Rory had seen a thousand fathers touch their sons. He wondered if his father had ever showed him love like that. He couldn't remember it. Something about that fatherly gesture made Rory look at Hex with new eyes. Maybe he could trust the strange magician after all.

"You are very kind, Bridget," Hex was saying. "Toy is all I have, now that my son is gone. He has been a great comfort."

A flash of pain flew across Hex's face. Rory felt pity tug at his heart.

"What happened to your son?"

Hex forced a smile. "That is a story for another day. I will tell you, I promise, but today is about you. People are looking for you, Rory. Including me. They've been looking for over a hundred years. Not for you in particular, just for someone with your talents. You are a very valuable boy. So valuable they compelled a Stranger to hunt those like you, and, believe me, it is near impossible to force a Stranger to do anything but eat."

Rory didn't want to be valuable. He wanted to be alive.

"Why don't they find someone else with my talents, then, and leave me alone?"

"There is only you, Rory. The rest of the Lights—that's what you are, a Light—have all disappeared. Taken by a Stranger like that one, in all likelihood. The one thing in our favor is that I believe the people who control that Stranger are not yet aware of you. Strangers can only be compelled so far. It was trained to react immediately to *any* Light it sees. If I injured it enough, we might have a little time before its master is alerted. Or perhaps not; Strangers can be as obstinate as bloodhounds. There is no way to tell. One thing I do know, whoever controls that Stranger will not be kept in the dark for long."

Cold panic gripped Rory.

"I don't understand any of this. Why does anyone care what I can see? Anyway, you seem to be able to see all of this crazy stuff just fine. Why do you need me?"

Hex put up a hand to stop the torrent of questions. He ran the other hand through his sparse hair as he tried to answer them.

"There is a world all around you that most mortals cannot see. We call it Mannahatta. Some say it is the spirit world, while others believe it is the city itself dreaming, or rather *remembering*. If something or someone was important enough, loved enough, feared enough, imagined enough, *remembered* enough, then it is reborn here in Mannahatta. In turn, Mannahatta overlaps the everyday world and whispers in its ear, keeping the memories of the city alive. If something big happens in Mannahatta, a fight between spirits perhaps, it can wash over into the mortal world, causing everything from mild distress to riots and blackouts. But though we watch over them, most mortals will never see Mannahatta. This might sound strange, but I believe it's because it is too *true*. People don't want to see the real truth. They'd rather live in a fog. They don't want to see the chips in the paint or the bums on the street. So they close their eyes to it, without even knowing it. But it's the nature of a Light to see through all illusion to the truth, to face the truth and point it out to others. So you, out of all the mortals in the city, can see through to Mannahatta. That is very valuable to many people."

Rory didn't want to hear any of this. He wanted to go back home where the worst thing he could accidentally see was his neighbor Mr. Little in his underwear.

"But I never saw anything strange before yesterday. Never!" he protested.

Hex arched an eyebrow. "Never?"

Something tickled the back of Rory's mind, but he ignored it.

"Never! You did this to me. With your stupid card trick."

Bridget hopped up on the couch, pulling a pillow up on her lap.

"How did you do that trick, anyway? If Rory can see through illusions to the truth and stuff."

"I didn't use illusion," Hex replied. "I used another method entirely. I'd heard of Rory from other magicians. The boy who sees through every trick. You're famous in their circles. But how had you not been discovered? Lights don't reach the age of twelve. They barely make it to three before they disappear. So I tracked you down. I followed you one afternoon and watched you stride by everything from a gang of rats beating up on a garbage monkey to a sidewalk seer speaking in tongues as she gave a reading to a living statue, all without blinking an eye. You didn't seem aware of any of it. But something bothered me. Your eyes would pause, just for a second, too quick for anyone to notice if they weren't looking for it. But I could see them flicker when you passed by these impossible beings. And that stuck with me.

"When your sister's birthday came around, I made certain I was the one hired. And sure enough, you saw through all my illusions without a problem. I knew there was definitely something going on. So I did a test, a trick you couldn't penetrate. I wanted to see how you would react to something that couldn't be real, but that you couldn't ignore. And, boy, you did not like it one bit. And ever since, you've been seeing the things you'd been ignoring, haven't you?"

Rory's head swam with all this revelation.

"How did I do it, then? I don't remember seeing any of those things you're talking about. I've never even heard of a garbage monkey."

Hex looked uncertain.

"I don't know how you learned to shut out Mannahatta. Obviously you don't remember it. But however it came about, it saved your life. The people on the lookout for the Lights never noticed you. You were hiding under their very noses all along."

"Until now."

"Yes. Until now."

"So you did this to me," Rory said. "I was doing fine until you snapped me out of it. You exposed me to things like that Stranger."

Hex nodded sadly.

"Which would you have wanted?" He said. "They would

have found you one day. No protection would have lasted forever. If I could find you, they could find you. Even if you were to leave New York, there are treaties between the cities, and one day a Stranger would appear at your door. You'd be a sitting duck, blinded or not. But I'm giving you another option, a chance to take control of your destiny. You can do what they're afraid you'll do—ruin all their plans—and then it will be too late for them. You'll do a great service to our city and protect yourself forever at the same time."

Rory didn't know what to believe. Could this be true? Cockroaches that waved to you while riding on rats were real? Indian girls with laughing eyes were real? It was all real?

"Who is this 'them' you keep talking about?" Rory asked. "And what kind of world is out there, anyway? What have I been making myself ignore?"

Bridget almost knocked all the couch pillows to the floor as she raised her arms in excitement.

"Is it a fairy world? With elves and swords and things?"

Hex smiled softly. He stood up and looked out the window, watching the empty street below.

"Not quite."

"Then what?"

He turned back to the two children, eyes dark beneath his heavy brow.

"Would you like to see?"

INTO THE PAST

Hex led them out the front door of his office and up the dark stairwell, which doubled back and forth above them. Bridget was beside herself with excitement. Her brother the superhero! Strange worlds filled with fantastic creatures! She sneaked a look back at Toy, who was silently following them like a Secret Service agent or a pet collie. A paper boy, just like in "Puff, the Magic Dragon"! When he'd come out of nowhere to save Rory from that horrible thing, she had almost died of relief. If Rory had died . . . she pushed that thought away. Next time she wouldn't just stand there and watch. Next time, she'd be ready.

As they rose up the stairs, Rory asked one of his sensible questions. "What are you going to show us, exactly?"

Hex glanced back over his shoulder, smiling apologetically.

"Well, I won't be showing you quite as much, Rory. I like to illustrate my tale with a bit of derring-do, but you'll be able to see right through that. So you're going to get more of the radio version, while Bridget gets the movie. But you won't be left out completely. There are still things to see as well as hear."

They continued to climb. Bridget took a look down the stairwell, which dropped away into darkness. "How tall is your building, anyway? We keep going up and up."

Hex shot her an enigmatic look.

"It's taller than it looks. Even to Rory. Here we are!"

Hex turned the corner, which opened up onto a landing with a small metal door on the other side. He strode across the floor to put his hand on the knob. Rory lay his hand on Bridget's shoulder, pulling her behind him.

"What kind of surprises are out there, Hex?"

Hex smiled impishly.

"Come on, Rory. There is no point in living if you're going to be a big scaredy-cat."

And with that, Hex opened the door and stepped out into the sky.

Rory and Bridget rushed forward, gazing out the doorway onto a frightening scene. The door opened onto nothing, high up in the air. Far beneath them, the city stretched out under the afternoon sky, cars and people flowing through the tiny streets like water through a sand castle built too close to the surf. Above it all, Hex stood in midair, somehow refusing to fall the hundred or so stories to the ground. Peering over the edge, Bridget discovered that the door seemed to be balanced on top of a long needle that in turn poked out of a skyscraper.

Rory gasped, immediately recognizing the mirrored peak. "We're on top of the Chrysler Building! What's going on?"

Whistling to himself, Hex walked a little ways out and dropped down on the edge of nothing at all, seemingly floating in the middle of the sky. Upon closer inspection, Bridget noticed that the patch of air beneath him was slightly bluer than the sky above, and that deeper blue extended back toward them like a walkway. She reached down, still holding onto the doorway, and tapped the tinted sky where it met the floor at their feet. A dull thump greeted her knuckles. She looked up at Rory.

"I think it's solid."

Rory put a heavy hand on her shoulder.

"Don't go out there."

"Why not? Hex is sitting right on the edge. He looks okay."

Hex was indeed seated on the tinted air, his legs swaying beneath him as if he were dangling off the end of a lakeside dock instead of thousands of feet up in the air. He beckoned to the siblings.

"Come on. You wanted to see."

Bridget squirmed under Rory's death grip as he stared down at the ground below and took a deep breath.

"I'm going first, Bridget. Wait for me to tell you to come out."

She was eager to rush out into the sky, but forced herself to wait her turn as Rory slowly stepped out into nothing. His foot fell through the air for an eternity before clanging onto the platform. Always the careful one, he dropped to his knees and crawled over to Hex, who smiled widely.

"Amazing, isn't it? Don't worry, there's a guardrail here. Hold on and swing your legs around. There we go!"

Rory did as asked and soon he, too, sat suspended above the city far below. His eyes teared as the wind blew past his face, whipping his hair around his forehead. He shouted back to Bridget.

"I don't want you to come out here. It's too dangerous!"

"Tough!"

Bridget bounded through the door unafraid, laughing as she walked on air. Behind her, Toy stepped out as well, but he stayed back at the door, watching. Bridget practically skipped over to Rory and plopped down next to him.

"This is awesome!"

She could see Rory wanted to shake her, but he settled for giving her his patented older-brother-knows-best look.

"Be careful, Bridget. This isn't a game! You almost gave me a heart attack running out like that."

Bridget made a face.

"Scaredy-cat."

Hex put up his finger.

"Oh no. Courage. You showed courage following me first, Rory. You didn't know what would happen. You don't know me or what I want. But you took a risk and showed great courage. That is what this city needs: courage. Someone has to slay the proverbial dragon. Someone has to sneak into the fortress and take back what's been stolen. Talent, no matter how impressive, is never enough."

What about me? Bridget wanted to shout, but then she thought back on that cold, frightened feeling that had come over her when she froze up in the alley. She didn't deserve to be called courageous. But she could be; she knew it.

Rory let out a whistle as he took in the city below.

"How did we get here? We were down in Greenwich Village, and now we're in Midtown. That's forty blocks north on the other side of the island."

Hex shrugged. "Not all roads go where you'd expect. Neither do all staircases. Great view, huh?"

Bridget put her hand out in front of her and smooshed all of Midtown between her fingers. She felt a hundred feet tall. Giant Bridget, crusher of cities.

"So why did you bring us up here?" Rory asked. "The view?"

Hex betrayed no annoyance with Rory's question. "Look north, toward the park."

They both turned uptown, where Central Park sprouted out of the middle of the city. Bridget heard Rory gasp before whispering in her ear.

"The glow . . . do you see it, Bridge?"

Once her brother mentioned it, she could see something. Gradually, a strange aura appeared over the park, blue and sparkling. Soon she could barely see the trees through the glow.

"It's like somebody turned Central Park into a giant bug lamp!"

"It's a shield," Hex said. "What most folks call the Trap. You can't see it when you're up close, but from way up here it shines. It's been surrounding the park for well over a century."

Rory looked away from the glow.

"Why?"

Bridget turned to see Hex regarding her brother with serious eyes.

"That's the story I want you to hear. The tale of the Munsees and the Gods of Manhattan."

Rory blinked in confusion.

"We have gods?"

Hex laughed. "I'd say. Mannahatta is lousy with gods, each of whom watches over his or her slice of Manhattan, big and small. Gods of everything from Justice to Sample Sales, Guilt to Jaywalking, Money to Street Construction—very equal opportunity."

"Where do all these gods come from?" Rory asked.

"When a mortal does something great, he is reborn in Mannahatta as a spirit. If his legend grows enough, he might be fortunate enough to ascend to godhood. Of course, it all depends on what they're remembered for. Mannahatta is littered with the spirits of famous gangsters, so very few of them become gods, since there's room for only so many gods of crime. But there aren't many contenders for the job of God of Alternate Side of the Street Parking, which is how Alan Tuddle rose to the position simply by being remembered as the guy who always got a spot. All told, there are thousands of gods here in Mannahatta, on top of hundreds of thousands of spirits, not to mention all the other creatures lurking about. They all have jobs to do—making sure Manhattan keeps sailing along smoothly, spiritually speaking. Though some work harder than others."

"So who's in charge?" Rory asked.

"That would be the Mayor."

"Wait a sec," Bridget cut in. "I thought gods had kings."

"Not in Mannahatta. Here we have the Mayor and his Council of Twelve, and he's elected. Though, the current Mayor has held his office for almost two hundred years, so make of that what you will. Those cursed incumbents always seem to win. . . ."

"So what's in that Trap thing?" Rory asked.

"Like I said, Mannahatta is ruled by the gods. But it wasn't always that way. See, these gods, they're newcomers in the grand scheme of things. They've only been here as long as the colonists who birthed them, four hundred years at most. For a thousand years before that, Mannahatta belonged to a different people. But I'm getting ahead of myself. We should start at the beginning. Ready?"

"For what?" Bridget asked.

Hex swept his hand into the air with a flourish.

"Take a look."

Bridget's heart skipped a beat as the world began to change. Buildings shriveled up, plummeting downward as if the island was sucking them back into itself. Even the Chrysler Building fell away, leaving them floating in midair above the disappearing concrete. Trees sprouted through the sidewalks, and ponds poured over the asphalt. Soon, the only buildings left lay far to the south, and they were small, ramshackle things barely standing. As she watched they, too, melted away, leaving forest behind to cover the island. Bridget clapped with delight.

"Do you see, Rory?! Isn't it amazing?"

"It's just the same old city to me, Bridget."

That's right, she remembered. *Rory can't see any of this, since it isn't real.* She described it all, trying to paint a picture that would make Rory see how beautifully the tall trees hung over sparkling brooks where just moments before there had been nothing but steel and pavement.

"So we're in the past," Rory said.

"Before the English, before the Dutch," Hex said. "When the only feet that walked on these ancient dirt paths belonged to those people."

He pointed, and suddenly Bridget was flying, soaring down toward a long path snaking in and around the trees from north to south. She laughed as the trees parted beneath her. Hex's voice spoke in her ear.

"This is Broadway. The oldest road. Very different from the wide avenue today, but still the same in all the important ways. No one knows who carved it out or why. But it has always been here, and it always will be."

Bridget landed on the dusty trail, reaching down to feel the dirt between her fingers. A noise prompted her to look up. Near a curve in the trail a small cloud of dust floated, followed by a familiar form.

"It's an Indian!"

Sure enough, a tall warrior rounded the corner, a copper spear in each hand and feathers in his hair. Behind him came a group of Indians, bare-chested and golden-skinned. The brave in the lead bore the tattoo of a wolf on his chest and a smaller wolf on his forehead. The others' bodies also carried various tattoos, though none as vibrant as the leader. Hex whispered, "These are the Munsees."

The Munsees passed Bridget as she lay in the dust, making little sound with their soft moccasins. Hex's voice continued in her ear. "This whole part of the continent, from the shores of Delaware Bay far to the south to the border of Connecticut just north of here, was once *Lenapehoking*, the land of the

Lenape Indians. The Lenapes were broken up into three clans, the Unalachtigo, who took the turkey as their totem and lived far to the south by the ocean; the Unami, who took the totem of the turtle and lived along the Delaware River up to Staten Island and the mouth of the Hudson; and the Munsees, who took the wolf totem and lived here around the Hudson to the Connecticut line. These clans were made up of many tribes, many of whom warred with one another as often as not, but their language gave them a common bond. And gradually as their numbers dwindled, they mixed together until here in the north, only the Munsees remained."

"But they're all gone now?" Bridget asked.

"Yes and no," Hex replied. "The Munsee people are mostly gone, forced to leave behind their homeland to the European invaders centuries ago. But their spirits, the souls of their tribes that were connected to the land, they remained. The island remembers them and gives them strength, even though they are without a living people. But now even the island can no longer feel them. Look out at the river, Bridget!"

Bridget found herself lifted into the air, soaring up from the path to rise above the trees. The sparkling river lay out before her, and right down the middle of it floated a small ship, its sails flapping in the breeze.

"Henry Hudson," Hex said, "coming to 'discover' Manhattan. As if the Munsees hadn't been here for a thousand years or more. Soon an idiot would sit some of the Munsees down and offer them trinkets in exchange for the island. And the Munsees would take them, and gladly. After all, in the Munsee world, there is no buying of anything, especially land. Only renting. In that sense, they really are the first New Yorkers. So the Dutch, see that's them down there . . ."

Bridget was flown to the south of the island, where small buildings were being raised inside a rough fort. Everything seemed so little compared to the skyscrapers of today. Even the people in their rough wool coats and dresses were shorter. She giggled at the thought that Rory could probably beat all of them in basketball, without really having to jump.

". . . the Dutch thought they'd bought the place, which they named New Amsterdam," Hex continued. "So they built and they traded and then they turned around and wondered why the Munsees were still there. There were issues, some fights between the settlers and the Indians, but that didn't stop the settlement from growing. By the time they sent in a governor to sort it all out, the small town had really started to take off, known throughout the world as a disreputable den of thieves and swindlers."

Suddenly, more houses sprouted up, and docks shot out into the rivers. Ships sailed into the harbor, one bearing the skull and crossbones of a pirate.

"Look at that!" Bridget exclaimed. "Rory, there's a pirate ship!"

"Yes, there were even pirates," Hex said. "There is said to be pirate treasure somewhere on the island, though I've never heard of anyone finding it. Anyway, the Dutch sent over a man named Willem Kieft to take charge and make the place respectable. He sailed in one bright morning determined to take the colony in hand."

Bridget flew in closer as one ship topped by a bright flag flapping in the breeze pulled into the dock. A tall, dark Dutchman with cold black eyes clomped down the gangplank and into the city.

"He looks mean," Bridget said.

"He was much more than mean," replied Hex. "He was a sorcerer, exiled to the New World in disgrace."

"*Come on.*" Rory's voice sounded exasperated. "A sorcerer? That can't be true."

"Listen to the tale, Rory. If you need any reminders of what's real and what isn't, just remember where you're sitting. May I continue?

"Kieft hated many things in this world. He hated his superiors for humbling him. He hated the settlers for reminding him of his exile. But most of all, he hated the Munsees. No one knows why, for sure. Some say it was because he attempted to learn their magic, and they looked into his soul and turned him away. Others say it was because he thought they should bow to him and they refused. For whatever reason, it was instant hatred—on both sides. The Munsees named him the *Gakpitschehellat*, and don't ask me because I don't have a clue what that means. But it wasn't nice.

"Kieft found reasons to fight war after war with the Munsees, often on the flimsiest of excuses. Finally, late one fateful night, he led a war party to attack a group of Munsees he claimed had come to murder the colonists as they slept."

The island went dark as the sun set, bringing out stars more brilliant than Bridget had ever seen. She floated above the fort as Kieft led a group of men on horseback out of the town, torches held high in their hands.

"What he didn't tell them was that those 'murderous savages' were in fact innocent refugees coming to beg for their protection. And so, in the dead of night, they fell upon the sleeping Indians and slaughtered them, every last one."

"They just murdered them all?" Rory couldn't believe it.

"It wasn't until morning that they discovered that most of them were old women and young children. By then the attackers didn't care. But the people of New Amsterdam did. They were horrified by what their leader had done. And some of the town elders were beginning to suspect that Kieft dabbled in the unnatural arts. So they exiled him from his exile, sending him home to Amsterdam to be tried for his crimes.

"But it was too late for the Munsees. Neither the Dutch nor the English after them ever found a way to truly live in peace alongside the island's original inhabitants, and gradually the Indians fled west. By the time of the American Revolution, almost all of the Munsees were gone, leaving their ancestral homeland to the invaders.

"Kieft never arrived in Amsterdam to stand trial for his crimes. His ship was caught in a gale off the coast of Wales, and all aboard sank to the bottom of the ocean. And so he wasn't heard from again, until he walked into City Hall to run for Mayor a hundred and fifty years later."

"Now hold on a minute!"

The illusions flew away, leaving Bridget sitting next to her brother on top of the Chrysler Building, the city once again laid out below them. Rory was rolling his eyes.

"Okay, maybe I can buy this whole Munsee story," he said. "But two-hundred-year-old guys running for Mayor? That's a little much."

Hex shook his head.

"No, no. It is here that we leave the story of Manhattan and move into the story of Mannahatta. Kieft had ascended to godhood; after all, nowhere is it written that a god must be nice. He ran for the post of Mayor of the Council of Twelve. Anyway, he didn't win. That dolt Alexander Hamilton ran away with it, he who'd only been a god less than a decade."

"Hamilton? The guy on the ten-dollar bill?" Rory asked.

"Yes, the guy on the ten-dollar bill." Hex made a face. "If ever a man didn't deserve immortality, it was Alexander Hamilton. But he got elected, and he's been Mayor ever since. Kieft did eventually wheel and deal his way into being appointed First Adviser to Mayor Hamilton, and the Mayor began following Kieft's lead in pretty much everything, especially with the Munsees."

"I thought you said they were gone," Bridget said.

"Their mortals were gone, but in the spirit world, in Mannahatta, the Munsee gods remained. Keep in mind, it had been their realm long before the European colonists had shown up; they had named it Mannahatta, in fact. Their connection with the island, with the *land*, was so strong that it remembered them long after their people had left. Unfortunately their relationship with the colonists' immortal gods was no better than the one their mortal counterparts had had with the colonists: neither trusted the other. Small skirmishes began to break out between the two peoples, gradually spreading throughout

Mannahatta as they fought over control of the spirit world. These fights would affect the mortal world time and time again, the worst of them causing the Draft Riots during the Civil War that almost burned the city to the ground.

"At last, the Munsees were weary of the conflict, as were we all, and so when the Mayor went to them with a compromise— Kieft's compromise, though the Munsees didn't know it—they took it. Their great sachem, Penhawitz, foolishly believed that the Mayor had always dealt with them fairly, though some others had not. But they knew nothing, because in truth no one hated the Munsees more than Mayor Hamilton, and he proved it when he sprung Kieft's great Trap."

"What was the Trap? Something in the park?" Bridget asked.

Hex turned to gaze north at the soft blue glow in the distance.

"Central Park *is* the Trap. The Mayor claimed he had it built as a peace offering to the Munsees. That was his supposed compromise. He gave it to them to live in a place where no god or man would bother them. But the minute the Munsees set foot within Central Park's borders, that blue barrier you see now leaped up and trapped them inside."

Bridget could see it in her head, the poor Munsees thinking they'd finally found their sanctuary, only to watch in horror as blue light shot up over their heads. They would have run up to the barrier, trying desperately to escape, but they could only beat hopelessly upon the walls of their new prison.

"That's horrible," she said, tears welling up in her eyes.

"The park was made by mortal hands, so the Munsees cannot feel the island anymore," Hex said. "They are cut off completely, trapped forever, which is ten times worse than being killed. The land searches for them and it cannot find them. And the consequences have been far worse than anyone suspected. I've come to believe that removing the Munsees has thrown the balance between our worlds completely out of whack. For the past hundred and thirty years it's been getting worse and worse. Haven't you noticed the weather changing? The long summers and short winters? The temperature shifting drastically from day to day? Worse, the people are getting restless. Many feel dissatisfied and lost without knowing why. This has led to riots and disorder in the past; it will again, and soon. I believe this will only get worse while the Munsees are imprisoned and the needs of the land are ignored. That is why you are so important, Rory."

"I don't understand."

"The Munsees need to be freed. I made it my life's purpose to do so, no matter what it may ask of me."

"What does this have to do with me?" Rory asked.

"The Trap was designed to be unlocked only one way, using four items together. All four items need to be used in conjunction for the Trap to open up. Only once in the last hundred and thirty years have these four parts even come close to one another, and that ended in tragedy. But I have tracked them down and I'm so close to finally bringing them together and tearing down the barriers. Then the Munsees can escape in peace and go where they will. We can finally put right the horrible events that began more than three centuries ago."

"What are the items?" Bridget asked, caught up in the grand adventure.

"The lock and the key, the belt and the power. I know where all four are. I can do this—with your help, Rory."

"What am I supposed to do, exactly?" Rory asked.

"You are the one with the power," Hex answered. "Only a Light can turn that key."

"That's why that Stranger thing was looking for me?"

"I believe so. And that's why you are in so much danger. Just as I want to free the Munsees, others want to make sure they never escape. Their power has grown since the Munsees were locked away and they are afraid of losing it again. So to my mind, you have two choices. Try to avoid capture for the rest of your life, always wondering when they will catch up to you, while the city of your birth heads toward certain catastrophe. Or break the barriers down for good and beat them before they can beat you.

"What do you say?"

6

THE SUBWAY SINGER

At the end of a small road called Stone Street, deep in the Financial District, stood a restaurant called The Old Winery. A small building dwarfed by all the huge skyscrapers around it, The Old Winery was actually not so old, having been built two years earlier on the site of another restaurant called The Old Vineyard. This fine establishment had also been liberal with the word *old*, being only five years in existence when it went under. Before that it had been The Old Grape, and The Old Bottle, and Ye Olde Sippe, and on and on, dozens of restaurants, none of which ever lasted longer than a few years before giving up.

This unbroken line of eateries went back much farther than any of their owners knew, since few records survived of the first tavern in the chain, built in the middle of the seventeenth century by a young Dutch soldier named Oloff Stevense van Cortlandt, who grew grapes in the back and made his own beer. In those days Stone Street was aptly named Brouwer—or Brewer—Street, and the short lane was lined with taverns. One stood above them all, however, roundly praised and fondly remembered as the finest tavern in the young colony, and so Oloff's Old Brewery remained, even after a fire burned it to the ground in 1698. No matter what business occupied that spot on Stone Street, if one were to wander through its back halls in just the right way, one might stumble into the main common room of the Old Brewery, which looked the same as it had three and a half centuries earlier. Only now the customers ran more to the fantastical: the nineteenth-century street-gang thugs and ghostly sailors on leave before their next voyage into the mist beyond the harbor. Sometimes their otherworldly voices leaked out into the present-day restaurant, giving the eateries a reputation for ghosts that drove them out of business sooner rather than later, but that wasn't Oloff's problem. He still tended his place as he had for hundreds of years. He didn't care what happened beyond the door. He had enough worries keeping his customers in wine and beer.

Not many gods frequented the Old Brewery, which was why the Rattle Watch frequently met there. The five of them sat silently at a table in the corner, heads hanging, until a tray of overflowing mugs crashed down, making them jump. Oloff gave them a grim look as he straightened up.

"I heard about Adriaen," he said, giving a gruff but kind nod to Alexa. "I'm sorry for your loss."

"Thank you," she said softly. She'd barely spoken since the Portrait Room. Nicholas couldn't tell if she was angry or sad. Probably a lot of both.

"You hear who they nominated to take his council seat?" Oloff continued, turning to the rest of them. They shook their heads. "John Randel Jr."

"What!" Nicholas exclaimed. "Johnny Jr.? He's a nobody! I can never even remember what he's a god of!"

"Street Construction," Albert said. "He's a nervous little guy. I think it's all the machines; they make him jumpy. I once gave him a piece of exploding gum, you know, just to be nice, and I swear he didn't stop running until he hit the Hudson."

Oloff laughed, a booming, joyous laugh that brought smiles to their sad faces.

"I wish I could have seen that!" he said, slapping his thigh. "Why doesn't your father come forward, Nicholas? He's a much greater god than this Johnny Jr."

"Father won't even leave his farm anymore," Nicholas said derisively. "He's too busy living in the past. The old coot has turned his back completely on his city. He could be doing some real good, but he's too busy moping around, blaming everyone but himself for losing the Mayor's job two hundred years ago."

"Well, that's too bad," Oloff said. "Johnny Jr. will sure have a hard time living up to Adriaen's legacy."

"He can't," Alexa said. "Dad was a god of justice."

"They just want someone they can push around," Lincoln said, balling up his fist. "I'll give 'em someone to push around."

"You do that," Simon said, rolling his eyes as he took a sip from his mug. "I'll keep your drink ready for when you get out of the Tombs in twenty years." His hand slipped and he spilled some liquid on himself, adding another mark to his already well-stained shirt.

"You're such a slob," Lincoln told him. "Do you ever wash your clothes?"

"One person's dirty shirt is another's work of art!" Simon

answered him, licking his fingers clean. "This is my tavern shirt. With every new stain, I blend in better, like camouflage."

"Why would anyone take us seriously with you two bumblers around?" Albert asked drily.

"Who cares, anyway?" Simon said. "It's not like there's a Rattle Watch anymore."

This caught them all by surprise. Simon shrugged at their startled faces.

"Don't look so shocked," he said. "Adriaen's gone. Without him, we're just a bunch of arrested adolescents, some of us none too bright." He pointed to Lincoln and then ducked to avoid the punch.

"You watch your mouth!" Lincoln shouted when he regained his balance. "We're not giving up now. We know who did this, even if everyone on the council is too thick-headed to see it."

Nicholas exchanged glances with Albert, who appeared to be giving the matter some serious thought.

"Simon's kind of right," Albert said to him. "It was fun while it lasted, but without Adriaen, we're nobodies. What can we do against someone like Kieft?"

Is that true? Nicholas thought. *Are we really powerless without Adriaen?*

"So what are you saying?" he asked. "That Kieft just gets away with murdering the only one who ever believed in us?"

"We're not gods, Nicholas," Albert answered. "It's that simple. I wish we were, but we're not. They won't even listen to us. They think we're a bunch of loudmouthed kids."

Nicholas turned to Alexa to see what she thought, but she wasn't even looking at them.

"Mind if I say something?" Oloff said. They all turned their attention to the barrel-chested innkeeper. "I remember the original Rattle Watch, from when I was mortal. They weren't much of a police force, just a bunch of volunteers, really. Regular folk, like us. And folks didn't always appreciate them running around New Amsterdam, rattling up a storm, warning of danger. Turned out to be some poor Indian out for a stroll more often then not. Most people just wanted to sleep the night. But sometimes . . . sometimes there'd be a big fire or a drunk crazy shooting up the place with his gun, and then we'd all be thankful the Rattle Watch was there to warn us. If not for them, this whole city might never have lived through its first few years. Anyway, I'm truly sorry about Adriaen. He was a good friend. I'll leave you to your beverages."

He gave them a little wave and headed back to his bar.

Nicholas didn't know what to do. Did he dare put up his little band of tricksters against the black-eyed man himself? A small voice cut in from the area around his boot, breaking his train of thought.

"Nicholas! Kids! Hello!"

He looked down. A cockroach was standing next to his shoe, holding his rat's reins in his insect hands.

"Fritz!" Nicholas exclaimed. "What are you doing here?"

"Can somebody give me a lift?" Fritz said sheepishly. "I hate talking to ankles."

Albert reached down, and Fritz hopped onto his hand. A quick ride later and the battle roach stood in the center of the table.

"I heard about Adriaen, so I came to find you," he said. "Rory is awake!"

This really shocked them. They'd all heard about the hidden Light, though they'd been sworn to secrecy.

"He's supposed to be blind to Mannahatta!" Nicholas exclaimed.

"He looked right at me," Fritz said. "Somehow, he's awake. And we've got to do something!"

They all looked to Nicholas. *What should we do?* And it suddenly never seemed clearer.

"This all means something," he said, thinking as he spoke. "The murder coming right when the only Light left wakes up? Something is going on here and we need to find out what it is. We knew when we signed on that this wouldn't be all fun and games. We just hadn't hit the hard part yet. Well, now it's hard. But we've got to grow up sometime. Might as well be today."

"Amen," Lincoln said, his face shining.

"Well spoken," Fritz added, nodding with approval. The others were nodding as well, their eyes lighting up as their leader inspired them. "So what do you think we should do about Rory?" Fritz asked.

"I have no clue," Nicholas answered him. "Maybe nothing, yet. Between the Light and the murder, I don't know what we should do."

"The Fortune Teller," Alexa said, abruptly coming back from wherever she'd been. "Father would ask her for advice. Maybe we should, too."

Albert rolled his eyes.

"Not this again. No one has found the Fortune Teller in decades, Alexa," he said. "Adriaen was a great man, but that is one story I just don't believe."

Nicholas did not scoff.

"Do you think you can find her, Alexa?" he asked.

"Father did, and I know I can uncover how he managed it from his writings," she answered.

"Then let's do it," Nicholas said firmly. "Fritz, go back and keep an eye on Rory. Make sure nothing happens to him. We can reveal ourselves once we know what we're doing. Albert, Simon, Lincoln, I want you to spread out. Ask questions and try to see if you can discover anything about the murder that we haven't heard yet. But stay out of the council's way! We don't want to tip off Kieft. Alexa, you and I are going to see this Fortune Teller of yours."

"I can't believe you're chasing after a fairy tale," Albert said.

"Hey, we're desperate, right?" Nicholas answered. "We might as well act like it."

The subway car raced north through the tunnels, bearing the Hennessy children homeward. Rory fingered the purple-beaded bracelet he now wore around his wrist, thinking about how he was so tired of hard choices. Bridget sat next to him, pouting, still mad that they'd walked away without promising to do anything. She poked him for the three hundred and fifty-sixth time (he kept count).

"I don't understand, Rory! The Munsees need us!"

"We don't know that. All I know for sure is that Hex wants us to break into a bank."

"That's where they're keeping the belt, he said. It's not like we're stealing money or anything. It's the good kind of bank robbery. The kind they make movies about."

"It's dangerous," Rory said. "And we don't know if it'll work. The bank is run by a god, for Pete's sake. And this Tobias doesn't sound like a happy, fun god, either."

"Hex is a magician, and you're a superhero. What could go wrong?"

A businessman sitting across from them glanced up, chuckling to himself at their conversation.

"I haven't decided yet," Rory replied. "I need to be sure."

"They're looking for you, he said. They'll find you."

"I've got this now." Rory held up his wrist, the bracelet dangling prominently. Bridget reached out to brush her fingers on the cool, purple beads.

"What did he call these again?" she asked.

"Wampum."

"It will protect you from the Strangers," Hex had told him seriously, handing over the bright jewelry. *"But it won't last forever. Nor is it all-powerful. It will keep you as safe as possible while you make up your mind."*

"What if something else finds you? Something worse? You could be killed."

"I just want to think about it," Rory said. "Now leave me alone."

Bridget looked ready to retort, but before she could, the door between the cars slid open and three tall black men entered. One had a salty beard and three teeth at most. The second stood shorter than the other two, with a large nose and bushy eyebrows. The third had a finely groomed pencil-thin mustache and the biggest smile in the world. He opened his mouth wide, flashing his perfect white teeth.

"Hello, ladies and gentlemen! We are the Troubadours, here to sing you the songs a' yesteryear! If you like what-cha hear, don't be shy 'bout showing your appreciation. And remember, we like the clink-clink-clink of coins, but our sing-ing sounds sweeter with the flit-flit-flit of the paper money. So here we go!"

And out came the prettiest three-part harmony Rory had heard in a long while. Rory's heart lifted at the sound. There weren't too many people on the subway car, but the Trouba-dours held everyone's complete attention until the song ended with a lovely, long chord.

"Thank you, my fellow New Yorkers. You are too kind. So don't be shy 'bout provin' it!"

They launched into a bouncier tune while they walked down the car collecting money. The smiling man held out his hat, a beaten-up fedora that quickly filled with an impressive number of bills. Eventually, he stopped in front of Rory and Bridget. Bridget pulled on Rory's arm, wanting him to toss in a dollar. Rory reached into his pocket and snagged one. He was about to drop it in the hat when the man grabbed his wrist. Rory looked up to see the man staring at him intently.

"Don't you worry 'bout that. Put your money back in your pocket. We don' take dollars from the likes a' you."

Rory pulled his hand back. The man still stared at him, with the other two coming up behind him. They all looked down at Rory knowingly. He shrank back.

"What are you talking about?"

The man with the grin winked.

"What do you dream 'bout, I wonder. I bet I know."

Rory started. "Who are you?"

The smiling man made a soothing sound. "Don' you be frightened, boy. We mean you no harm. The Troubadours are your friends, you can count on that. And maybe one day you can be our friend, too."

"I don't know what you mean."

"It's all in the eyes," the smiling man said. "Anyone can see it, if they're looking for it. You'd do well to remember that. I'll be seeing you soon, I'm sure. After all, you can't hide. Not anymore."

He poured the money from his hat into a little bag at his belt and placed the hat back on his head. He gave a little mock tip of the cap and then turned to walk on. The other two Troubadours followed suit, tipping their caps. They began to sing a catchy tune about the city, snapping their fingers as they disappeared through the door at the end of the car.

Rory didn't say another word for the rest of the ride home. He kept picturing the singer's eyes as he told Rory he couldn't hide. Shuddering, he pulled at his bracelet. It was okay. He was safe. For now . . .

They reached their apartment without any more adventures. Night had fallen, but Mrs. Hennessy still hadn't come home from work. Rory immediately locked himself in his room, leaving Bridget to talk to him through his door. But though she tried to needle him into telling her what he was going to do, she was met with silence.

Giving up, Bridget skipped over to the bathroom. She washed her hands and stared at herself in the mirror. Hex's plan seemed pretty simple. They'd break into this bank where the belt was being held. Hex said he knew where the other items were, the key and the lock, and he'd pick them up on the way. When everything was brought together, Rory would put on the belt, turn the key, and let the Munsees free. Then no one would want him anymore and he could go back to his normal life. Easy as pie. If it was up to her, they'd already be on their way to that vault, off to the rescue. She pictured those poor frightened Indians waiting to be freed. They'd be staring at that blue shield, wishing it would fall. Then suddenly there'd be a rumble and a loud flash. When the smoke cleared, lo and behold a huge hole would appear right in the center of the Trap. And standing in the middle, smoking megagun in her hand, would be the most beautiful girl in the world: Bridget the Brave.

She smiled at this mental picture. She wondered where she'd find a megagun. Hex probably had one. You didn't go on a rescue mission without a megagun. That's just standard operating procedure. She'd better be allowed to fire it. It was what she was good for, after all.

Sure, she was jealous. Rory had these great powers. And she couldn't even move when her brother was attacked. You always rush to help your companions when they're in danger. Once again, it's standard procedure in the hero business. She'd seen all the sword and sorcery flicks like *The Lord of the Rings*. She loved space epics like *Star Trek* and even ancient classics like *Star Wars*. But her absolute favorite was *Charlie's Angels*. Pretty and butt-kicking at the same time. Just like her.

Bridget did a karate chop with her hands. She let out a blood-curdling yell and swung a death blow through the air. The yell turned to a whimper of pain as she accidentally slammed her palm into the electric-toothbrush holder. She hopped around the bathroom, waving her hand frantically. Stupid.

Still rubbing her palm, she left the bathroom, went into her bedroom, and closed the door. Flopping on her bed, she reached over and picked up her only Barbie doll. She normally didn't play with such girlie things, but her brother had given it to her for Christmas and so she'd decided to keep the doll but give it a Bridget-style makeover. She'd wrapped a bandanna around the Barbie's head and taped a huge double-edged sword from one of Rory's old toys to her hand. This was Malibu Death Barbie. A fashion-conscious dealer of justice. The last thing her enemies saw before their horrible dismemberment was a flash of pink lipstick and a really big knife.

Why couldn't she be like Malibu Death Barbie? If only she could see what Rory saw without his help. She wouldn't be any help if she couldn't even see what was coming until it was too late. She scanned the room intently, peering into every nook and cranny. Nothing. Not even a pixie.

She dropped her head to the pillow. She was useless. No wonder her dad had left. He probably looked down at her crying in her crib and decided that he couldn't take being around such a useless, stupid baby. But she really didn't believe that. She could see him smiling in his photos and she knew he'd never just abandon them. She turned onto her back, thinking.

She'd always believed that he was out there fighting to get back to them.

And now there was a whole world of danger and magic around them. Maybe he was caught up in it! Maybe he was just like Rory, with special powers and a need to do what's right. Maybe he was out there right now, fighting down in the subways and through the alleys, trying to make sure justice was done. Her eyes shone at the thought.

She'd be strong, like her father and Rory. Her brother was going to need her, she knew it, and when that day came she'd be ready. She wouldn't let him down again. She would come through, just like Malibu Death Barbie would. She'd come through and then some.

～～∧～～

That night, Rory dreamed of his father. As always, his dream was vivid, almost more like a real experience than a dream. Mr. Hennessy towered over him, tickling him to make him laugh, though Rory squirmed as he tried to get away. A younger Mrs. Hennessy sat at the table in the corner, baby Bridget laughing in her arms. Bridget loved to laugh as a baby. But Rory didn't feel like laughing. He knew something was happening.

Mr. Hennessy stood up and pulled his jacket over his big shoulders. Mrs. Hennessy looked up from feeding and asked him to pick up some cheese and juice while he was out. He smiled and promised that he'd be back in a jiffy. The smile never reached his eyes.

Mr. Hennessy made a face at baby Bridget. She laughed,

taken in by him as always. He looked down at Rory sitting on the floor and threw him a smile, too. He'd be right back, he promised. With gummy worms from the store just for his little soldier. But Rory suspected that this was a trick. He'd learned from a young age that Mr. Hennessy loved to play tricks—on Mom, on Rory, on everyone. Mr. Hennessy was the king of tricks, and Rory expected no less this time around. What kind of trick this new one would be, he had no idea. He'd have to wait and see the big finish.

But then something else caught his eye, down on the floor, by the heating vent. A cockroach, standing up, waving at him. He waved back. Mr. Hennessy's smile slipped a little. Rory laughed as the cockroach waved again, its tiny antennae wiggling. His smile gone completely, Mr. Hennessy gave Rory one last strange look before opening the door and striding through it, closing it behind him firmly with a dull thud. Rory knew he was gone for good. His daddy's last big trick was a disappearing act. Rory didn't even cry. He felt anger, so much anger. He ran up to the window and called for his secret friend at the top of his lungs. He called him to make it all go away. . . .

Rory awoke in a cold sweat. The moon still shone through his window, and his clock informed him it was the middle of the night. Mumbling to himself, he turned over and fell back asleep, never noticing the small form on the windowsill, watching him from the darkness.

THE GHOSTLY SHIP

The moon shone down as Alexa hurried up the walk to the little town house with the small, gated lawn that sat at the end of the alley, hemmed in on both sides by soaring skyscrapers. She pushed through the gate and knocked on the door, glancing behind her to make sure no one was watching. Eventually, she heard a latch turn. The door opened to reveal Councilor Whitman, God of Optimism.

"Alexa! What a magnificent surprise!" he exclaimed, showering her with exclamation points, as usual.

"It's nice to see you, too," she said, smiling wryly at the god's enthusiasm.

"Come in, come in," Whitman said, ushering her through the door. He led her to his small study, where she plopped down on an overstuffed chair. "What can I do for you?" he asked.

"Father would always stay with you when he went to council meetings. He'd often say that you and Caesar Prince were the only two councilors he trusted, and with Caesar it was more of an understanding than trust."

"Well, Caesar is an odd bird," Whitman admitted. "But he was the only one besides your father on the council who maintained that the First Adviser was up to no good. Without any proof, of course."

"You can't tell me you think Kieft had nothing to do with my father's death!"

Whitman sighed.

"Perhaps he did, perhaps he didn't. But bringing it up again and again will only close people's ears to your warnings. Kieft bound a lot of people to him when he sprung his trap on the Indians. I think deep inside their hearts many knew it wasn't right, but they were frightened of the Munsees and so they went along with it, and not reluctantly, either. To believe that Kieft is an evil murderer now would be to admit that they did a horrible wrong back then, and no one is prepared to do that. Not yet, at any rate. But I'm not blind. I can see that more and more longtime councilors are being replaced by low-level lackeys. Johnny Randel Jr.? It's an outrage, a disservice to your father's memory. But you need proof, not baseless accusations. And the fact that no god can be a party to another god's murder is a strong mark against your case. But that being said, I know everything will work out swimmingly, you just wait and see!"

Alexa almost snorted. The irrepressible god just couldn't go more than a few minutes without looking on the bright side. It was more than a little annoying.

"Father once told me that he stayed with you so often, he began leaving some of his books here," she said. "I was hoping to go through them."

Whitman pointed to the stairs.

"He left scores of books in his room upstairs. You're welcome to them. I'm sure you'll find something helpful!"

Rory hadn't slept well, and so he had no patience the next morning when Bridget burst into his room.

"We can be there by noon if we hurry!"

"I'm not going anywhere," Rory said. "And neither are you."

"But the Munsees . . . you have to do it!"

"I don't have to do anything. They're not family. It's sad, but that doesn't mean I have to risk your life and Mom's life and mine for them."

"But the balance."

"How do we even know Hex is telling the truth?" Rory asked. "We don't know him. Anyway, he said there will be other Lights. Let one of them grow up and take care of this."

"They won't grow up! They'll be taken." Bridget was hopping up and down she was so mad.

"I wasn't taken by anything. If I survived, they can survive."

"But . . ."

"Look, I haven't made up my mind yet. Maybe I will do it. Maybe I'll go risk my life and our family's future based on some crazy magician telling me I have to save some Indian tribe I've never even heard of before. Who knows. But Hex doesn't need you either way. The last thing I want to do is explain to Mom why another member of the family is never coming home. So no matter what I decide, you can just forget about coming along."

Bridget got right in Rory's face.

"If it were me—"

Rory exploded.

"Well, it's not you. It's me. And you're not going anywhere near Raisin Street. That's the way it's going to be."

"You can't tell me what to do," Bridget replied. "You're not my father!"

"Well, the next time you see Dad, you ask him what he thinks you should do! Until then you do what I say!"

Bridget burst into tears and ran out of the room. Rory felt bad, but he couldn't risk her. It was too dangerous.

Even Mrs. Hennessy noticed something was wrong. At breakfast she sat through the silence between her two children. After trying in vain to get a conversation started, she made an attempt to get to the bottom of it.

"Is something going on between you two?"

Rory shook his head while Bridget glowered.

"No," he said. "Why?"

"I could store frozen turkeys in here, it's so frigid. Did you guys have a fight?"

Bridget looked sideways at Rory.

"Rory won't take me out. I want to go . . ."

She trailed off, remembering her vow of silence.

"Where, honey? Where do you want Rory to take you?"

Trapped, Bridget thought quickly.

"Shopping. I wanted to go shopping, and Rory wouldn't take me."

Rory stepped in quickly.

"We don't have the money right now."

Mrs. Hennessy looked pained.

"What do you need, honey? Maybe I can pick it up for you on the way home from work."

Bridget shrank, hating that money had come into the conversation. Rory felt ashamed for his part in bringing it up. There was never enough money. They all knew it, and they never mentioned it.

"It's not important," Bridget said.

Mrs. Hennessy wouldn't have it.

"We can go shopping today. I've barely taken a vacation in two years. Mr. Corgin can give me a day. I'll get you whatever you want. My treat."

Bridget smiled bravely, caught. She couldn't say no now.

"Sounds great."

"It'll be just us girls. It'll be fun!"

Mrs. Hennessy went back to eating. Bridget and Rory exchanged a glance, feud momentarily forgotten in their concern. They'd have to be more careful from now on. No matter what happened, their mother was to be left in the dark.

Mrs. Hennessy got her day off, though it didn't sound like her boss was happy about it, which made everyone nervous. But she never wavered, rushing Bridget through breakfast to get them on the subway and downtown before the morning slipped by. Rory watched them go, glad to get his sister out of the way. He sat in the empty apartment for a while, trying to figure out what he should do. Not getting anywhere, he pulled on some old sneakers, grabbed his basketball, and ran out the door into the brightening morning.

The basketball courts where Rory played cut into Inwood Hill Park, which was right around the corner from his house. A lifelong resident of Inwood, Mrs. Hennessy loved to point out that Inwood Hill Park was home to the only primeval forest still left on the island of Manhattan. Only here did anything remain from the beginnings of New York; the rest had been cut down and paved over long ago. The trees grew tall and dense along the cliffs of Inwood Hill Park, where small paths led toward the top, looking down on the two rivers bleeding into each other far below. Rory had wandered along the trails a few times as a boy, but he never liked the way it felt under the ancient trees. It was as easy to lose your way on the ancient paths as it was deep within the winding streets of Greenwich Village. There were many stories of young lovers getting lost and being led astray. First they'd hear strange sounds, then far-off laughter. The trees would rustle above them, limbs bending under the invisible weight of something stalking them from up high. Frightened, the couple would bolt, heading for safety. Thinking they were running back toward the tame park around the pond, they'd instead find themselves bursting out of the trees into the nothingness high above the Hudson. They'd grasp in vain for the cliff face behind them, and no one would hear them scream as they fell into the raging river below. This forest was small but mean, like a tiny pit bull on a leash. Admired from a distance, but approached at your own peril.

The area at the base of the cliffs by the river had been

cleared to make room for several playing fields, including a
section dedicated to basketball. Rory grabbed a court with an
old rim at the end. It had been bent from a few too many hanging dunks, and he had to adjust his angles to make his shots.
After fifteen minutes or so, he was hitting baseline jumpers
and kisses off the glass like always. He sure could shoot, if
he did say so himself. Even the homeboys from Washington
Heights were impressed by this little white boy knocking down
fifteen-foot jumpers like nothing. He worked on that jumper as
his mind ran through Hex's proposition.

The plan seemed pretty dangerous. They'd break into this
bank where the belt was being held. Hex said he knew where
the other items were—the key and the lock—and when everything was brought together, Rory would put on the belt, turn
the key, and let the Munsees free. Then no one would want
him anymore, and he could go back to his normal life. A little
danger in exchange for his life back. Was that so bad?

He set himself to take another shot, but just as he launched
the ball into the air, a horn blared loudly nearby, startling him
into sending the ball over the backboard and into the trees. He
looked around, but no one else seemed to have noticed. He'd
heard that horn before, back when he first saw the Indian in
the trees. But he didn't see any Indians now. Shaking his head
to clear it, he walked over toward the trees to grab his ball.
He bent over to pick it up but almost dropped it again when
another horn note sounded, this one almost in his ear. Rory
straightened up quickly to look around, but he didn't see anyone with a horn. He turned toward the river, and what he saw
through the trees drove the horn right out of his head.

Slowly gliding down the river toward him was a ship. Or at least the tattered remains of one. It sported three tall masts with ratty sails billowing out despite the huge holes ripped through them. Battered crow's nests sat atop the two taller masts, and Rory could just make out a small figure up on one of them, pointing out toward the Hudson. Rotted wood hung from the hull of the ship, forming huge gaps in the side that should have sunk the boat, but somehow the vessel stayed afloat. Cannons poked out of the side, some half-hanging over the water. It looked for all the world like a pirate ship falling apart. But it couldn't be. *What was it?* Maybe it was Old Broken-down Ship Week at South Street Seaport.

"Finally you have heard me. Did Peter send you?"

Rory whirled around at the sound of this new voice. He came face-to-face with a man in an old-fashioned black wool jacket with a white collar. The man held a trumpet. Rory stared.

"Was that you blowing the horn?" Rory asked.

"Of course, young squire," the man said. "I am the Trumpeter, after all. So Peter didn't send you? What is the use of posting me here to give warning when no one heeds me? Things have been run very poorly, if you ask me. Danger is approaching, and I am blowing my trumpet and no one hears!"

"I heard you. And I heard you the other day. That was you!"

The Trumpeter gave a snort.

"And now you stroll up, two sunrises later, like you are out on a morning constitutional. Why do I even bother? Why should I kill myself watching out for danger if you're all just going to ignore me? I slave for you people, working myself half to death, or at least it would be half to death if I wasn't already dead, and I get nothing in return. Nothing! Not even a pie! I don't know why I bother!"

The Trumpeter sputtered out. Already dead? Rory didn't want to think about that one, so instead he smiled apologetically.

"I'm sorry. I didn't know what it was."

"It's not hard. It's a trumpet. See?" He blew the horn, almost bursting Rory's eardrums. "I mean, it's obviously not an oboe."

"Please," Rory said, putting his hands over his ears. "I'm here now. You don't need to blow it again."

"Fine," the Trumpeter said. "So is Peter coming?"

"I don't know who that is."

"You don't know Peter? Ol' Peg Leg Pete? Don't tell him I called him that. He hates it."

"I don't know who you're talking about," Rory said.

"Well, if you see him, tell him about the danger."

"What danger?"

The Trumpeter pointed out to the ship.

"The *Half Moon* is sailing. That can only mean one thing. A storm is coming. It only sails before a storm."

Rory watched the ghostly ship sailing closer, a shudder running down his spine.

"What kind of storm?" he asked.

"It's not my job to figure that out," the Trumpeter replied. "That is for those more important than myself. But I know danger when I see it, and that's why I'm blowing my horn, just like Peter told me to."

"Is that why you blew it two days ago?" Rory asked. "Because of this ship?"

The Trumpeter shook his head.

"Oh no. I saw someone chasing Van der Donck over the river, so I sounded out to warn the citizenry. But no one heard me, as usual. Do you think Peter has forgotten about me?"

Something in the Trumpeter's sad voice got to Rory.

"Nah," Rory replied. "And if I see him, I'll be sure to tell him."

The Trumpeter brightened.

"You do that! You just go and do that! Everyone must be warned! And tell ol' Peg Leg Pete I like blueberry. For my pie, I mean! I don't think a pie is too much to ask, do you?"

With that he turned and ran into the trees. Just before he disappeared, he spun around and blew his horn.

"That one's for you, young master!" he cried. "Danger!"

And then he was gone.

Rory smiled ruefully. He knew he was in danger, all right. He didn't need a trumpet to tell him that. The ship had just about reached him, and he wanted a closer look. So he walked down to the shore, not noticing the black shadow that danced behind him before disappearing into the trees.

8

THE STRANGER

At the northern tip of the island, the waters of the Harlem River Ship Canal dipped into the land, forming a salt marsh that stayed calm as the deeper waters behind it surged past under the ugly blue metal of the Henry Hudson Bridge and out into the Hudson River. Rory walked down to the waterline, keeping his eyes on the impossible ghost ship as it passed. He could hear strange voices on the breeze, yelling sailing instructions as the ship sailed by. He could make out faces now, of all races, bobbing up and down with the ship's movement. Who were these ghostly mariners? Were they trapped on the ghost ship? A face turned to him on the deck, and suddenly all those thoughts flew from his head.

It couldn't be! It was impossible!

Rory sat down heavily on a bench by the water. He blinked, and when his vision cleared the figure that had shocked him so had disappeared. He had no idea if the sailor had seen him or not. *It was nothing*, he told himself. The more he thought on it, the more convinced he became. It was nothing at all.

Rory was so focused on denying what he thought he saw

that he didn't notice the shivers at first. It took an involuntary shake of his shoulders to snap out of it, his eyes finally noticing the goose bumps on his arms. The base of his spine felt cold and numb, a creeping chill climbing up, one vertebra at a time. Looking around wildly, he searched the park for signs of shadows, but the trees and benches seemed normal and clear. Another shiver ran through him and he knew. *A Stranger is here.*

Where was it? He twisted in his seat, trying to find some sign of those searching lights. It had found him. Somehow it had found him. The chill was overpowering now, causing him to shake uncontrollably. It must be close. But where? There was no place around him to hide. His vibrating arm accidentally slammed into the hard wooden bench. Suppressing a shout of pain, he clutched his elbow to his stomach. Stupid bench. His eyes widened. Slowly, he looked down between the wooden slats into the darkness underneath. A pair of glowing eyes stared back at him as a child's pink finger reached up to graze his ankle.

"*Come.*"

Rory flew back away from the finger, falling off the bench in a heap. He could see underneath, where the familiar small boy, the Stranger, knelt on its hands and knees, beckoning to him.

"*Come.*"

"I don't want to come with you. Leave me alone!"

Rory scrambled to his knees as the Stranger climbed out from the shadow. Rory looked around wildly for help, but no one was paying attention. The creature with the glowing eyes ambled over to him.

"*Come!*"

Its small voice sounded put off. It didn't like being denied. Rory sat on the path around the inlet, frozen in fear as the child-thing came closer.

"Leave me alone!"

The Stranger stopped a foot away, regarding Rory with its head cocked to the side like a puzzled puppy. It smiled, showing teeth that were larger than they should have been for such a small mouth. And so much sharper. The light glinted off those tiny white knives as it answered Rory's plea.

"*No!*"

The little boy-creature's eyes glowed as its smile turned evil, the lights within screaming up and out of the sockets. Rory had just enough time to raise his arm before the boy was upon him, mouth open as it brought its sharp teeth down on skin.

Wszzp!

Light blazed out for a moment, sending sparks up into the air from Rory's wrist. The bracelet! The wampum bracelet! The boy-creature stumbled back, rubbing its burning mouth. The purple beads glowed for a moment longer before fading back to a dull shine. Rory felt a wave of relief run through him. It worked! It really worked! The relief did not last long as the Stranger shook off the pain, its eyes as fierce as ever, and advanced on him once more. This time its gaze was locked on the source of the shock, the circle of wampum around Rory's wrist, and it raised its hand to reach for it.

"*Take it off! Burns. Take it off!*"

"No! Go away, or I'll burn you again! Leave me alone!"

Rory scrambled back as the child-thing kept coming, hand

stretched out before it. Rory wasn't fast enough as the Stranger reached out and grasped the bracelet. Light flared from the jewelry, scorching its skin, but this time the creature refused to let go. The Stranger tugged on the bracelet, trying to pull it loose. Horrified that the bracelet wasn't stopping it, Rory kicked the child-thing away as he pushed himself to his feet. The child stared up at him with a look of contempt.

"Never stop. Take it off you. Then bite, bite, BITE!"

Rory backed away, trying to figure out what to do. The Stranger stood between him and the exit to the park. He had only one option, little though he might like it. Gathering his strength, Rory spun around and sprinted off down the path toward the worst place he could go. Toward the cliffs.

He reached the edge of the trees and ran up the path. Afraid to look behind him, he kept running and running, to save his life. The ancient trees arched over him, covering him from all eyes. It felt like a horror movie, where the victim ignores all common sense and heads down into the basement to get away from the killer. But what else could he do? He could only run.

The path ahead split in two, with the paved section going forward and a dirt path bending off to the right. Without thinking, he veered right, crashing through the brush up the dirt trail. The trees now closed completely around him, leaning into him, scratching him with their branches, but he was too frightened to care. A vivid picture came to him of the edge of the cliff approaching and his body shooting out of the trees and onto thin air, falling to the same death as the young lovers from the tales. But he couldn't slow down. Then it would catch him and he'd be gone, bracelet or not.

The choice was taken out of his hands by a root, which slipped over his foot as he ran, bringing him down to the earth in a loud crash. He quickly rolled over, ready to fight off the devil. But nothing came. The trail behind him was empty, stretching off into the distance with no sign of anyone. He lay there, stunned, listening to the slight rustle of the wind through the leaves. Somewhere in the distance, a bird sang, and he realized that the forest sounds and his heavy breathing were the only noises he could hear. Where were the cars rolling across the bridge? Where was the bridge, for that matter? All Rory could see were trees and more trees. The small swath of primeval forest didn't go particularly deep—definitely not deep enough to block out all sights and sounds of civilization. So where was he?

Sure he'd lost his pursuer, Rory slowly sat up. He'd torn his jeans in flight, ripping the fabric on the knee. He gently rubbed his ankle, testing to see if it was twisted. It felt all right. The air smelled different, cooler and fresher. Sweeter, somehow. Everything felt so calm and quiet. It should have made him feel more at ease. Instead, he was surprised to find a knot of fear in his stomach totally unrelated to the Stranger. It was this forest. Something in this forest scared the life out of him. But there was nothing there.

A breeze ran through the trees, mussing his hair and making him shiver. After a moment the breeze died down, but the shivers did not. A cold chill shot up his spine, and he had just enough time to turn around before the Stranger was upon him.

It leaped out of a small shadow behind a rock by the side of the trail. Its teeth had blackened, but they were still sharp. The creature landed on Rory's stomach, pushing him back down to the ground. It pulled at his wrist with superhuman strength, and Rory could barely hold his own. Hot breath dripped down on his face from the Stranger's tiny mouth, smelling of rotted garbage and street sewers. Rory struggled to throw the boy-creature off, but he couldn't make it budge. Finally the creature hooked a finger underneath the bracelet and sat up on Rory's chest, ready to yank it off. Rory braced himself for the bite. But instead, the child-thing froze. After a second, Rory could see why. A spear had suddenly appeared in the center of its chest.

The Stranger brought both hands up to circle the spear, its eyes disbelieving. A thick thud announced the appearance of a second spear right next to its brother. The boy-creature fell back, clutching at the shafts with an uncomprehending look in its alien eyes. It landed in the dirt, the smooth wood sticking up like goal posts. Then the creature began to break apart, opening up like an overstuffed chair, spilling darkness and shadow all over the forest floor. The shadow sank into the earth until nothing remained but the two spears that fell over with a loud clatter.

Shocked, Rory crawled over to the fallen spears. No trace of the Stranger remained. He was reaching out to touch the wooden shafts when a rustle behind him sent him scrambling away toward a nearby rock. A pack of golden dogs bounded into view, falling over one another as they rushed into the clearing. They saw him and let out a howl. Rory tried not to panic as they surrounded him, fighting to get to him. They were just about to leap upon him when a sharp whistle set them back on their hind legs at perfect attention. Behind them, out of the shadows, stepped a tall man with light brownish-red skin. His head was shaved except for a thick mohawk of dark hair that split his scalp in two. His chest was bare, as were his legs, with only a brown loincloth covering his middle and soft moccasins on his feet. Unlike the Indian in Central Park, his cheeks were bare of tattoos.

Rory's heart skipped a beat as he recognized the Indian from the other day, standing underneath the trees. *And from my dreams.* That thought bubbled up in his mind as the Indian walked by Rory without a glance, absently petting a dog or two as he passed, and then knelt down to retrieve his spears. As he looked over the bright copper tips for damage, he spoke.

"Are you well?"

Rory didn't know if he was in more danger or not, so he thought it best to answer politely.

"I'm okay. Thank you for killing that thing."

Now the Indian did turn, and his eyes gave Rory a jolt. Deep and green-brown like the forest, but so sad and wise, they felt more familiar than the man's face. The Indian spoke again, his voice soft with a slight English accent.

"There are many more. The *Tschepsit* have always fed on the unwary. Though this one hunted bolder than most."

"It was after me."

The Indian nodded slowly. "I know, Rory."

Rory felt a shock.

"You know me?" he asked.

"Of course. And you know me. Come, we must attend to the wampum before another *Tschepsit* finds you."

He pointed to Rory's wrist, where the bracelet rested. Rory fiddled with it nervously.

"It burned its mouth."

The Indian shrugged.

"Burning is not killing. It would have taken you, bracelet or no bracelet. This wampum must be made strong again. Come."

"Are you a Munsee?"

The brave looked surprised.

"I had thought that word forgotten. Yes, young one. I would call myself a Munsee. There is much we need to speak of, now that you can see once again."

He whistled to call the dogs to him as he turned to head deeper into the forest, but Rory held back a moment.

"What is your name?" he asked hesitantly.

The Munsee turned and smiled.

"You do not remember? Wampage. I am Wampage. Come."

Wampage. That name rang familiar in Rory's head. He'd known this man once. But when? And how had he forgotten? Only one way to find out.

"I'm coming."

Picking his way carefully through the brush, Rory followed the Munsee and his dogs deep into the dark forest.

THERE'S A ROACH
IN MY SHOE

Macy's on 34th Street overflowed with people. One could barely squeeze through the throng, which was just the way Kaylee Morton liked it. It made it less likely anyone would notice her as she happened to grab some pretty clothing and walk out without paying. Glancing around, she couldn't see any security guards, so she went for it, snatching a bright scarf and tossing it in her bag with one quick motion. Without waiting to see if anyone had noticed her crime, she slowly made her way to the exit doors, not drawing attention to herself. Another day's work done well.

Kaylee didn't see the smiling girl sitting on the handbag display, even though she walked right by. In fact, *no one* noticed the girl with the impish eyes and quick hands who went by the name of Jenny Fingers. She'd earned that name back during her mortal days, so far in the past she could barely remember. She'd been Jenny O'Toole, she knew that, until her skill at stealing earned her the nickname Jenny Fingers. She became famous on the street for her talent. Stories sprung up in her wake. A shopkeeper could keep his eyes on her the whole time she skipped through his store and he would swear she took nothing, but once outside and around the corner she would always pull out the store's nicest piece of merchandise and run off laughing. These tales became legend, so after her death she was reborn as Jenny Fingers, the Goddess of Shoplifting, looking after the quick-fingered scamps who'd rather run than pay. Kaylee was one of her favorite disciples, since she was so quick on her feet and never got caught.

Jenny practically lived at Macy's. Its huge glass doors and the masses of people going through them made it very hard for her followers to get pinched. Jenny opened the large bag by her side and placed a ghostly scarf inside, laughing as it disappeared into the darkness within. Closing it with a tug, she hopped down from the display table, her mind already on other items to stick in her bottomless sack, but she never had a chance to steal them. A dark form stepped up behind her and a long arm snaked around her throat, pulling her down to the floor. A bright knife flashed through the air, ending Jenny Fingers forever. As Jenny fell, an unseen security guard stepped out and grabbed Kaylee right before she could leave the store, placing her under arrest. Her otherworldly guardian was no more, leaving Kaylee on her own.

As Kaylee was led away, hungry fingers pulled Jenny Fingers under the table, snatching the glowing locket from around her neck. Then the dark form disappeared, leaving the body of the goddess alone on the floor, the light in her eyes gone forever.

Unknowingly passing by the table under which poor Jenny Fingers lay, Bridget followed her mom through the huge store, struggling to keep her in sight. They reached the escalators, where Mrs. Hennessy took her daughter's hand.

"Down one floor. You ready? Isn't this exciting? Mother-daughter day, just you and me. I hope you know the type of shoes you want. Don't let the saleswoman try to sell you on something you don't like. Be firm. Ready? Here goes!"

They stepped on the escalator. Bridget was getting excited. Shoes! Pretty new shoes! But what kind of shoes? Open-toe? Sandals for the beach? Sneakers? There were so many choices.

She thought about Rory's face that morning. She'd already forgiven him for their fight. She just hoped he didn't get into any trouble without her there to save him. He wasn't good with trouble. He was more of a thinker. Bridget was the butt-kicker in the family. She was the muscle; he was the planner. She just wished she knew what he was planning. . . .

They reached the kids' shoe department. As always, the sheer number of shoes took Bridget's breath away.

"So beautiful . . ."

Mrs. Hennessy looked down at her daughter's shining face and smiled.

"Now try not to get distracted. Go!"

Bridget rushed down the aisles of shoes, leaving her mother to shop another section. Her head swam with all the choices. She saw a lovely pair of flip-flops with a big yellow sunflower over each big toe. She looked at a wonderful pair of pink sneakers that had tiny little zippered pockets on the sides just large enough to fit a single dime—as useful as plastic fruit, but so *cute*. A juicy pair of Pumas caught her eye. She lifted them off the shelf and almost screamed. A cockroach stood inside the left one, waving two of its brown insect legs.

"Hello! Bridget!" it said.

"You're a talking cockroach!" Bridget said loudly. Another shopper looked at her oddly and moved away. She leaned in and whispered, "Rory said he saw something like you."

The roach sat on the lip of the shoe as it cursed to itself.

"You can see me. I knew it! I thought Rory might have begun using his gift to point out Mannahatta to other mortals and I was pretty sure he'd start with you. Looks like you're already at the point where you don't need Rory's help at all to see into our world. A little girl like you wandering around Mannahatta? My head aches at the thought of it. Do you mind?"

The roach reached up and lifted its head up and off. Under the insect shell there was a flash of pink as a small human face was revealed. Bridget gasped.

"You're a little man!"

The man-roach pointed a leg at her disapprovingly.

"I'm a roach. I'm no man."

"But you have a head!"

"This is what roaches really look like. This is our armor."

He knocked his chest, which made a hollow sound.

"So you're a guy in a suit!" she said.

"Battle armor! This is our battle armor."

"Do you do battle a lot?"

"I am a battle roach. I've been fighting since before your mother's mother was even thought of. We used to fight for the Mayor, but we had a bit of a falling out. Now we're on our own."

"The roaches are out on their own?" said Bridget, trying to understand.

"Not all of us. Not even most of us. Just me and my people. Where are my manners? I haven't even told you my clan name. I'm Fritz M'Garoth of the M'Garoth clan."

"I'm Bridget."

She reached out to shake his hand but pulled back when she realized the physical impossibility. Fritz snorted.

"I know who you are." Fritz looked over her shoulder. "Is your mother nearby?"

Bridget looked around. Mrs. Hennessy stood on the other side of the walkway, looking at sweaters.

"She's way over there. She can't hear us."

"She can't hear *me* no matter what. I just don't want her thinking you've gone loony. Put the shoes down and pretend to look around."

She replaced the Pumas on the shelf and made a big show of checking out the plain brown sandals next to them.

"Are we like spies or something?"

"Try not to move your lips too much. Where's your brother?"

She moved down to a ridiculously ugly pair of Birkenstocks, trying to keep her lips closed.

"E's ack ome."

She heard Fritz snort.

"You can move your lips more than that. You look like a bad ventriloquist."

She pouted, giving Fritz a mean look.

"I said: he's back home."

"That's good. I was hoping he'd stay put today. I've been watching over him since he was a baby, and I've watched you both grow up. But now he's in great danger. My friends and I didn't want to contact Rory before we knew more—he's probably freaked out enough as it is—but we really have no idea what's going on with him. So I decided to follow you and introduce myself. Get a little information before revealing myself to your brother. At least find out how he woke up. Can you help me with that, do you think?"

Bridget knew she had no reason to trust this little roach-man, but something about that honest, open face put her at ease. So she explained about Hex and his magic tricks. Then she went on to talk about the Munsee rescue mission. As she spoke, Fritz's face drained of all color.

"That has been tried before," he said. "A long time ago we sent in a team to turn that key. It ended in disaster. Everyone died in the attempt. This Hex person may mean well, but this is much too dangerous for Rory."

The shoes in front of Bridget blurred as her eyes filled with tears. And she'd tried to push Rory to help Hex. Fritz paced inside the Puma.

"But Rory is in great danger, anyway," he said, talking to himself. "The Strangers will come back. There has to be a way to keep him safe."

Bridget brushed her tears away and stood up straight.

"So what can I do?"

Fritz pulled his helmet on, becoming a full cockroach once again.

"Don't do anything. I'll talk to my friends and come back tonight. Tell Rory not to do anything until I arrive! Okay?"

"Okay."

The cockroach saluted and crawled away. Bridget looked at the Pumas. Cute. But even though she knew now that the cockroach was just a suit of armor, it still gave her the willies. So no Pumas for her.

"Any luck?"

Fritz had left just in time. Her mom walked up behind her. Caught off guard, Bridget looked around at the remaining shoes wildly. She had no idea what she wanted. Then she saw them.

"Those. I like those."

Mrs. Hennessy wrinkled her nose.

"But those are boots, honey. I think they have steel tips. I don't even know why they make them in children's sizes. Are you sure those are what you want?"

Bridget nodded, grabbing them from the shelf.

"Absolutely. They're perfect."

No matter what might pop up in the future, at least she'd be ready to put a dent in its head.

10

WAMPAGE

Alexa led Nicholas down a dark alley on the Lower East Side. He cursed as he stumbled over a fallen garbage can.

"Are you sure it's here?" he asked crossly, kicking the garbage can away. Alexa turned and put a finger to her lips.

"Be quiet!" she hissed. "Remember where we are. This was the only entry I could decipher, or we would have gone after a different door, believe me. Now try not to call attention to yourself."

She continued leading them down the alley. Nicholas made a face at Alexa's back. He had searched many times for the Fortune Teller, and he'd never found anything but rumors. Alexa had always maintained that her father visited the Teller the three times allotted, but after studying her father's journals through the night, she found reference to only one of the doors. It was just their luck that the door was in such a bad part of town.

This section of the Lower East Side had once been filled with tenements, poorly constructed apartment buildings with no bathrooms or electricity that were so tightly bunched together that no sunlight could peek through. Children grew up inside these foul structures without ever seeing the light of day. Death and misery were the daily companion of the tenement dwellers, and their lives were often painfully brief. Their plight was eventually discovered and publicized by the great crusading photographer Jacob Riis, and the tenements were torn down and the people within given help. But the memory of their suffering was so strong that the shadows of the tenements remained here in Mannahatta, filled with the angry, lost souls who had once called them home.

Looking around at the dismal place, Nicholas began to regret sending Albert, Lincoln, and Simon out into the city for news. He'd feel a little more comfortable with a few more eyes watching his back. A moan made him jump.

"I hate this place," he complained. He knew whining wasn't heroic, but he couldn't help it.

"Me too," Alexa said. "Father brought me here once, to show me why we must never forget who we fight for. I couldn't wait to leave. And I heard that some of the gangs have been hiding out here."

"I heard that, too. If you don't mind the cold hand of a damned soul on your neck, it's not a bad place to lay low."

Alexa shuddered. "Let's do this quick and be free of here."

They hurried down the thin, dark alley. Above them, shadows moved past the darkened windows. Nicholas tried not to look, for he did not want to attract any more attention from those miserable creatures. Alexa finally pulled up in front of a dirty, rusted iron door.

"Here we are."

Nicholas crept forward, gazing intently at the run-down entrance.

"Are you sure?"

"It's where Father said it would be. One of the three doors."

Finding the Fortune Teller was not meant to be easy. There were only three doors, and seekers were only allowed to pass through each door once. After a door was used, it would be closed to the seeker forever. The location of these doors had always been a closely guarded secret known to very few, and those who had guarded that secret had long since faded away. So now no one knew where to find the doors. Somehow Adriaen had tracked them down, through study or long years of searching. If he had not left a clue to the location of at least one of the doors, the knowledge would have been lost with his death. *That is, if this really is one of the doors,* thought Nicholas with no small measure of doubt.

They stood there a moment, frozen, each unwilling to be the one to turn the knob. A moan from far above finally spurred them to reach forward and open it together. The scent of exotic spices and sweet smoke drifted out of the open doorway. They quickly ducked inside, closing the door on the misery outside.

The room they entered was smoky and dim, lit by only a few candles along the walls. A small couch sat across from a folding table with a cardboard box underneath and a single folding chair behind it. Sitting on the folding chair was an enormously fat woman in a bright red and gold dress, smoking an equally fat cigar. She turned and spat in the corner before addressing them.

"You here to donate your clothes?" she asked in a low growl.

Confused, Nicholas and Alexa exchanged a glance.

"Um, no," Nicholas answered.

"Furniture, then?" The woman looked past them, trying to see what they brought. "Bring it up here. I don't have all day. It better have all its legs, whatever it is! No three-legged tables, can't move 'em!"

Nicholas and Alexa were thoroughly confused.

"Um, we don't have any furniture," Alexa said. "We thought . . . that is . . ."

"Out with it!" the woman boomed. "It's not old board games, is it? If I see one more Monopoly board with only a shoe and Park Place left, I'm gonna scream."

"We're not here for that," Nicholas said, completely lost. "We wanted a seeing."

A look of understanding dawned on the woman's face.

"You came through *that* door. I didn't notice. It's been such a long while since anyone has come through *that* door that I don't even pay attention anymore. So no donations, huh? It's fortune-telling for you. Hold on a second . . ."

She leaned down and rifled through the cardboard box. She lifted out various odds and ends, looking for something. There seemed to be far more items in the box than should have been able to fit inside. Finally, she pulled out a dirty old crystal ball. Plopping it down on the table, she dusted it off.

"There we are. Go on, pull up the couch."

They grabbed the couch, dragged it over in front of the table, and sat down. The couch proved both low and extremely uncomfortable, but they made no complaint. The Fortune Teller gazed down at them, puffing on her cigar.

"So, you have payment?"

Nicholas pulled out an old knife from his jacket and handed it over.

"My father gave me this knife and taught me how to whittle with it," he said, giving it a sad look. "It is the only gift, both the knife and the skill, I remember getting from him."

"Well, hand it over, hand it over," the Fortune Teller said. "Old knife, a little dull, but maybe still useful."

The covetous look on her face told Nicholas that the gift was more than just useful. She turned to Alexa. "And you, dear?"

Alexa reluctantly pulled out a small ribbon and handed it over, though not without a last sorrowful caress.

"It was my mother's," she said simply and left it at that. The Fortune Teller took the ribbon and placed both gifts in the box at her feet.

"So let's take a look, shall we," she said, gazing into her ball. The two Rattle Watchers leaned in. Eventually, the Fortune Teller began to speak, and what she told them turned their blood to water. It was so much worse than they'd imagined. . . .

Rory struggled to keep up with Wampage as they made their way through the trees. He stumbled over fallen branches and scratched his arms on brambles. He asked the tall Indian question after question, but Wampage refused to speak. They walked for a long way, much farther than should have been possible, the dogs running ahead and then bounding back again and again. All of Inwood Hill Park couldn't have been much larger than a half hour's stroll, but they never seemed to reach the end of the trees. Finally, Rory spied a clearing up ahead. Expecting to come out at Dyckman Street, Rory was surprised to step into an open area in the middle of the forest. A small cave jutted out of the ground, the smoldering remains of a fire in its mouth. More dogs waited, barking as they greeted their fellows back from the hunt. But what drew Rory's eye was the large mound of white in the center of the clearing.

"What is that?" he asked.

Finally, Wampage spoke.

"It is a shell pit. Come closer."

Stepping up, Rory could see that the mound was in fact made up of thousands of shells of all shapes and sizes, most white but some purple or black. He reached out to pick one up.

"Do not touch!" Wampage shouted, and Rory pulled his hand back quickly.

"Why not?" Rory asked.

"It is not for you to touch."

"But they're just shells."

"These are not just shells, little one. This is what makes a Munsee. Give me your bracelet."

Rory pulled off the string of beads and handed it over. Wampage laid it carefully atop the pile, and to Rory's surprise, the bracelet began to glow.

"What's happening?" he asked in wonder.

"Your wampum was weak. This will make it strong."

"Is that what those shells are for? To make wampum strong?"

Wampage shook his head.

"No! This is where wampum comes from, where the weavers would work to make our jewelry and amulets. This was the source of our strength, this and the others like it, which have since been lost. But now the Munsees are gone, and only I remain to protect this last shell pit."

"Could you make another bracelet?" Rory asked. "For my sister?"

"I am sorry, Rory," Wampage replied. "If you come across more wampum, the bracelet will let you know, but I cannot make you new pieces. I am not a weaver. All those with the knowledge are trapped within the Blue Abomination. I remain to protect the shell pit, but I have no power to help my people. Not anymore."

"Why aren't you in the Trap, too?" Rory asked.

Wampage's eyes grew distant and sad.

"When we received word of the Mayor's offer of Central Park, I did not trust it. I was shocked when our sachem, Penhawitz, agreed to take the Mayor's gift. His son, Tackapausha, convinced him that this was the only way to end our endless strife. Tackapausha had always been a peaceful man, and he believed the Mayor's promises. I did not trust so easily, not after centuries of blood. I was the fighter, Tackapausha the diplomat, and Penhawitz would usually hear our arguments and find a middle road to follow. So on the eve of my people's journey to the park, I made my case against Tackapausha, he who was my brother in all but blood, before Penhawitz and the elders of my people, begging them to turn away from this mad course of action. But Penhawitz would listen only to his son, and brushed aside my warnings. I am ashamed to say I gave in to my anger. I cursed their gullibility and left in a rage. I came north alone to calm myself. Soon, I was surprised to find dogs pouring into camp. They were the dogs of my people; why were they leaving the dogs behind? Who would protect the tribes?

"I rushed back to see what was happening, but it was too late. I could not get in, and they could not get out. I heard them crying, but I could not see them. I sent them dogs, but the dogs would not stay where they could not feel the land. I spoke to them, but I could not help them and their cries tore at my heart. Penhawitz commanded me through the barrier to leave and save what I could. I am ashamed to say I did not argue. I was glad to escape the sound of my people's tears before it tore my sanity away like bark from a dead tree. The guilt still plagues me. If only I hadn't lost my temper that last meeting before the elders. . . . If I had found a way to convince Penhawitz of the plan's folly instead of stomping off like a spoiled child, maybe I could have prevented my people's tragedy. Instead, I am exiled. All I can do is remain here to protect our last great shell pit and await the end of days."

Rory looked around the small camp and felt pity for this once-proud warrior.

"How did I meet you? I don't remember any of it."

Wampage sat down by his fire and poked at the embers with a spear, absently scratching the neck of a dog lolling at his feet with his other hand.

"Why should you? I took that memory away. After all, you asked me to."

This simple statement rocked Rory.

"What?" he cried. "I *asked* you to? Asked you to do what?"

"To take away your sight. I met you when you were but a small babe. Your mother would push you through the woods and you would see me. So I knew you were *Sabbeleu*, what the newcomers call a Light. I had not seen one in so long. I made your mother sleep, and we would visit. I took you here to see the shell pit, and I told you many stories of my people. We were . . . friends."

"I don't remember any of that," Rory marveled. "I do dream about you. I just can't remember much about what happens in the dreams."

"Maybe one day you will remember our talks," Wampage replied. "I would like to think those stories will survive."

"What happened?"

"You cried my name one night, and I came at your call. I never leave the woods, but your voice held such pain, I crossed over the streets and climbed to your window. You tearfully told me of your father and his betrayal of your family and said over and over that it was because of you. Because you were different, that was why he left. He fooled you into thinking he cared, but he never did because you were not like him. So you begged me to make you normal, to take away the world only you saw. Not in those words, of course—after all, you were only three or four. But I understood you, nonetheless. I know what it is like to feel alone and different, the only one of his kind, and I did not see why you should feel that. So I helped you. I took away your sight, so you could have what you wanted, to be like those around you. It was my thank-you for those moments of friendship."

Rory felt his eyes tear up.

"You saved me. I would have been taken away by a stranger if you hadn't helped me."

Wampage shrugged.

"Perhaps. I do not know the truth of such things. I only heeded the cries of a young boy who showed friendship. I can see, however, that someone has broken through my gift. How was this accomplished?"

Rory told the Munsee about Hex and his mission. Wampage's face remained impassive as he listened, betraying nothing.

"This Hex, do you believe him?" he finally asked.

"I don't know," Rory admitted. "It sounds really dangerous."

"Will you do it?"

Rory hesitated. He didn't want to anger his new friend. But at the same time, he couldn't bring himself to lie.

"I don't know. Why does it have to be me? Don't I get a choice? I owe you, I know, but you're the only Munsee I've ever met. Should I risk my life for them? Hex talked on and on about the balance and all that, but New York has lasted a hundred and fifty years with the Munsees trapped. Why should it fall apart now? I can't help thinking that somebody else would be more qualified to do something like this.

"I don't know why I'm telling you this. I should lie and tell you I can't wait to help your people. A good person would want to help."

Wampage shook his head.

"It is good you do not lie. You are *Sabbeleu*. Truth is your meat and your air. To deny that would be to risk much."

Really? Rory wondered if being a Light meant more than Hex was telling him.

"What is *Sabbeleu*?"

"I am not a medicine man," Wampage replied. "My answer would be poor and misleading. I am sorry."

Rory hung his head. "I don't know what to do."

A smaller dog pushed its face into Rory's hand, making the boy pet him.

"They can sense your pain," Wampage said. "That is what makes them such valuable allies and protectors. If you cannot truly feel the anguish of others, you cannot truly join with them. I would love for my people to be free. But you cannot do it for my sake. You must do it for more than that. You must open yourself to those you would save and join with them in your heart. Otherwise, you will fail."

Wampage stood up and walked over to the shell pit. Picking Rory's bracelet off the top, he handed it over to the boy solemnly, as if it were a great sword. The purple beads glowed brighter, but softer, now. Rory could feel its power as he slipped the bracelet back over his wrist. Wampage looked down at him, his eyes deep and unknowable.

"You stay apart. I have seen you," he said. "You play your games alone. Your sister keeps you company at times, but too often you are by yourself, waiting for something, though I know not what that something is. I have also remained apart, for many, many years. It is lonely, Rory. It is lonely."

Rory looked around the campsite, thinking of the centuries Wampage spent keeping a solitary watch over the last remains of his people, and a cold shiver ran up his spine. But Rory wasn't alone. He had his family. Wampage was wrong there. He was anything but lonely.

NIGHT VISITORS

A stor Place is one of the busiest squares in the East Village. Not two, not three, but four streets intersect there, along which thousands of cars and people stream by, headed in every direction. One of those streets, Lafayette Street, had a much more sedate history. Though it now led all the way down to the Brooklyn Bridge, over a century earlier it had only lasted a few blocks before reaching a dead end. But what an exclusive few blocks they were.

Then named Lafayette Place, it originally led directly to a beautiful mansion built for John Jacob Astor, once the richest man in New York. If you were to stand next to the ornate subway entrance on the small island in the middle of the square, you could still see the street sign for the forgotten dead end road hanging from the lamppost. It points out across the busy streets of present day, obviously just a relic from old times.

But . . . if you were to stand under the sign and face in the direction it pointed, you might, if you tilted your head just so and looked very carefully, catch a glimpse of that old, lost street with its cobblestones and flowering trees lined up neatly along each side. And if you were particularly adventurous, you could step forward, ignoring the cars screaming along 8th Street, and, if you stepped correctly, your feet would land on those old cobblestones. Then you could walk along the pleasant cul-de-sac toward the towering mansion that was demolished so many years before but still remains at the end of Lafayette Place. You could walk up to the front door and step inside the house of a god.

John Jacob Astor, God of Excess, was not at home. He was at the council meeting, as were all the members of the Council of Twelve, which was why Fritz and the Rattle Watch felt comfortable meeting in his study. Though *comfortable* was a strong word.

"What if one of his men comes back to grab something?" Albert asked, clearly unhappy to be meeting in the old god's home.

"Daddy is completely wrapped up in this meeting, kiddo," Simon Astor said, insolently tugging on his lacy shirt. "You worry too much."

"Be civil, Simon," Fritz said, irritated by the youthful fop's attitude. "This isn't a game."

"I know," Simon replied, not looking like he cared what Fritz was saying. "That's why I'm wearing my conspiracy shirt. I only wear it when there's a lot of whispering to be done."

Simon's conspiracy shirt was bright red with orange trimming. It was actually one of the quieter shirts he owned.

Albert shook his head. "You are an idiot, Simon."

"Ooo, big, mean words!" Simon said, waving his hands in mock fear.

"Where are they?" Fritz asked, looking around. "They should be back by now."

"They'll be here," Albert replied. "Meanwhile, you know what I heard? Caesar Prince has disappeared."

This caused an uproar. The God of Under the Streets was one of the oldest gods in the city.

"When did this happen?" Fritz exclaimed, motioning for everyone to quiet down.

"I don't know. He didn't show up for the council meeting and ignored all summons. They went to his home to force him to attend, which I guess they've done before, and he wasn't to be found. The guy was just gone!"

"Come on," Simon said. "Caesar's always been crazy, living underground with his subway trains. He probably licked the third rail or something and is sleeping it off."

"Or he's dead," Albert said.

There was a moment of silence as they thought this through.

"What is Kieft up to?" Fritz wondered. "Killing gods? What is going on here?"

"I think we might have some answers to that question," a new male voice said. They turned to the door to see Nicholas and Alexa entering.

"Don't tell me you actually saw the old broad!" Albert said, astonished.

"What did you have to pay her? A finger? Two?" Lincoln asked as he and Simon tried to get a good look at Alexa's hand. She shot them an irritated look.

"It doesn't concern you," she said. "It's what she told us that matters."

"And what was that?" Fritz asked.

Nicholas held back a moment as his mind returned to that dingy, dark room. He and Alexa had waited breathlessly as the Fortune Teller ran her fat, ring-covered fingers gently over the crystal ball. The ball had begun to glow gently as the round old woman looked deep inside. Then she spoke.

"You are at a crossroads. What you do now will change your lives forever, and the lives of everyone you love. Sorrow and heartbreak await you no matter which road you choose to walk. And the biggest choice is not yours to make—"

The Fortune Teller had gasped, her eyes flinching. "A knife. I see a terrible knife!

"I see death for our people," she had said, her voice quivering. "This knife brings death to us all."

"How do we stop it?" Nicholas had asked, proud that his voice didn't shake too much.

"There is a Light," she had said. "A hidden Light. He must come into his own. He will make the choice. You cannot make it for him. If he chooses well, then truth will be revealed. This I foretell."

Then she had lapsed into silence, and nothing he nor Alexa could say would force her to speak again.

As he and Alexa filled the Watch in, Nicholas hoped this Light came through. He hated trusting the welfare of Manna-hatta to some unknown mortal boy. *You better come through for us, Rory Hennessy,* he thought. *Our lives are in your hands.*

Rory was thankful to come home to an empty apartment. The worst thing that could happen would be to walk in on his family and have to explain where he had been. Bridget would pounce on any lie and the minute he thought of his mom as clueless was always the minute she would notice something was wrong.

He'd barely sat down in the living room before the front door opened. Bridget bounced in, jumping into the other chair, while Mrs. Hennessy brought dinner—Chinese—into the kitchen.

"What did you do, Rory? I got some great new shoes. Wanna see? Wanna see?"

"Sure."

Bridget rummaged through her bag and pulled out the steel-tipped boots. Rory was taken aback.

"What are those?"

Bridget smiled wide.

"Butt-kickers."

Rory's eyes narrowed in suspicion.

"Whose butt do you plan on kicking, exactly?"

Bridget's face was the picture of innocence.

"No one. Just good boots to have. In case a burglar breaks in or the Con Ed guy tries to read the meter."

She stood up, opened her door, and tossed the boots inside her room. They landed with a loud crash. Rory could see right through her. She couldn't wait to walk into the fire with him. Steel-tipped boots . . . what use are they against shadows?

As Bridget rushed into her room to see what she'd crushed,

Rory realized what he had to do. Another Stranger would find him, or something worse, and this time Bridget wouldn't freeze up. He could picture her rushing the creature, ready to kick its head in with her new boots, but she would be the one hurt—or worse. He couldn't risk her or his mother. He had to end this before his family suffered.

Mrs. Hennessy caught her son staring off into space. "You okay, honey?" she asked.

"I am," he answered her. And he was. Or would be soon.

"Look after Bridget tomorrow," she said. "I have to go to work extra early, on a Saturday and everything—and I'll be back late. My reward for taking the day off, I guess. I won't have time to look in on you, so take care of food and stuff. Think you can handle that?"

"Sure," he answered. This was even better than he'd hoped. If he had to do something tomorrow, his mom would never know. Satisfied, Mrs. Hennessy tousled his hair before turning her attention to dinner.

He made sure his mom was busy in the kitchen before grabbing the phone from the wall and disappearing into his own room. He pulled out the card from his pocket and dialed the number. Hex answered on the second ring.

"If I help you, are you sure they'll leave us alone?" Rory asked him. "This Kieft guy or whoever will stop sending creatures after me and my family?"

"There will be no more reason for him or anyone else to want you," Hex answered.

"Then I'm in," Rory said, an odd mixture of worry and relief washing over him as he said the words.

"Thank you, Rory," Hex said. "You're doing a great thing."

"What happens next?"

"We meet tonight outside the bank and do the job."

"What! Tonight! That's crazy!"

"We caught a break. There has been an incident at the bank involving a giant pig. Don't ask. So the bank security will be in disarray for the next day or so trying to clean up the mess. Which means we should be able to slip in unnoticed. But we'll have to do it tonight."

Rory's head was spinning.

"But that's no time at all. I'm not ready."

"There's not much to be ready for. We sneak in, you turn the key, we get out. It's not going to get any easier if we wait. This is the moment, Rory. I know it's sudden and so much to decide so quickly. But that's the way it has to be."

In the end it wasn't much of a decision. His family was more important than anything.

"What's the plan?"

"What's the plan?"

Rory was pretending to get ready for bed when Bridget's whispered voice cut in. He turned to see her stepping into his room and quietly pulling the door closed. He purposefully turned his back and flopped into bed.

"There is no plan. Go to sleep."

Bridget knelt next to the bed.

"Come on. When do we hit the bank? Are we seeing Hex tomorrow? By the way, I almost forgot, there's something I need to tell you—"

Rory cut her off, determined to nip this in the bud. He had to be harsh, to protect her.

"You're not coming with me, Bridge."

"What are you talking about—"

"You'll slow me down and get in the way."

Bridget's eyes welled up.

"I would not!"

"I won't let you tag along! You're a little girl. You should be playing with your dolls. So stay out of it. This is for the big boys, not the little babies."

Bridget bit her lower lip to keep from crying.

"Fine! See if I care what happens to you."

She ran out of the room as Mrs. Hennessy's voice drifted in.

"Quiet down, you two! Go to sleep!"

Rory lay back in bed, knowing that sleep was not in the cards for him. Not tonight.

Bridget woke up suddenly. She looked around her dark room, wondering what could have startled her out of sleep. Her clock radio showed the time: quarter after eleven. She'd been asleep for less than two hours. She relaxed back into her bed. She was still mad at Rory, she guessed. Maybe she should learn meditation or something. Take up Buddhism. She could hike out to some obscure mountain somewhere, seek out an ancient monk.

It would take three years before he would even look at her, and two years after that before he'd say good morning. Eventually, he'd break down, agreeing to teach this young Westerner all his secrets. After months and months of training, Bridget would finally be able to reach inner peace and fight in mid-air like in those kung fu movies. For, with self-awareness and inner peace, comes the ability to kick some serious heiney.

She turned to check her clock again. And almost screamed. She whispered angrily, "I may know you're really a little man, but a roach by your clock is still pretty scary!"

Fritz put up his little legs, gesturing for her to stay silent. He got down off his rat.

"Simmer down, Bridget. You don't want to wake up your mother."

Bridget shifted uneasily.

"Could you take that helmet off? I hate seeing my reflection in your little eyes."

Fritz reached up and lifted off the helmet, revealing his white face grinning sheepishly.

"Battle armor is supposed to terrify the opponent."

"And make them reach for a shoe."

"Don't make me crawl on you. Neither of us wants that." Fritz wiped his brow, absently feeding his rat a small piece of cheese. "This is my steed, Clarence. Clarence, say hello to the little lady."

Clarence ignored them both, chewing on his cheese. Fritz smiled apologetically.

"He's a little temperamental. I want to introduce you to another friend. This is Nicholas."

A young man stepped out of the shadows. He was dressed in eighteenth-century clothing and wore a long ponytail.

"Hello, Bridget."

Bridget sat up, pulling her covers around her.

"Who are you? How'd you get in?"

Fritz sighed.

"I told you we should have brought Alexa," he said.

"Bridget, we need to talk to Rory," Nicholas said calmly. "I'm here to help."

"I don't care about him," she said, sniffing. "He's stupid."

"What are you talking about?" Fritz asked, bemused.

"He called me a little girl!"

"You *are* a little girl," Nicholas said with a fine taste for the obvious.

"He didn't have to go saying it," Bridget muttered.

"We need to talk to him, anyway," Fritz said. "It's very important. I think you should introduce us, quietly, so you don't wake up your mother."

"Fine," said Bridget petulantly, rolling her eyes as she hopped out of bed and put on her slippers. "You should sit on his face or something, to scare him. It'll serve him right."

Bridget led them through the living room, wincing at every squeak. It sounded like she was stepping on mice. Nicholas seemed to make no sound at all, which annoyed her even further. *Stupid boys,* she thought. She reached Rory's door and opened it slowly. His sleeping form lay on his bed. She tiptoed up to him and reached for the covers to reveal his head. She pulled back and gasped. Fritz crawled up onto the nightstand and took a look as Nicholas looked over her shoulder.

"This is not good," Fritz said.

Under the covers where Rory's head should have been lay a mannequin head. Lord knows where he'd found it. Pillows rounded out his fake body. Rory was gone. Bridget sat down on the bed.

"I don't understand."

Fritz hopped over to sit beside her.

"He's gone AWOL. That's obvious. Where would he go?"

Bridget shook her head, mad at herself.

"He went to talk to Hex. And he didn't tell me."

Nicholas leaned up against the wall heavily.

"He wanted to protect you, I take it," he said.

"That's why he was being so mean to me! He's so stupid!"

Fritz began to pace along the edge of the bedspread.

"Why would he leave in the middle of the night? Unless—"

Fritz stopped, his face frozen in a horrible realization.

Bridget felt a chill run down her spine. "What?"

"Pushing you away. Acting so mysterious. It all makes sense. He's gone to First City Bank. And if we don't get there soon, he'll never come out again."

THE BACK WAY

City Hall was filled with tiny rooms, some hardly reachable anymore, some forgotten completely. Much knowledge had been lost in the centuries since the hall had been built, and many of the early gods had created little hidey-holes for themselves, only to pass onward without telling anyone where these secret spaces lay. The room John Jacob Astor now stood in had belonged to Sven Jorgen, an early Swedish settler and once the God of Fur Traders. Unfortunately for Sven, the animals his followers preyed on soon died out, and the fur trade died with them. Sven held on for a while, trying to attach himself to the high-priced fur merchants on Madison Avenue, but he had no chance, losing out to a beautiful new goddess of expensive fashion halfway through the last century. Forgotten and irrelevant, he faded away, leaving behind only his portrait with its dead eyes and this small room with beaver carcasses hanging from its walls.

Astor didn't know how many of these dead-god rooms lay scattered throughout the building, nor did he care to find out. He didn't enjoy the reminder that even gods fade. He was certain that Kieft chose these rooms on purpose to make him feel uncomfortable. Kieft could do anything he wanted down here, and nobody would know . . . Astor pushed the frightening thought from his mind and finished recounting his news to the twitching creature in front of him. *Just remember the rewards,* he told himself. *Soon they will crawl before me and these little distasteful moments will be but unpleasant memories.*

"Interesting," Kieft said. The god himself wasn't there, of course. Kieft was always careful not to be seen with any of his coconspirators, as far as Astor knew. Instead, Kieft used some of that blasted sorcerer mumbo jumbo of his to speak through one of Astor's minions, one of the many luxury-loving spirits that flocked to the God of Excess. The spirit stood stiffly, his mouth moving under Kieft's power while his eyes darted about, terrified at the invasion. "We can use this to our advantage."

"Tell me that Nicholas upstart will suffer," Astor growled. "He forgets his place far too easily."

"He and his watch are proving themselves irritants. But this . . . this will break them. We have a trap to lay, Astor. Tell our new assassin I need to speak with him."

"About our new assassin," Astor said, shifting uncomfortably. "I'm not happy about using him like this."

"Your reservations in my choice are duly noted, John." The spirit's mouth curled into a frown. "Do not question me again."

Astor resisted the urge to press. He didn't want to push Kieft too far.

"What are you going to do about the Light?" he asked, changing the subject. The spirit did not respond right away, and Astor wondered if Kieft had heard him.

The spirit's mouth moved finally, and the voice within did not sound happy. "What Light?"

"I know something you don't know? How pleasant, and yet disturbing," Astor said, feeling only the latter. "The Rattle Watch used my home as a meeting place, foolishly believing I wouldn't find out. They spoke of a Light, some boy who had somehow escaped detection. I thought you knew."

"I hadn't. No one told me."

His dead tone made Astor's stomach clench.

"I'm sorry," he said, proud of his nonshaking voice. "I assumed—"

"Enough," Kieft cut him off. "Concentrate on the Watch for now. Leave the Light to me. But if you ever keep something from me again . . ."

The voice trailed off. Astor nodded his head eagerly until the body the spirit was in collapsed to the ground. That was the one side effect of being used as Kieft's mouthpiece: it drained the essence out of the luckless creature entirely. Lost in thought, Astor barely noticed the dead spirit as he stepped over it on his way out. He'd never truly been afraid of Kieft before. He'd respected his power and ruthlessness, but fear . . . Astor was a god, he feared nothing. Nothing, that is, until Van der Donck's death proved that Kieft had discovered a way to sidestep the divine rules they all must follow. Nothing until that knife. The black-eyed god had promised that his weapon would only be brought to bear on their enemies, but the knife's very existence was a threat Kieft would undoubtedly use to keep Astor and his fellow conspirators in line. The sweat dripped down his forehead as he realized that he would never feel truly safe again. But it was worth it, he told himself. The power he would wield when the herd of Mannahatta gods was thinned would be immense. Of course it was all worth it. . . .

* * *

Rory sat on the bus, heading downtown. He'd had no problem sneaking out. The door closed behind him a little louder than he'd have liked, but no harm done. The city outside seemed livelier now than during the daytime. Groups of kids hung out on the street corners, tossing around basketballs while trying to act five years older than they were. Old men sat in their chairs outside the little convenience stores, white hair glowing under the harsh neon storefronts. If they only knew what Rory knew. . . . He kept his eye out for anything odd, but it all appeared normal. For all the crazy things he'd seen, nothing much seemed to have changed about the city as a whole. The buildings were the same. The people didn't look any different. Were the really strange creatures only in the alleys or underground? Or was Manhattan so weird to begin with that the nightmare creatures just blended in?

He'd thought about taking the subway, but he didn't want to run into those strange subway singers, so Rory stuck to the buses. Thankfully, no one bothered him and before he knew it he was stepping out onto Broadway across from City Hall. He looked around. Things seemed a little quieter down here than uptown. Not too many people lived in the Financial District that filled the bottom tip of Manhattan. It was all office buildings, banks, and City Hall. He looked up at City Hall, which loomed menacingly above him. Something about it made his head swim. Like he was looking at two buildings at once. The more he stared, the queasier he felt. Two buildings, one large, one impossibly huge, occupied the same space, fighting for his attention. Finally, he had to look away. He headed over to the corner where Hex was waiting, Toy right behind him.

"You're here! Good! How are you holding up?"

Rory shrugged, trying to look brave. Hex took his shoulder and pointed diagonally across the street.

"There it is. First City Bank of Mannahatta. Established by Alexander Hamilton, taken over by Tobias when Hamilton was elected Mayor, and run by him ever since. Bankers don't create, they speculate. To be honest, it's the only true bank in New York. The mortal banks are just children that he allows to play pretend. This is where all the money of Manhattan comes and goes."

First City Bank of Mannahatta was a large marble building on the corner of Broadway and Vesey Street. Though taller steel buildings towered over it, the bank somehow seemed larger and grander. It radiated power. Where a church would have had statues and murals of saints and angels on its walls, First City celebrated a different religion: money. People holding it, people loaning it, people taking it back. The carvings all worshipped money. And in the center, right above the door, a larger stone statue loomed. It watched the people traveling in and out of First City from above: a round, stern man dressed conservatively, arms crossed as if to say, *How dare you have money! It doesn't belong to you! It belongs to me! Now fork it over!*

"Quite a statue, huh?" Hex said. "Looking down like the Messiah himself, judging everyone who passes under him? That's him. The great T. R. Tobias."

He spit this out and Rory couldn't blame him. One look at that statue curdled his stomach, as well. Rory turned his attention to the side of the bank, where a large chunk of wall had been somehow dug, almost *eaten*, away.

"What happened there?" he asked.

"I told you, an incident with a giant pig. Duck!"

Hex pushed Rory behind some bushes in the park. Rory peered through the small branches at the bank entrance.

"What's wrong?"

Hex glanced over at Rory.

"You can't tell me you don't see them."

Rory looked again. And bit back a cry.

"What are those!"

Hex smiled grimly.

"The famous guards of First City. The Brokers of Tobias. Loyal, dim, strong, and quite formidable. We would do well to avoid them."

Rory couldn't look away. Out of the front door of First City, with big bags of money gripped in their enormous hands, walked two of the ugliest, largest, and scariest beings he'd ever seen. Their skin gleamed like steel, but it was as green as the money they protected. Red eyes shone from under huge, heavy brows. Not a hair sprouted anywhere on their spiked skulls. Large silver teeth, like sharpened quarters, filled their oversize jaws. They towered over the few people who walked around them, unseeing.

Rory shivered. "How many of them are they?"

Hex shrugged. "Who can say? As inflation goes higher and higher, they just seem to multiply."

The two creatures reached an armored car. They opened

the back and climbed in, still clutching their bags of money. Hex smiled grimly.

"I'd hate to be the thief who tries to rob that car."

Rory sat down on the concrete.

"How are we supposed to get past them?"

Hex looked down at him, eyes bright.

"Don't worry. They'll all be up here by the giant hole in the wall, making sure no one sneaks in. Tobias thinks the back way is guarded enough for one night. Fool. Why don't you take this, Rory? I'm sure you won't need it, but it's good to know what you're looking for."

He handed Rory a folded piece of paper. Rory opened it to discover one of the drawings from Hex's wall, the crude child's rendering of a white circle.

"The belt, right?" he asked.

"Yes, that's the belt. I brought it in case you needed a reminder."

"It shines in my dreams," Rory whispered, tracing the circle with his fingers. "Who drew this?"

Rory heard a soft sigh.

"My son."

Rory glanced up at Hex, whose eyes were glistening. Something occurred to him.

"Was he like me?"

Hex nodded slowly. "Yes, he was a Light."

"What happened to him? Did a Stranger get him?"

"No," Hex replied, shaking his head slightly. "I protected him from the Strangers. He grew up to be about your sister's age. And then . . ."

"Then what?"

Hex reached out to touch the drawing with his long fingers.

"It's not your worry, Rory. It is my sorrow, not yours. I'll tell you all about it someday, I promise. Right now my heart isn't up to it."

Rory heard the pain in the magician's voice. Even Toy's eyes softened at his master's suffering. How much had the old man sacrificed?

"Why are the Munsees so important to you?" he asked the magician.

Hex's voice grew fierce. "It was a great wrong, the greatest wrong, to shut them away. It threw the world out of balance, that is how great a wrong it was. I must make it right. I must!"

Hex's eyes blazed and he clenched his fist as he spoke. Rory didn't know that someone could care this much about people he'd never met. He wondered if he ever could. *Probably not,* he thought ruefully. If not for the threat to his family, he wouldn't be here.

Toy, who'd been watching the street, held up his hand. Hex gazed over the bushes and pulled himself to his feet.

"They're gone. Come on. We don't have time to linger."

Hex led them down a side street that circled around to the rear of the bank.

Eventually they came to the corner across from the back of First City. Instead of large, impressive columns and intricate carvings, the back of the bank seemed plain and blank. Rory couldn't see any doors.

"Where do we get in?"

Hex pointed down at their feet.

"Right there."

Rory could see only pavement.

"Right where?"

Hex smiled slyly.

"It's magic, my boy."

He knelt down and felt along the asphalt.

"What are you doing?" Rory asked.

"Just finding the right spots. There we go!"

Hex pushed down with his finger in three spots, one after the other, and to Rory's amazement an entire section of the street dropped down to reveal a ladder leading underground.

"That's the secret way in?" Rory asked. "Isn't it kind of easy to open up?"

"Not at all," Hex replied, lowering himself down into the hole. "You have to press in just the right sequence. It'd be practically impossible for someone to hit the right spots by accident. So that weeds out the innocent passersby."

"What about people like us?"

"He's not worried about us getting in. He's certain we'll never come back out."

Hex dropped down into the hole. Toy followed, disappearing into the black.

Rory called down. "Hex? Hello? I hate the dark."

Muttering to himself, Rory lowered himself down into the hole. After a moment, the pavement rose back up. No cracks remained to show it had ever moved, leaving the street empty and quiet.

13

THE BRITISH
ARE COMING

Dark surrounded Rory, pitch-black in every direction. A click sounded at his side as a light flared up, making him wince. Hex had pulled out an electric lamp, which he shone down the passageway.

"Well, here we are," he said.

They were standing at the beginning of a tunnel that led away into the dark distance. The walls were red brick, like an old town house. Dust lay on the floor a half an inch deep. Rory took a step, sending a puff of dirt up into the air.

"Looks like no one's used the back door in a while."

Hex nodded, checking his watch. He gestured toward the tunnel.

"Come on. Let's get going. Time's wasting!"

He headed off down the passageway, his light growing smaller as he walked ahead. Rory hurried to catch up. The air smelled stale, like no one had ever inhaled it before. He could feel Toy following right behind. Hex moved smoothly, not to mention quietly. The only footsteps Rory could hear were his own. He tried to make his footfalls softer, but there was only so much he could do with the cold concrete beneath him. Practically tiptoeing, Rory moved deeper into the dank shadows.

The tunnel curved left then right. The walls changed as they wound their way inside. The bricks on the wall became more irregular and individually shaped. Rory's footsteps changed as the concrete floor melted into wood, shifting from *clop* to *thump*. He moved up to Hex's ear.

"Are we in the bank yet?"

Even that soft whisper echoed loudly. Hex winced.

"We've been in the bank for the last twenty minutes. This place has been here a long time and the tunnels reflect that. Keep your eye out!"

Worried, Rory turned his attention back to the passageway in front of him. He couldn't see anything but dark, and beyond that, more dark, and a little farther on, even more dark, and after that, black. He wouldn't be able to see anything until it jumped on his head and ate his face. Wonderful.

Hex outlined their plan as they walked.

"As I think I told you, fifty some odd years ago a small group executed a raid on this bank to do what we're trying to do right now. They had the lock, they had the key, and they needed only the belt to bring down the Trap."

"And they had a Light?" Rory asked.

"Yes, they did. A strong one. They made it past all the obstacles and into the vault, where disaster struck. There was an argument, and somehow the Brokers were alerted. They all perished, except for one small warrior. He escaped with the key and the lock, though the belt was too large for him to carry."

"Too large? How big is this belt?"

Hex chuckled.

"Too large for him, anyway. He was a cockroach, after all. His name was Sergeant Bertold of the M'Garoth clan, and he dragged the lock and the key behind him as he ran. He knew he'd never outrun the Brokers and the last thing he wanted was to let Tobias capture the items he carried, so he hid them along the way before expiring."

"Um, Hex. If this cockroach died, how did you get all this information?"

"He was found before he succumbed to his wounds and so the knowledge did not die with him. But as far as Tobias is aware, no one escaped the botched raid. And since he is such a world-class cheapskate, he hasn't even changed most of his traps. So we can follow the same plan they did."

"But if they didn't succeed, why do you think we will?"

Hex turned and smiled.

"But they did succeed. They passed through all the rooms safely, which is what we will do. They just fought amongst themselves at the end; that was why they were caught. We will not have that same problem."

"Why did they fight?"

"Bertold didn't know. He arrived last to the vault, which was how he was able to escape. But I'm not worried. We are not they. We are of one mind. We're going to do this, Rory. We will not fail."

The wooden floor soon became dirt. The brick on the walls turned into large, irregular stones mortared together like a farm wall. The ceiling came down closer, until Hex was forced to hunch. No one spoke. They heard the dripping of water somewhere in the distance. The tunnel they moved through looked like it had been dug down deep into the bedrock, the bones of the island. Suddenly, Hex stopped. Rory had to halt to keep from running into him.

"What is it?" he asked.

"We're at the first room," Hex replied. Sure enough, they'd come to a door at the end of the tunnel. Rory stepped up to it, touching the moldy wood.

"What's the first room?"

"It's a memory," Hex said. "A moment from the past forever repeating. There are three rooms leading up to the vault, and the first one is a memory room. We have to stay focused, find what we came for, and get through."

"I don't understand," Rory said. "Will I be able to see this?"

"It's not an illusion. It's an actual moment in time, bottled up and replayed over and over again. Nothing you do will actually affect that point in time, since it's been taken out of its place in the order of events. Kind of like a live-action video recording. But this room is very dangerous, because Tobias picked a moment where certain death awaited anyone who stumbled into it. And that is final and very real."

This didn't sound too promising.

"Then how do we get out alive?"

"This path was designed to allow Tobias to enter from the back way undisturbed, so there is a way through. It's a door that only opens seconds before certain death. But I know where to look, so I'm not too worried about that."

That doesn't sound too bad, Rory thought.

"What I *am* worried about," Hex continued, unfortunately for Rory's stomach, "is the fact that we have to search out the lock. Sergeant Bertold hid it in this room somewhere, and we have to find it before the door opens, or this whole mission will fail. And if we search too long . . ."

He trailed off, but Rory didn't need him to finish. If they searched too long, they'd die. Rory mustered up a bravado he didn't really feel.

"Sounds peachy. So what does this lock look like, anyway?"

Hex put his hand on the doorknob.

"Just like a normal padlock. If you see something like it, call me over and I'll tell you if you've found it. Ready?"

"Wait! Where should I look?"

"Everywhere, kiddo. Look everywhere."

With that, Hex opened the door and they stepped into the past.

"Duck!"

Hex pulled Rory to the ground as something whistled overhead. The sound of something crashing behind them made Rory jump. He looked up and was astonished by what he saw.

They seemed to be in some kind of fort. The wooden walls that surrounded them were dotted with cannons firing into the distance. Soldiers, or what he guessed were soldiers, ran back and forth, loading shots into the cannons and firing over the walls with their guns. They didn't seem to be wearing any uniforms, just dirty rough clothes and tri-cornered hats. Bullets whistled through the air; cannonballs flew overhead. Rory could barely hear over the noise.

"Where are we?" he asked.

"Fort Tryon, not too far south of you up in Inwood."

"You mean Fort Tryon Park? This doesn't look like a park."

"That's because it's not a park. Not yet. It's November 16th, 1776, and the British are attacking. Come on!"

He pulled Rory to his feet and dragged him over to the wall. Toy followed, dodging bullets and soldiers who were racing to defend the fort. A loud whistle sounded, followed by a thud, and Toy looked down at the lead musket ball that had sprouted in his shoulder.

"Stay down, Toy! You'll get blown to pieces!" Hex shouted.

They hid behind a piece of wall that had a small hole blown right through it. Rory chanced a look through the hole to see what was going on outside. They seemed to be on the top of a hill overlooking the island, but instead of the buildings and streets of his day, there were only a few farmhouses and lots of trees. But the trees weren't what grabbed his attention. That was reserved for the thousands of soldiers in red coats firing up at them.

Hex's voice yelled in his ear. "Those are the British and the Hessians. The cannonballs are coming from their fort in Queens and from a ship out on the river. They're trying to take Fort Washington, which is the large fort behind us, and they're going to succeed. It will be the biggest military defeat for the Americans in the Revolution, costing thousands of lives by the time the last prisoner dies. And it's all due to the pride of General Greene, who thought he had enough strength to push back a far superior force. Such an imbecile! Thousands died because of his hubris. After this battle, the Revolutionary Army will be kicked out of New York, not to return until after the war. Half the city will burn to the ground before the war is through. Such a waste."

A woman ran by carrying a cannonball in her hands.

"Was that a girl?" Rory asked.

"Margaret Corbin, Revolutionary hero. Her husband went down, and she kept fighting. She gets seriously injured in this battle, so stay away from her! Stay near the wall and try not to get shot! We're looking for the lock. Remember, it looks like an everyday padlock. It should be around here someplace."

Rory looked around at the chaos surrounding him. The lock could be anywhere.

"This is impossible."

"No it's not! It was hidden in plain sight, so if we look hard enough we'll find it. Go!"

Rory hugged the wall, watching the soldiers fire their muskets over the wall. As he watched, one man was hit, flying back from the wall to land heavily on the ground. The man pushed himself to his feet, holding his side, and ran for cover.

Rory couldn't ignore the facts any longer. If he stayed here he was going to die.

Desperate, he began to look around for anything resembling a lock. Instead, all he could see were wounded soldiers and musket balls. He yelled back at Hex.

"I can't find anything!"

"Keep looking. We've still got a little time."

Rory came upon a door in the wall. He wished he could just open it and run away. Maybe he'd survive here in the memory of 1776. He could be a fife boy or something. But no, the door was locked. He could see the padlock on the handle. Padlock . . .

"I think I found it!" he shouted.

Hex ran over, followed by Toy. Rory pointed to the lock. Hex let out a cry of triumph and smacked him on the back.

"Good boy! Actually used as a lock! How that little cockroach got that lock all the way up there, I'll never know . . ."

"Retreat!"

The call came from behind them. Rory turned to see the American soldiers running away, carrying their wounded out a gate in the back of the fort. As he watched, two men ran by carrying the woman he'd seen earlier. She was covered in blood but still moving.

"Don't worry, she survives," Hex said.

"Where are they going?"

"To Fort Washington. It won't help them. That fort will fall in a few hours and most of them will either die in the fighting or on the prison ships. It doesn't matter to us. We can't follow them. We can't leave the fort, except by the door Tobias provides. Not that it matters, since we found the lock with a little time to spare! Come on, grab that crowbar over there. We can pry off the handle."

Rory walked over and picked up the crowbar lying near a cannon. A thought occurred to him.

"If they're running away out that gate, where does this door go?"

"It looks out onto the front. It doesn't matter; the British are about to overrun the fort anyway."

"Which door are they coming in through?"

Before Hex could answer, the door shook, as if something had slammed into it. He backed away.

"This one," Hex said unnecessarily.

"So that lock is the only thing between us and the British?"

Hex sighed.

"Bertold must have replaced the original lock with our prize. This is a toughie."

The door shuddered again. They could hear shouting on the other side.

"What happens when this door opens?" Rory asked.

"The British kill whoever they find in the fort."

"Wonderful."

Suddenly, Hex pointed. Fifty feet along the wall, a light had appeared, outlining a doorway.

"There's the doorway! We're out of time! We've got to chance it."

He picked up the crowbar and tried to pry off the handle, but it wouldn't budge.

"How long does that doorway stay open?" Rory asked in a panic.

"Not long!"

Suddenly, Toy pushed Hex out of the way and with a mighty heave, ripped the lock off with his bare hands. He pushed hard against the door as the soldiers tried to force it open and handed the lock to Hex, gesturing toward the glowing exit.

"Come on!" Hex yelled and took off for the way out.

"What about Toy?" Rory yelled, following him.

"He'll be along."

Just then, the door Toy had been barricading flew open, sending the paper boy flying. Hex reached the glowing doorway and practically tossed Rory through it. Rory landed on the tunnel floor and quickly turned to stare back into the fort. Toy had risen to his feet and was running as fast as he could. Hex stood in the doorway, beckoning at his paper companion.

"Run, Toy! You're almost there!"

The glow began to fade, and Hex stepped into the tunnel, but Toy was not yet to the doorway. Then, just before the glow disappeared, trapping him in the memory forever, a musket ball hit Toy in the back, propelling him forward through the doorway just as it closed. He landed heavily on the floor of the tunnel. All the noise of war was gone, replaced by Rory and Hex's rough breathing. For a moment, no one said a word. Then Hex patted Toy on the back, pausing to pull out the musket ball.

"That wasn't too bad," he said.

And onward they walked down the long, dark tunnel.

A NEEDLE IN A
GOLDEN HAYSTACK

I am trusting you with a great task. The most important task. You are my hand out in the world. Fail, and you will be punished. But succeed, and you will rise . . ."

Kieft's words rose up in the mind of the dark figure stalking the shadowed streets of the sleeping city. Kieft had come to him not long after the Council of Twelve had discovered Van der Donck's fate. Before that, he had been just another of Kieft's sleeper agents, hidden deep among the gods and spirits like tiny bones in a fish. Easy to miss and ready to choke. But Kieft had picked him out of the crowd, granting him the ultimate of honors by appearing in person to give him his orders. The old assassin was dead; a new one must take up his mantle. Kieft then placed an ugly metal *thing* in his palm. Crudely made, more scrap iron than weapon, the knife sat heavily in his hand. The gnarled hilt bore no carvings or sigils. Just rough, barely shaped steel. But the knife's edge was more than sharp enough to end a life. Beauty was not the intended purpose for this weapon. Kieft had forged it to deal death and end hope.

Kieft had wasted no time in giving his new assassin a task. Not long after that first meeting, Jenny Fingers lay dead under the table at the department store. Her murder had come easily enough to the assassin. It was the murder that awaited him that gave him trouble: the death of the Light.

He felt a flash of unease. He'd recently discovered the Light's existence on his own but had decided against mentioning it to Kieft. He told himself he was biding his time until the boy awoke and proved to be dangerous, but deep down he knew the truth. He feared that if he spoke up, Kieft would ask *him* to end the boy's life. He had no problem slitting the throats of pompous, overbearing gods, but a kid was another matter. He'd hoped Rory would stay blind until he was old enough for the assassin to kill him without getting the blood of a child on his hands. But events moved past him. Rory awoke, Kieft found out, and now the assassin had to stain his soul with a boy's blood before the night was through.

This had to stop. He couldn't do his job with these guilty feelings weighing him down like this. . . . A thought suddenly occurred to him and he unconsciously caressed the knife in his belt. *Of course.* A sharp smile flashed across his face. He knew exactly how to get rid of his guilt. Kieft wouldn't mind if a little more divine blood was spilled; it would add to the fear rising in the hearts of everyone in Mannahatta. Just a little detour, to get rid of his pesky conscience. And then he'd be able to do his job and kill the boy. He raced down the dimly lit alleyway, relief on his face and murder in his heart.

As Rory followed Hex deeper into the dark tunnels, a question popped into his head:

"How did the first party get out of there alive?"

"You saw the doorway, correct?" Hex asked in reply. He didn't even wait for Rory's nod before continuing. "Of course you did. Because of your talents. The first party had a Light as well. I, also, am able to see the door due to my own particular skills. That gives us the edge where most people would see no way out and perish. I wouldn't wish to be the poor fools who attempt a break-in without someone with our skills in tow."

Rory felt a moment's relief, glad he'd left Bridget at home. After all, she couldn't even have seen the way out. He took a closer look at the lock. It seemed perfectly ordinary, like a rusty old padlock you would find in somebody's toolshed.

"How do you know this is the right lock?" he asked.

"I know," Hex replied without looking over his shoulder. "That's the lock, all right. And this is the next room!"

They stopped in front of another door, identical to the first. Hex took back the lock and placed it in his pocket.

"We're looking for a small white key," he said.

"That sounds harder to find than the lock."

"Don't worry, my boy. Just keep your eyes peeled and don't touch anything unless you have to."

He opened the door and stepped through. Confused, Rory followed, muttering to himself. "That doesn't sound good."

Rory found it hard to breathe as he looked around the room he'd just stepped into. In all directions, as far as he could see, was gold upon gold upon gold. Gold statues and gold weapons and gold armor and gold rods and plain old gold bars lay stacked against one another all around them, along with piles of diamonds and other jewels, paintings and sculptures, and hundreds of other obviously valuable items. Above them the ceiling had disappeared, replaced with a soft glow that illuminated the huge room, reflecting off all the bright, shiny precious metal. It had to be the most wealth ever gathered in one place. Rory turned to Hex, his voice tinged with awe.

"Is this another memory?"

Hex shook his head, his eyes shining. "No. This is all in the present."

"So this is the vault."

Hex chuckled.

"This is just his storeroom. The vault is for the really valuable stuff."

Rory didn't know what could be more valuable than all this treasure. One little bauble could set his family up for life. He leaned in to take a closer look, but a hand on his shoulder pulled him back.

"Don't touch anything, Rory," warned Hex. "That's Tobias whispering in your ear. This is all too well-guarded. We wouldn't make it too far."

Rory looked around wildly.

"Are those Broker monsters around?"

"No. They wouldn't do for this work. There is . . . another guardian. But nothing we have to worry about. After all, we're not here for money. We're here to find that key!"

Rory stared out at the huge room.

"I hope it's a big key," he said, not really kidding.

"About the size of a quarter. But don't worry, it's not gold, it's white, so it should stand out."

Rory couldn't see how anything could stand out among all these mounds of shiny gold.

"We're never gonna find it, Hex!" he said. "This place is huge!"

"Don't get discouraged," Hex said calmly. "We know that Bertold was not large, and that he stayed on the path from that door over there to the door we entered by." Rory could barely see the other door all the way across the room. "So it has to be along the way. We'll find it in no time."

"How can we look if we can't touch anything?" Rory asked.

"You can touch the treasure. Just don't hold on to it long. I mean it, Rory. Tobias protects what's his, and you don't want to run afoul of his guardian. So put anything you pick up back down as soon as you move it. Okay?"

"Okay," Rory said, certain their quest would stop here. There was no way they would find one small key amid all this treasure. Hex and Toy immediately began shifting through the piles by the path, looking through each piece. Rory walked a bit down toward the other door to start from that end. He couldn't help staring at all the gold just lying there, begging to be pocketed. One small gold spoon seemed especially inviting. It all seemed so unfair.

About three quarters of the way to the far door, he felt his wrist getting warmer. Looking down, he noticed his wampum bracelet was getting hot. Alarmed, Rory looked around for any shadows that might conceal a Stranger, but he saw nothing. Continuing to walk, he felt his bracelet grow warm until it was almost burning his skin, and then it suddenly began to cool again. He reached the far door, and his bracelet became room temperature again. Strange.

He shifted through some of the gold by the door, careful to drop anything he put his fingers on. After ten minutes or so, the frustration threatened to take over. He kicked the plate he'd just moved and stood up. There was no way he could possibly find that tiny key in the middle of all this stuff! This was crazy! He stomped back toward Hex, determined to tell him this was all a wild-goose chase. But he hadn't walked more than ten feet when his wrist began to warm up again. Touching his bracelet, he felt the heat rising, more and more, as he walked. Something was definitely going on here. But he could see nothing that appeared dangerous. He reached the point where it burned hottest when a thought occurred to him. Dropping to his knees, he began to shift through the pile at his feet. He pushed a gold figurine to the side, and a gold necklace, a gold bar, and three gold chess pieces. Finally, he caught a flash of white.

"Amazing," he muttered.

Lifting a gold letter opener out of the way, Rory revealed a small white key nestled in the middle of the pile of riches. He never would have found this on his own, not without hours and hours of searching. But this key, with its smooth white surface, had called out to him. Where had he seen something like this before? He whistled as he realized the truth.

"It's wampum," he whispered to himself. Of course. Wampage told him that his bracelet would help him find wampum. He hadn't known how important that help would be. He picked up the key and took a closer look. It had been carved out of smooth white shells, maybe from the very pit Wampage now guarded. He heard footsteps behind him.

"You found it," Hex said. "I knew you would."

Rory looked up at the magician, who stood behind him with Toy at his side, both appearing to be completely unsurprised.

"How did you know?" Rory asked.

"Lights often see things hidden to everyone else. I was pretty sure this would be one of those things."

Rory stood up, bringing the key with him. It hung from a long silver chain that dangled from his fingers. A soft breeze made it sway gently. He wondered briefly where the breeze was coming from, but then the thought slipped away.

"You could have said something," he muttered, unhappy to have been kept in the dark.

"I didn't want to mess with your head and have you over-thinking things," Hex replied. "It all worked out. We're almost there— Where is that wind coming from?"

Shrugging that he had no idea, Rory turned to head toward the door. He hadn't gone two steps before he heard Hex gasp behind him.

"What's that in your other hand!" Hex demanded.

Rory looked down at the gold letter opener still resting in his palm, and for a moment he could only stare dumbly.

"Drop it, Rory!" Hex yelled. "Before it's too late!"

Finally, Rory reacted and tried to open his hand to drop the letter opener, but before he could release it the soft wind he'd felt earlier picked up, growing almost immediately into a full-force gale. Quickly, a fog rose from the floor and wrapped around him, forcing his arms to his sides and trapping the letter opener between his palm and his leg. He tried to shift his hand to let the golden piece drop, but the wind pushed into him, making it impossible to move. He could barely hear Hex shouting over the roar of the air around him. The fog pushed into his nose and mouth, rushing into his body, choking him. He tried to scream, but he could make no sound as the wind crushed him from both inside and out. He gave his hand one last desperate shake before the tornado overcame him and he fell into darkness.

"Wake up, Rory. Please wake up."

Rory became aware of someone shaking him. He opened his eyes to see Hex and Toy bending over him. Hex let out a long, thankful sigh.

"You're alive. I was worried for a moment there, Rory."

"What happened?" Rory croaked. His throat was dry and scratchy, while in his chest it felt like his lungs had tried to blow up like a car air bag. Hex poured some water into Rory's mouth while he explained.

"You held on to that gold letter opener for too long and you awoke the guardian. It almost suffocated you. If you hadn't somehow managed to fight the wind and let the gold fall to the ground right before you blacked out, it would have killed you. But instead, the wind let you go the moment you dropped it. A gold letter opener. What a stupid thing to die over."

"Am I okay?" Rory asked, sitting up. He felt dizzy and a little shaken but otherwise all right.

"Your chest may ache a bit for a while, but I think you'll be fine. I told you not to hold on to anything! You are a stubborn boy, Rory Hennessy."

"Sorry about that."

"Well, no harm done, I guess. We'll move on when you're ready."

Rory sat quietly for a moment, still shaken up at how close to death he'd come. He was frightened to head even farther into danger. But eventually he pushed those fears away and stood up. After all, he had a job to do.

They left the treasure room behind and headed through the new door into another dark tunnel. They hadn't gone far before a sound stopped them short. Hex covered the light, revealing a glow coming from around the corner. Hugging the wall, Rory made his way down toward the light. As he got closer, the light grew brighter, until he could see that it came from some kerosene lamps hanging from the ceiling. Under the lamps lay a teenager, asleep, dressed in rags and wearing a stovepipe hat just like Sly Jimmy's. As Rory watched, the boy rolled over in his sleep. Rory looked around the rest of the small room. An underground stream bordered one side, making its own tunnel through the darkness. He could hear faint splashing in the distance. A card table was set up in the corner, a deck of cards lying on it, neatly stacked. Beyond the sleeping teenager, a large wooden door stood closed. Rory took this all in and rushed back to Hex and Toy to report.

Hex cursed to himself. For the first time since the break-in began, he appeared uncertain.

"Plug Ugly. He's no illusion. Neither are his knives. Damn you, Tobias. Why'd you have to go and splurge on a guard!"

"What's a Plug Ugly? He looks only a few years older than me."

"A few years plus a hundred and twenty. He's a member of the Plug Uglies gang. They're a lot like the B'wry Boys that Sly Jimmy belongs to. They worked the streets back in the late nineteenth century. Out of Five Points, mostly, where China-town is today. Some of the Mayor's advisers have their own gangs to do their dirty work. Kieft uses the Forty Thieves. Tweed uses the Whyos gang. Tobias uses the Plug Uglies. They're mean as dogs. We have to be careful."

"So what do we do?"

"Maybe we can sneak by. We just have to be extremely quiet."

A splashing up ahead interrupted them. Hex's face drained of color.

"Oh dear. I hope that isn't what I think it is."

He took a few steps forward and peered around the corner.

"Things just got a tad more interesting."

Rory sidled up next to Hex and looked around the corner. The gang member was waking up as a white shape crawled over toward him. Rory could see the lamplight reflect off of hundreds of scales, rough and ridged. He blinked.

"Is that an alligator?"

Hex nodded slowly. Rory looked again.

"*He* doesn't seem too scared."

Hex nodded again, even slower this time.

"That's because he's an alligator rider. That is his mount."

Sure enough, the Plug Ugly was scratching the alligator's ridges and smiling. He pulled out a small piece of meat and tossed it to his gator. The large animal chomped it down and rubbed up against his leg. Rory shuddered.

"He rides that alligator? Where?"

"Through the sewers. They're an elite group."

"Since when are there alligators in the sewers?"

"Have you ever heard of the Albino Alligator?"

Rory blinked. His neighbor Mr. Little had told him and Bridget stories of the great white alligator that lived in the sewers beneath the city streets. Those tales had kept them up nights until Mrs. Little made her husband stop and assured them it was all made up.

"That's a myth."

"Try telling that to her children. There are dozens of them roaming the waters under the city."

Rory looked back toward the light.

"So what do we do now?"

Hex leaned in.

"I'm going to do something. Give me your hand. It's important that you trust me. Do you trust me?"

Rory nodded slowly, holding out his hand. Hex took out a pin and pricked Rory's palm.

"Ow! Jeez!"

"Don't be a baby, it's just a little pinprick. Now rub the blood on your forehead."

Rory followed instructions. Hex reached down to the floor and scraped up some dirt. He wiped the dirt into the blood on Rory's forehead. He murmured to himself with his eyes closed. Finally, he clapped lightly and opened his eyes, admiring his handiwork.

"Perfect!"

Rory looked down at himself.

"What? I don't feel any different."

Hex chuckled.

"But you look completely different. You now blend in perfectly with whatever is behind you. Don't touch! You'll rub it off. And now to do me."

Hex repeated the same trick on himself. After the final soft hand clap, he stared at himself, nodding in satisfaction.

"Perfect."

Rory could see Hex just fine. His own forehead was starting to sweat, but he made himself not think about it. Hex was bending down for more dirt.

"Now for Toy. He's inanimate, so he needs a slightly different magic."

Toy glared at him, apparently unhappy to be called inanimate. Hex finished his incantation and looked satisfied. To Rory, however, nothing looked any different.

"Are you sure we're invisible?"

"Yes. Now don't touch it!" He slapped Rory's hand away before he could wipe off his sweaty forehead. Rory reminded himself to be careful.

"We have to be ridiculously quiet," Hex said. "Just follow me to that door."

Rory looked closely at the closed door.

"What's behind it?"

"The entrance chamber to the vault. It's a huge room, empty except for the guardian."

"What is the guardian?"

"The last thing between us and the belt. We'll deal with that when we get to it. Just get ready to creep like a mouse."

The Plug Ugly, a scruffy-looking kid with a scraggly beard, sat down at his card table and picked up the pack of cards. He called down to his alligator mount.

"You wanna play some poker, Hamish? You got the perfect poker face for it."

He laughed at his own joke as Hamish stared back up at him impassively. Hex gestured with his hand and began to sneak down the tunnel. Rory and Toy followed, trying to stay as quiet as possible. Scraggly Beard dealt some cards.

"Hamish, you got some hand! Look at that! You gonna call or what?"

Hamish didn't answer. Scraggly Beard took this as a yes and tossed some pennies onto the center of the table. Hex reached the table and slowly slid by, holding his breath. Rory was right on his heels, almost passing out from not breathing. He looked down at Scraggly Beard as he slipped by. The Plug Ugly didn't even twitch, he was concentrating so hard on his cards.

"Hey!"

Rory froze in terror. Hex turned swiftly, his face alarmed, but he quickly relaxed. Rory turned to see Scraggly Beard waving a finger at his mount, who still hadn't moved.

"No peekin' at the cards!"

Trying not to shake, Rory resumed creeping. Hex had reached the door and stood there waiting for the other two to join him. Rory stepped up beside him with Toy right behind. Sweat began to pour down Rory's face in earnest. Scraggly Beard's back was to them, so they had a chance at opening the door and slipping through without him noticing. Hex put his hand on the knob and was just about to turn it when a small growl stopped him cold.

"What is it, boy?"

They turned back to see Hamish beginning to move, a small grumbling coming out of his reptilian snout. To Rory's horror, he was making his way right for them. Scraggly Beard knelt down beside the alligator.

"Where are you goin'? There's nothing there. Just that door, and I ain't openin' that, no matter what they pay me."

The sweat ran thicker down Rory's forehead, stinging his eyes. And that's when he did it. He didn't mean to; it was a reflex. But reflex or not, it was the worst possible thing he could have done. When the sweat dripped into his eyes, he reached up and wiped it clean with the back of his hand. He heard an intake of breath. Looking at the back of his hand, he could see a large smudge of reddish mud.

"Who are you! Where did you come from!"

Rory wasn't invisible anymore. He'd wiped his protection off with the back of his hand. Scraggly Beard stared at him in disbelief, reaching to his side and coming back with a knife. He jabbed it in Rory's direction.

"Answer me! Where'd you come from!"

Hex didn't waste another minute. He quickly opened the door and stepped through. Scraggly Beard jumped.

"How'd you do that?"

Toy stepped through the door, and Rory backed up after him, finally answering.

"Magic. Don't follow me or you'll get it worse."

Scraggly Beard looked past him, through the door.

"Oh, I ain't followin' you. You couldn't pay me to go in there. I'm just here to make sure you don't get back out."

Unnerved, Rory backed through the door and Hex closed it. The last image he had was of Scraggly Beard looking after him with an odd mix of satisfaction and pity.

And then the world turned white.

Scraggly Beard (whose real name was Michael O'Shea) stepped up to the door once it closed. He didn't know where that kid had come from, and he didn't want to know. If the boss ever found out he let someone sneak by, he'd get it bad. Not that the boss would ever find out. Nobody ever came out of that room next door. Not even the remains of people were ever seen again.

Glad it wasn't him, Michael sat back down at his card table and looked over his cards. They were awful. He considered trying to bluff, but you can't pull one over on an alligator. So he folded. Hamish stared back at him with that same empty stare, but Michael thought he saw a small hint of satisfaction in his eyes. Ah well. He'd get him next hand.

THE CAVALRY IS
RUNNING LATE

Don't you know how old these are! They've been in the family for generations!"

Dylan Arnold looked down in shame as his mother screamed at him. She pointed over and over at the large glass case holding her prized possessions, one of which now lay in pieces on the floor.

"These are china! China plates!" Mrs. Arnold shouted. "My great-grandmother, your great-great-grandmother, brought them here from Munich! How could you disrespect your ancestors like that?"

Dylan knew how old those china plates were. His mother never missed a chance to point it out, telling him to be careful every time he got within ten feet of them. It wasn't his fault he was a clumsy boy. You try being six foot two at fifteen years old, he wanted to yell at her. But he kept quiet, his eyes on the floor and his stomach in knots as Mrs. Arnold continued her tirade.

Sitting on the dining room table, unseen by either of the Arnolds, Hiram Greenbaum couldn't help but laugh. Mrs. Arnold was one of his favorite disciples. It really wasn't Dylan's fault he tripped over the rug in the dark and knocked one of those precious plates to the floor, where it shattered into a hundred pieces. It was just bad luck. But it gave Mrs. Arnold a chance to shine, and Hiram Greenbaum's belly grew warm with all the sweet guilt that flowed through the room. Dylan's hands were shaking, which meant a tearful apology could be only moments away. Hiram Greenbaum, God of Guilt, leaned in with anticipation.

He never even heard the soft footfalls of the assassin behind him, nor saw the knife. But once his dead body hit the floor, everything changed. Dylan suddenly straightened up.

"You know what, Mom?" he said, cutting her off. "I don't care about your plates! So, why don't you save your breath!"

He turned abruptly, carelessly brushing up against the glass case. Two more plates went tumbling to the floor, smashing into tiny shards. Dylan didn't even turn around, he stomped out of the room, leaving his mother behind, speechless. Her god had deserted her. The assassin leaned over the body of Hiram Greenbaum and yanked the small locket from around the dead god's neck. Nodding in satisfaction, he looked up . . . right into the eyes of the terrified god sitting on top of the china case. Though Mrs. Arnold was oblivious to the murder done in her presence, Jean Pierre Le Grand, God of the Good China, had seen everything. Squealing with fear, he dropped to the ground and dived straight through the floor, heading for the basement. The assassin sighed, gave his knife a quick wipe, and swiftly followed.

At first, Fritz hadn't wanted to let Bridget come after Rory with him. But she quickly disabused him of that particular notion.

"You need me!" she said, pulling on her boots defiantly. "Do you think Rory's gonna listen to some strange cockroach popping up out of nowhere? If I'm not there, why would he listen to you?"

Fritz reluctantly saw the wisdom in that, and soon they were on the subway heading downtown. At one point, Nicholas stepped out between the cars with Fritz in his hand and, from what Bridget could see, they started arguing about something. She was so intent on watching them, she didn't even notice the singing until it was coming from right behind her. The old doo-wop song finally caught her ear, however, and she turned to look right into the eyes of the same subway musician who'd spoken to her and Rory the day before. He was alone this time, and he seemed to be singing just for her. He finished his ditty to applause throughout the car and swept off his fedora to collect the money. While doing so, he threw a wink in Bridget's direction. Unsure of what to do, she pulled out some money to drop in his hat.

"Keep your quarters, child. You're gonna need 'em," he said, closing her hand back around the silver.

"Um. Okay." Stung, Bridget put her money back in her pocket. "For a street singer, you sure do turn down a lot of money."

"It's late for a girl like you to be out and about, ain't it?" he asked her as the train pulled into a station, the doors opening silently to let off passengers.

"I'm going to meet my brother, and I know kung fu," she

replied. "And don't you be sayin' something weird about my dreams or something or I'll, I'll, I'll step on your toes!"

He looked down.

"I like your boots."

Bridget glanced down at her steel-tipped clompers.

"Thanks."

"Nice sword, too."

Bridget blushed, trying to hide the cardboard sword she had brought with her. It made her feel like a hero to be carrying Buttkicker. "I like it."

"You just need one more thing," he said, grinning widely.

"What?"

He reached out and tapped her forehead. Her eyes closed briefly and she shivered, feeling something race through her.

"What was that?" she demanded. But the door was closing behind the grinning black man, who'd somehow made it outside during the second her eyes had been shut. She was still shaken when Fritz and Nicholas returned. She told them all about it. They exchanged a look.

"Was that who I think it was?" Nicholas said thoughtfully.

"Could have been," Fritz replied, worry on his face. "I wonder what he wanted."

"What are you talking about!" Bridget demanded, but they wouldn't explain. They didn't want to worry her, they said. Which was pretty stupid, she thought, since she was probably more worried being kept in the dark. An old woman across the way gave her a weird look and she realized how crazy she appeared, talking to invisible people on the subway, so she lapsed into a pouting silence. Nicholas joined her in her pout, so he must not have liked the decision he and Fritz had come to out between the subway cars. After a moment, she put her hand over her mouth and whispered down to Fritz.

"Can you at least tell me what's so scary about this bank?" she asked. The woman gave her another disapproving look, so Bridget stuck out her tongue at the old lady, who sniffed and went back to reading her magazine. Fritz leaned up against his rat, Clarence, and started to explain.

"About fifty years ago, my clan was approached by a man named Tom Hill and his son, Jason. They wanted to release the Munsees by breaking into Tobias's bank to get to this magic belt he had stashed away in his vault. Our clan leaders forbid it, but a few of us decided to help anyway. Four battle roaches went into the bank with Tom and his son, and I hold their names dear to my heart: Captain Lymph, Lieutenant-Captain Pieter, Sergeant Bertold, and Private Tieg. I would have gone as well, but my wife begged me not to, and out of love for her I stayed. So six went in, but only Bertold came back out. I found him lying on the pavement outside the bank and he died in my arms, but not before he warned me of a monster."

"What kind of monster?" Bridget whispered, her heart beating fast.

"He died before he could say. But we're going to catch up to Rory before he meets this monster. Don't worry."

This tale of horror made Bridget doubly frightened for her brother, but something else tugged at her.

"Wait a second. That was fifty years ago!" she said, louder

than she intended. The old woman across the way got up and quickly moved to the other end of the train. "Cockroaches live like a week. That's impossible."

"Is that the truth?" Nicholas said, breaking his own silence with a small smile.

"I am over a hundred years old," Fritz said patiently. "We roaches last forever. We're hard to kill. Even when you think we're dead, we're usually just pretending so you'll flush us down the toilet and we can make our way back home. You humans don't know everything you think you do."

The train arrived at City Hall, and five minutes later they were out on the street. The reason for Nicholas's unhappiness was revealed when Fritz sent the young man on his way, refusing to let him risk being caught in the bank.

"They catch me, I'm just a renegade with a grudge," Fritz said. "They catch you, and the whole Rattle Watch will end up in the Tombs or worse, especially after that business with the sandhog. It's better to be safe than sorry. I'll send word the minute we're out."

"Protect him," Nicholas answered. "But don't forget, we don't know yet what he's supposed to do. Maybe this is it."

"Maybe," Fritz answered. "But I won't let him face it alone."

After one last worried look, Nicholas turned and disappeared down a side street. Bridget turned to Fritz, who was staring thoughtfully toward the corner.

"I thought I saw a rat," he said.

"Well, it *is* the city," Bridget replied. "We have a lot of rats."

"You're right," Fritz said, shaking it off. "I'm just on edge."

Fritz led them around to the back of the bank. Bridget

followed after him, her new steel-tipped boots sending loud echoes through the deserted city streets.

"No one here now," he said, looking around the empty corner. He turned Clarence around and rode up the street. Bridget ran after him.

"Where are we going?" she asked him. "Do you remember how to get into the bank?"

"I wasn't ever let in on that particular secret. So I'm gonna ask for some help."

"What kind of help?"

"You'll see."

Fritz headed to the far corner of the block behind the bank. As they approached the side of the building, Bridget could just make out a statue near the wall. Gray as concrete, the statue was of a young woman in a long evening gown. Her gray hair was piled up on top of her head while one gray-slippered foot balanced a bit forward, toe pointing down, as if she were about to pirou-ette. As they came closer, Bridget was struck by how lifelike the statue appeared. If not for its complete stillness, it could almost be one of those performers in Times Square, the living statues that would appear to be stone but would suddenly move at the drop of a coin in their bucket. In fact, now that she stood right in front of it, Bridget could swear it was a real woman, standing on this dark street corner in the middle of the night waiting for a stray tourist to wander by and make her dance. But her skin did not appear to be painted; it seemed to be hard stone.

Bridget whispered down to Fritz. "Is she real?"

"A real what? Human? No. Statue? No. Do you have any quarters?"

She pulled the quarters she almost gave the subway singer out of her pocket. Fritz gestured to a small bag at the statue's feet.

"Toss one in."

Bridget dropped a quarter in the bag. Immediately, the statue sprang into motion, stepping forward daintily on her front toe and dipping into a curtsy. A light but raspy voice flew out of her stone mouth.

"I'm a living statue, little girl. Alexandria Haverford is my name. I am not human, nor am I statue. But I am indeed made of stone."

Alexandria finished speaking and ceased moving all at once, locked in her curtsy. Bridget asked another question.

"Why are you back here in the middle of nowhere?"

Alexandria didn't respond. Trying to move things along, Fritz gestured to the bag. Bridget dropped in another quarter, launching Alexandria into action. She lifted out of her curtsy and rose to her toes, her arms arched over her head like a ballerina.

"This is where I rest. No one bothers me here. The worst that can happen is a little spray paint, and the street cleaners are kind enough to scrub me clean. During the day I am out in the park, collecting coins and delighting the children as my kind are made to do."

She froze again, impossibly balanced on her tippy-toes. Fritz tapped his foot impatiently.

"Are we done chatting? We need some information. Have you seen a man and a young boy come by here in the last half hour?"

Bridget tossed in another quarter. Alexandria dipped down again, her back leg lifting high into the air.

"I spied a man and two boys not fifteen minutes ago."

"Great, we're not that far behind!" Fritz exclaimed. "Where did they go?"

Bridget dropped her last quarter in the bag, prompting the graceful statue to reach out with her arms imploringly, pointing to the road.

"They disappeared into the middle of the street like magic. This has been quite a night for magic; I'm not used to all the excitement. I'll be glad when you're all gone."

She ceased to move, locked with her arms outstretched. Fritz gestured to Bridget, who was looking through her pockets.

"Come on, let's check it out," Fritz said. "What are you doing?"

"I'm looking for a quarter so I can say thank you."

"There's no time. Come on!"

And they rushed off, leaving the statue behind. Bridget shivered. How awful it must be to be trapped in stone like that. So cold. They reached the center of the street where the statue had pointed. Fritz studied the ground.

"There has to be something here. A trapdoor, something."

But neither of them could find anything. Finally, Fritz threw up his hands in frustration.

"I don't understand it. Maybe this Hex is a better magician than I thought."

"Come on! Rory needs us!" Bridget cried. She banged her fist against the ground three times, showing how angry she was. Suddenly, a section of the street fell away, opening a hole right underneath Fritz, who barely had time to look surprised before falling down into it. Bridget peered over the edge.

"Fritz! What did I do? Are you all right?"

A small voice drifted up.

"I'm good. Dusty, but good. You'd better come down here."

A few moments later, Bridget was standing in the tunnel, lowering Clarence to the ground just as the hole above them closed up, leaving them in darkness.

"Awful spooky in here," she said.

"It sure is."

There was a pause.

"Did you bring that flashlight?" Fritz asked finally.

"Oh yeah."

Embarrassed, Bridget pulled out the flashlight and turned it on. The light revealed an old passageway leading off into the distance.

"Somebody was here, all right."

Fritz pointed down at the dust, where she could plainly see footprints. Fritz climbed on Clarence and started to ride ahead. Bridget followed carefully. Fritz looked back at her.

"You have to be the luckiest girl alive, finding that trapdoor."

She shrugged.

"I'm Malibu Death Barbie."

They walked forward, following the footsteps in the dust, hoping that they could catch up with Rory before it was too late.

THE LUCKIEST GIRL
IN THE WORLD

Bridget moved through the passageway quickly, forcing herself to slow down when she left Fritz too far behind. The footprints went ever ahead, even as the walls and the floor changed. She listened as she walked for any voices floating back toward her, but the air remained stubbornly silent. She had no idea how far ahead they'd gotten. The tunnel led onward, endlessly. Then, suddenly, she came upon the first door.

"What's this?" she asked.

"I don't know," Fritz answered, catching up to her. "I guess we go in. Stay behind me!"

"You're three inches tall."

"Just do it! Now open the door."

Bridget reached out and turned the knob, stepping into 1776.

The sound of gunfire made Bridget cry out. She whirled around, taking in all the soldiers and the cannons.

"What is this?" she screamed.

"It's the past! This must be a memory room! Get down!"

Bridget dropped to the ground by Fritz as a cannonball landed behind them, sending up a shower of dirt.

"What do we do?" she asked him.

"There has to be a way out. Get behind those barrels!"

She crawled over to some barrels of grain, hiding behind them to escape the musket balls. Fritz joined her.

"Some memory rooms are designed to keep you inside them forever. Others are just supposed to kill you. I don't know which this is. Hopefully the first kind."

"I don't want to be stuck in here forever!" Bridget cried.

"Rory might be here, too," Fritz answered her. "I'm going to take a look. Stay here! I didn't bring you along to let you get shot!"

He rode off. Bridget watched as a woman ran by holding a cannonball. A girl soldier! Keeping low to the ground, Bridget ran up to her.

"Excuse me? Lady? Have you seen a magician and two kids?"

The woman turned to her, her face shocked to see a little girl.

"Get away, little one! This is no place for a child! The British are at our throats!"

Suddenly a cannonball landed right on the barrel Bridget had been hiding behind, destroying it completely. The woman shook her head.

"You are a lucky one. Go!"

She ran off toward the cannons. Bridget made her way to the wall opposite a door in the fort. Looking closely, she could see that the latch had been pulled off, leaving the door hanging partly open. Someone really should have stuck a lock on that thing. . . .

"Retreat!"

A voice yelled out the command. Suddenly everyone began to run away. Bridget watched as the woman soldier was carried by two of her fellows, her shoulder bloody. Bridget hoped she'd be okay. Fritz rode up.

"I think we should follow them. Maybe we can find a place of safety and figure this out. Come on!"

He began to ride off, followed by Bridget, when suddenly the door behind them flew open, and soldiers in red coats streamed in, guns pointed right at them. Bridget put up her hands, backing up, as Fritz did the same.

"Are they taking us prisoner?" she asked.

"I don't think so," Fritz answered.

The soldiers raised their guns and prepared to fire. Bridget stumbled back, throwing up her hands in front of her face. It wasn't supposed to end this way. She was Malibu Death Barbie! She had a sword! She wasn't supposed to get shot! Bridget braced herself for the pain, falling back as the guns rang out—

She landed with a thud. Confused, she felt all over her chest—no holes. Spinning around, she was more than a little surprised to find herself in another tunnel, looking through the wall at the fort, where a group of very confused solders stared in her direction. Fritz and Clarence suddenly leaped through the hole, landing at her side. The hole faded, leaving behind a plain wall.

"You are something else," Fritz said admiringly.

"What happened?" she asked.

"You stumbled back and just fell through the wall. You must have happened upon the doorway by mistake. You okay?"

Bridget pushed herself to her feet.

"Yeah. I think I am."

She noticed that Fritz was staring up at her thoughtfully.

"Have you always been this lucky?" he asked.

Bridget thought it over.

"I guess. I mean my dad left when I was a baby, my mom can barely afford to buy me new shoes, and my brother is walking into a death trap."

"So this is recent," Fritz said.

"What are you trying to say?"

"Nothing. I just think it's interesting. That's all."

He urged Clarence to continue forward. Bridget gave herself a good shake, a smile peeking through her lips. She was something else, wasn't she? She brandished her sword before her and strode forth, ready to take on whatever came her way.

Bridget found it hard to keep track of time as they moved through the dank tunnel. They didn't seem to be gaining on Rory. They couldn't hear anyone up ahead at all.

"Do you think they got out of that last room?" Bridget asked, her lip trembling at the thought.

"Look down. What do you see?"

Of course. Footprints in the dust.

"We'll catch up, Bridget," Fritz promised.

"Okay. I know."

But she didn't know that; the thought made her stomach hurt.

Eventually they came to another door, and pushed their way through to a beautiful sight.

"Look at all this treasure!" Bridget gasped. She gazed around in wonder at all the piles and piles of gold and jewels surrounding her. Fritz gestured impatiently.

"Come on. We're not here for money. Just follow the footprints!"

Clarence leaped forward, scurrying toward the exit. Bridget lingered behind, dazed by all the rich stuff. Just one little piece of gold could put the Hennessy family on top! She reached out to grab a particularly shiny necklace lying by her feet. At the last minute she stopped herself. Her mom would wonder where Bridget found such expensive jewelry, and she didn't want that. She walked on, trying to ignore the call of the gold in her head. Fritz yelled over to her.

"Bridget! I found the exit! Come on!"

She hurried to follow after him. Just before she left, a flash caught her eye. It was a small gold spoon. So tiny, hardly anything really. Who would miss it? But it could pay for so much. She'd tell her mom she found it in the park. Without stopping to think any further, she reached down and snatched it up.

"Bridget!"

She raced out of the treasure room, putting the spoon in her pocket. After a moment, some of the lighter golden items began to move gently as a breeze began to blow.

Bridget and Fritz found themselves in another tunnel. After a few moments of walking, Fritz put up his hand, coming to a stop. Bridget leaned over next to him.

"What is it?"

"There's light up ahead. See?"

Sure enough, a soft yellow flicker crept in from around the corner. Bridget dropped her voice to a whisper.

"Do you think it's them?"

"Better to be safe. Do you feel a breeze? We might be near the surface. Come on."

They slowly made their way to the bend in the tunnel. Bridget and Fritz snuck a look around the corner.

A teenager with a scraggly beard dressed in old-fashioned clothes was sitting at a card table, muttering to himself. Beyond him lay an underground stream and a door. Fritz looked up at Bridget and mouthed something. Bridget answered him in confusion.

"Lug Buggy?"

Fritz's eyes flashed impatiently as he whispered back.

"Plug Ugly. Gang member. Gator Rider, but where's the gator?"

As if to answer him, a large, white-scaled reptile crawled into view. The teenager leaned over and scratched his eye ridges.

"I warned 'em. Can't say I didn't warn 'em, right, Hamish? And now he's dead. Ah well, good riddance. Stupid boy."

Bridget's face drained of all color. Were they talking about Rory? Rory wasn't dead! *No!* She stepped into the light before Fritz could stop her.

"Take it back!"

The boy leaped to his feet.

"Who are you? A little girl? What's going on here? How did all these kids get down here?"

"He's not dead! Take it back!"

She kept walking toward him, her cardboard sword held out before her. He took a step closer.

"What's that in your hand? A dolly?"

He soon found out that it was, in fact, not a dolly. Bridget reached him and immediately hit him over the head with the cardboard sword. It left a small paper cut down the boy's cheek. His hand flew up to his face.

"Son of a— That hurt! What's wrong with you? Are you some kind of crazy girlie?"

"Take it back!"

She proceeded to whack him again, this time on the other side of his face. An identical paper cut appeared on the other cheek, making it look like he had quotation marks around his nose. He squealed again, backing up.

"What are you? A vengeful spirit come to punish me?"

She kicked him with her steel-toed boots. He screamed in pain.

"Ow! Stop it!"

And again. And again. She would not stop. The Plug Ugly backed up as she whacked him in the face and gave him nasty kicks to the legs. Fritz watched in amazement. It was like seeing a bear get whipped by a hamster.

"Ow! Stop that. I'm serious!"

Bridget never let up smacking and kicking. The teen kept backing up.

"Okay, you know what? I'm gonna take that thing away from you right *nowaaaaggghhh*!"

He grabbed the sword out of her hand right as he hit the edge of the underground river. The sword waved in the air as he fell backward. *Splash*. The water moved quickly along the stream. The Plug Ugly flailed about, trying to keep his place, but the flow of the current proved too strong. Finally it swept him and Buttkicker away, far into the distance, until even his shouts became echoes before fading entirely.

Bridget looked back at Fritz, her face drawn and frightened.

"It's not true."

"Watch out!"

The alligator, angry about this mistreatment of his master, rushed Bridget. She backed up in fright, until the door to the vault stopped her. She didn't even have a sword to protect her anymore. Without thinking, she pulled out the spoon and held it in front of her, hoping the shiny surface would distract the beast.

"Stay back!"

The alligator snapped, and Bridget barely got her hand out of the way as the gator swallowed the spoon whole. The gator opened his mouth again, this time to rip Bridget in two.

"Bridget, look out!"

But the snap never came. The breeze she'd been feeling picked up, becoming a gale. The gator stopped in confusion.

"What's going on?" Bridget gasped.

"I don't know," was all Fritz had for her.

A fog poured in from the tunnel. It swept by Bridget and surrounded the alligator, diving into his snout. The gator began to shudder, like he was suffering a violent seizure. His eyes rolled back as he gave one last huge shudder and fell still. The fog poured back out, seeping from the reptile's eye sockets and nostrils. The beast's mouth opened, and out flew the gold spoon. It soared through the air, held up by the fog as it headed back down the tunnel, toward the treasure room. The spoon disappeared around the corner, carried by the retreating wind, leaving Bridget, Fritz, Clarence, and a dead alligator behind.

After a moment, Fritz was finally able to speak.

"Where did you get that spoon?" he asked slowly.

"I picked it up from the treasure room."

"I guess they don't like it when you take things."

"I guess not."

"You are, without a doubt, the luckiest girl in the world. Do you know that?"

Bridget didn't answer. She just hoped her luck held.

BEETLES AND
BANK NOTES

The assassin warily approached First City Bank, looking in every direction for some sign of his quarry. It had taken him longer to arrive than he'd hoped, and now he feared that he was the last one to the party. With Hiram Greenbaum, God of Guilt, dead, the assassin no longer felt an ounce of remorse about disposing of the Light. Actually, he didn't feel guilty about anything at all, not anymore. Entranced by this new feeling, he'd enjoyed running past the locked-up houses, the pale faces of various spirits and gods peeking out from behind the curtains. They were frightened, frightened of *him*, though they didn't know it. Soon he'd be even more powerful and they'd truly have a reason to fear. The thought warmed his heart. But those happy daydreams had slowed him down, and now he was paying the price.

The idea to send little Sally after Fritz had paid off, but the information his rat spy had brought him meant nothing if he couldn't catch up. He'd arrived at the bank—where he suspected they would try to gain entrance—and sure enough he saw signs of them on the ground. But where had they gone?

How did they get in? Casting about for an answer, his eyes fell on a dark figure on one of the street corners. A living statue. Such creatures saw everything. He pulled out his knife, which despite its grim night's work still shone clean in the moonlight. But then he stopped. He had no time to hide the body, and Tobias would not be happy if a dead statue was found near his bank. What to do—wait! She was pointing at something. Something in the center of the street behind the bank.

The assassin quickly searched the street at the other end of the living statue's finger. Eventually, he stumbled upon a circle in the pavement. It must be some sort of trapdoor. But he had no idea how to open it. Glancing at the sky, he could tell that the night was slipping through his fingers. Another task awaited him at dawn, so time was short. He had to choose.

Unsure, he pulled out a gold locket and ran his fingers lovingly over it. Such a small, trivial thing, and yet filled with so much power. When Kieft had told him the secret, he hadn't believed it. At first he hadn't known why Kieft had approached him at all, but certainly the powerful god knew him better than he knew himself. The promise of all that power—of finally pulling himself up to the level he'd always known he deserved—it overwhelmed him. All it took was one of these little lockets. And the only way to gain a locket was through murder. A small price to pay, in the end.

So he bowed before Kieft, like they all would soon, and later, when asked, he became his assassin. All for this lovely little trinket, and all the others like it. Kieft forbade him from wearing it, for now, since people would sense the changes it would bring. Be patient, he had said. The assassin had dutifully waited for this day to arrive, when he could finally reach out and take the prize, though he waited still to claim it as his own. Patience rewarded him every time. So he would be patient again.

He sent Sally ahead, to scout out the sewers for signs of their quarry. Then he fell back into the shadow of the building behind him to wait, his eyes always on the small circle in the pavement. If Tobias caught Rory, then his job would be done for him. If not, the boy would have to come back out the way he'd gone in. And then the assassin would be waiting, and this time his hand would be steady as he wielded the knife without a tinge of conscience.

Rory and his companions stood with their backs against the door and gazed around the room in which they now found themselves trapped. It was huge and white, with an impossibly tall ceiling. At the very top of the room was a large stained-glass window depicting a group of Indians meeting a couple of old-fashioned-looking men who were handing over jewelry and trinkets. Across the room, a small metal door stuck out as the only break in a long white wall that stretched on into the distance.

"What's the danger this time?" Rory whispered.

"This one has been changed. They killed the guardian fifty years ago, so Tobias had to replace it."

"With what? I don't see anything."

"Something is in here with us, I can feel it. Stay by the

door. Just take a look around. Look closely. Something will jump out at you."

Rory struggled to calm himself, forcing his breathing to slow. He could sense something in there, too, and it didn't feel friendly. Trying to remain calm, Rory slowly scanned the huge white room. Hex nudged him.

"Try relaxing your eyes. There's something here, so there has to be something to see."

Rory did as asked. He forced his eyeballs to look at nothing, until everything in front of him doubled. As it was all just white, anyway, it didn't really change much. Except now he could see something moving ever so slightly.

"Do you see that?"

Hex looked intently in the same direction.

"No. What is it?"

Rory kept his eyes defocused and tried to make it out. It looked like a long line, a string for a balloon or a piece of tinsel hanging from some far-off limb from a Christmas tree. He tried to point it out to Hex, who stared intently into the white.

"What's it hanging from? Is it attached to anything?" Hex asked.

One end of the string went down toward the metal door. Following the other end led Rory upward, where it seemed to be hanging from the ceiling. Trying one last time, he relaxed his eyes again. And then it leaped out at him. He gasped, causing Hex to look up at the ceiling.

"What is it?"

"It's on the ceiling."

"Well, what does it look like?"

"Like a man-eating monster. A bug-shaped, man-eating monster."

Hex peered up at the ceiling.

"I see it! It's a giant snow beetle."

Rory relaxed a little. A beetle didn't sound too bad. Beetles climbed onto your finger and let you stroke their backs. Beetles weren't scary. Of course, Hex wasn't done yet.

"It's a fire-breather. Territorial. Cooks them and eats them, I guess you'd say."

Rory stopped relaxing in a hurry.

"A fire-breathing *beetle*?"

"They occupied these lands when everything lay frozen under a large glacier, thousands of years ago. They would burn their way into the ice to make their nests. The Munsees trapped a few of them long ago and used them to guard their sachem burial ground."

Rory gazed up at the huge death beetle clinging to the ceiling far overhead.

"Are you guys invisible to it?" he asked. "Maybe you can make a break for it."

"Nope. That sucker can see right through my little spell. It's far older than my magic."

"So we're doomed."

Hex patted his shoulder in reassurance.

"Don't worry. It's not a man-eater by nature. It attacks only because it's tethered. The old Munsee shamans used to chain them somehow. Maybe if we release it, it'll just fly away."

"Release it? You want to let it go wild?"

Hex nodded briskly and then scratched his chin.

"Can you see where the other end of the line is attached?" Hex asked.

Rory focused on the metal door, trying to see where the line led. He could just make out something flapping at the base.

"It's tied to some kind of paper."

"Newspaper? Tissue paper?"

"Just a piece of white paper."

"We need to find out what's on that paper. Which means we need to get across this room somehow without getting burned and eaten."

As he finished speaking, Hex's eyes had come around to rest on Toy. Toy stared back up at him, his face shiny and blank.

"Toy. Toy, I need your help."

Toy didn't respond in any way. Hex knelt down next to him.

"Flavio made you flame-retardant. He told me. He hated it when kids would set his piñatas on fire. Don't worry, I'll make sure nothing happens to you. I swear it."

Toy's face didn't change. Rory shifted uncomfortably.

"Hex, maybe this isn't such a good idea."

Hex took Toy's chin in his hand, putting his other hand kindly on his shoulder.

"Please, Toy."

Toy slowly nodded. Hex bent over and kissed Toy on the top of his head. Toy accepted the kiss without moving. Hex stood up straight.

"When Toy gets the beetle's attention, we need to run across the room as fast as we can. Toy, make sure to lead it to the other side, so it isn't looking in our direction. Let's hope this works. You ready, Rory?"

Rory nodded once.

"All right," Hex said. "Here we go. Ready, Toy? Go!"

Toy darted out into the wide-open room. The beetle reacted with terrifying speed. It dropped down off of the ceiling, a huge white oval with big buzzing wings and long white legs that hung down ready to snatch its prey. It had been trapped in this room for far too long, and now someone would pay the price. Finally, its eyes picked up Toy and it opened its mouth wide. A long blast of fire shot out, ripping through the air toward tiny Toy. The flames engulfed him, burning the air around him for a moment.

Rory couldn't see how anything could survive that blast. But after a moment, the flames died down and there Toy stood. His skin had blackened a bit, the paper bubbling in parts, but still whole. The beetle hung in the air, uncertain why its prey was still moving. Toy, having gotten its attention, ran toward the opposite end of the room. The beetle turned to follow him. Hex grabbed Rory's arm.

"Okay. That's our cue. Run!"

Hex took off. Rory hesitated a moment then ran after him. Hex never glanced over toward the hovering beetle, but Rory couldn't look away. It chased Toy and let out another lick of flame. This time, Toy leaped to the side, and the flames missed him. He jumped again, narrowly escaping being impaled by the beetle's thrusting claw. The beetle had apparently decided that since fire wasn't working, it was going to have to do this by hand. Toy moved from side to side, avoiding the striking claws while trying to keep the beetle's attention away from the metal door.

Rory was so caught up watching the struggle that he tripped, landing hard on the ground.

"Get up! Quickly!" Hex hissed.

Rory pulled himself to his feet and in a blind panic scrambled the rest of the way. He ran right into Hex, who was kneeling beside the door. Rory's shoulder brushed up against Hex's face. As it came away, a large mud stain appeared on his shirt. Hex's forehead had been wiped clean. Hex sighed.

"Well, there goes that spell. Where is this piece of paper?"

Rory pointed to the paper, and they both bent over to read it. It said **BANK OF FIRST CITY** in big letters, with the words CREDIT EXTENDED underneath. At the bottom was a number written in slightly smudged ink. It read $4.27. Hex grew excited.

"It's a debt. Leave it to a banker . . . someone must have loaned this beetle to the bank for four dollars and twenty-seven cents. And judging by that number, it was a long time ago."

"So what do we do?"

"He's trapped by debt. Tobias is so cheap, he didn't even pay up front. He owes this money. Maybe we can pay off the debt. Then we can do what we want with the beetle, and *Tobias* would owe *us*."

Rory didn't follow any of this. All he knew was that Toy was running out of time.

"So what do we do?"

"We buy the debt. Quick! Empty your pockets! Do you have any money?"

"What about you?"

"I don't carry money. There are a lot of thieves in this city."

Rory patted his pockets. In his front pants pocket he pulled out three wrinkled singles. From his other front pocket he pulled out three quarters and three nickels. His back pockets came up empty. Hex groaned.

"That's not enough. Check your jacket!"

Rory searched through his jacket pockets, turning up a dime, a nickel, and finally a penny. Hex let out a long breath.

"That's still not enough."

"That's all I have."

"There has to be more!"

Rory threw up his hands. He looked toward Toy, who was being backed into a corner. Soon he'd be trapped. It was hopeless. *Why is it always about money?* He never had enough. He slumped in defeat. And that's when he saw them. Right in the middle of the floor: glittering silver and copper coins. They must have fallen out of his pocket when he tripped. Rory pointed them out to Hex, who let out a worried sigh.

"Perfect! So who's gonna get them?"

Rory looked back at the giant beetle, floating above Toy and ready to kill.

"I'll do it. I'm faster than you."

Hex didn't argue. He clapped Rory on the shoulder.

"Just run out, grab the money, and run back. Don't stop for anything. Okay? Go!"

Rory leaped out into the open floor, heading full speed for those tiny, shiny dots. He heard Hex gasp behind him.

"Rory, the beetle sees you. Come back!"

But he couldn't come back. Even though he could hear the buzz of those huge wings coming closer, he couldn't stop now. Skidding to a halt, he bent down and grabbed the coins. He straightened up just in time to see the beetle hovering directly above him. He screamed before he could stop himself.

The huge black eyes stared at him as the mouth opened wide. Rory could smell the sulfur in the air. He could imagine what came next. The bright tongue of flame would rush over him all at once. He'd be burned to a crisp. To his surprise, however, the mouth slowly closed again. Evidently the beetle decided that Rory must have been like Toy, impervious to flame. So instead of being burned alive, he'd be impaled on one of the beetle's front claws. Wonderful. Rory stared upward, frozen, waiting for the strike to come. The front leg came shooting down, headed for Rory's chest. It was just about to plunge into his heart when a small blur leaped toward him, pushing him out of the way. The leg crashed into the floor, a small body impaled on it. Toy. The paper boy turned his head to Rory, and for the first time, sound breathed out of his paper mouth.

"Oooooo!"

Go. Rory scrambled to his feet and raced back to the door. The beetle rose behind him, Toy still impaled on its front claw. Rory reached the door and grabbed the rest of the money. He turned to Hex.

"What do I do now?"

Hex stared out at Toy dangling from the beetle's leg with horrified eyes, frozen by the sight. Rory struck his shoulder.

"Come on! What now?"

Hex sprang to life.

"Place the money on the paper."

Rory dumped his fistful of money onto the paper. The bills began to fly around the coins, twirling like a hurricane. The coins began to swirl as well, until all the money spiraled like water going down a drain. It spun faster and faster before sinking down into the paper, leaving no trace. Hex breathed out slowly.

"Somebody's bank account just went up by a tiny bit."

The paper came free of the door, falling into Rory's hand. It was his. Thinking fast, he reached up and untied the string, which quickly pulled free.

Rory turned to look up at the beetle. It darted around, waiting for the line to tug it back. The string whipped around behind it, flapping loosely. Finally, the beetle discovered it was free. With a blinding rush of speed, it rose toward the stained-glass window in the ceiling. Crashing through, it sent small glass shards raining to the floor. Then it disappeared through the black hole in the ceiling. Falling with the glass was a small shape, which thudded to the ground in front of them. Hex and Rory ran up to it. Toy looked up at them from the ground, feeling for the large hole in the middle of his chest.

Hex kneeled down beside him and spoke tenderly. "You're all right. You're almost there! You did very well."

He leaned over and kissed Toy on the forehead again. Toy struggled to his feet, his hand dangling from his wrist. His paper skin bubbled in places, with small black cracks running through the scarred surface. His skin tone no longer shone pink, but rather yellow and brown from where the flames had covered him. He stood, swaying slightly. Rory looked at Hex.

"Is he all right like this?"

"Don't worry. We'll fix him up. Everything will be all right soon enough."

Toy staggered toward the door and tried to turn the big metal wheel in the center. Hex walked up to him, gently pushing him aside. He gave the wheel a big spin. It twirled around before stopping with a click. Hex turned back toward Rory.

"Magic time."

He pulled the door open and stepped inside the vault. Toy hurried in after him. Rory folded the paper and placed it in his pocket. He gave the white room one last look before rushing over to step through the door . . . where he saw the very last thing he expected, even in his darkest dreams.

TOY'S SECRET

Cars buzzed by the northern edge of Central Park despite the late hour, but inside the park it was quiet. Soft yellow streetlamps lined the paths that twisted along the man-made hills and valleys, giving the still park a magical, otherworldly feel. One of those paths opened out onto the sidewalk that ran along the northern edge of the park. A dark figure loped up to this opening from the street outside and peered in. A car passing by lit the figure for a moment, but the driver could not see the Indian crouched down, leaning up against thin air as if it were solid, pushing but not able to step through the seemingly open entrance. Wampage, for it was he, turned to the panting dog that had followed him.

"Find her," he said. The dog yipped once, not wanting to enter the park. Wampage knelt down and stared into the dog's face.

"Please. Find her."

The dog licked Wampage's hand and took off, rushing through the entrance and quickly disappearing into the trees.

His face pained as if this were the last place he wanted to be, Wampage sat back against the wall to wait.

The moon had long set by the time a rustle in the bushes on the other side of the wall roused Wampage from his vigil. He turned just in time to catch the leaping dog in his arms, pulling back as the canine licked at his face. He listened to the wind blowing gently from the park, but he could hear nothing else. He set the dog on the sidewalk.

"Thank you for trying," he said sadly to his companion's eager face.

"Wampage?" a voice called out from the other side of the wall. Wampage rushed to the entrance, leaning up against the invisible barrier with his ear to the air.

"Sooleawa?" he said. "Is it you?"

"It is, Wanderer," her voice answered. "You sent that brave hound to fetch me, and here I am. I have missed you, old friend. We all miss you."

Sooleawa—the sister of his oldest friend, Tackapausha. Medicine woman and one of the wise, her voice carried much weight among the Munsees. Sachem Penhawitz had taken no wife in the spirit world, leaving his daughter to speak for the women. Her knowledge of magic was unrivaled, and she led them all in their rites. Wampage had called to her since he valued her wisdom above all others. He leaned his forehead against the invisible wall, his stone facade cracking at her voice.

"It is beyond suffering to be left behind."

"What did I tell you about blaming yourself?" Sooleawa's voice said sternly. "Now why did you call for me? Not that I am not glad of it, but we have not heard from you in a century. Is the last shell pit in danger?"

"It is safe. You will make wampum there once again, I promise. I bring news. About a young *Sabbeleu*—"

"Is this the young man spied strolling through our prison grounds yesterday?" Sooleawa interrupted.

"Yes. Rory is his name."

"Rory. I will tell Soka. She spoke with him, you know. I think she is enamored, though it is hard to tell with her. She calls herself levelheaded, but she is like a bird flying from want to want."

Wampage had never met Sooleawa's daughter, Soka, nor her brother, Tammand. They both had been born after the Trap. He had only heard about their birth during those first years when he still came down to the Trap for news. Would he now finally get the chance to see his dear friend's children?

"Who was the one who shot at Rory?" he asked.

"Oh, that was Tammand. He meant only mischief; I do not think he would have hit the boy. My son has fallen in with bad friends. He is very angry. He does not realize that there is no hope in his path. Only destruction. But he is not alone in his feelings. In fact, you would be surprised to know who has turned to such dark thoughts as the years pass and we remain imprisoned."

"That is my news," Wampage said. "I believe that the *Sabbeleu* is attempting to free you as we speak. A mighty newcomer has discovered the way to unlock the Trap, and I believe Rory is going to attempt to help him. I do not want to give any of us false hope, but there is a chance you might be freed very soon."

"What!"

Wampage was surprised to hear fear in Sooleawa's voice rather than the joy he was expecting.

"Can he truly accomplish this?" she asked.

"Yes, I think so."

"Then you must stop him!"

The vault looked nothing like Rory expected. For one thing, there was hardly anything in it. No gold bars, no piles of money or jewels, not even some old baseball cards. Instead there stood a simple glass case in the middle of a small room the size of his family's living room. The walls were an ugly gray with a large, impressive door across from him that he decided must lead to the bank proper. Inside the case was the white belt, gleaming in the dim light. He recognized it from his dreams. But that wasn't what grabbed Rory's attention. What shocked Rory was the small skeleton lying at the base of the glass case, dressed in a tattered shirt and jeans.

Toy let out a piercing cry and ran over to the skeleton, throwing himself at its feet. He threw back his head and out of his mouth came a sound that turned Rory's stomach into water. The anguish and the despair that poured from the small paper boy tore Rory to pieces. Handing the lock and the key to Rory, Hex ran up to Toy, his eyes wild.

"It's too late! We can mourn later. Quickly, Rory, put on the belt!"

Hex swung and smashed the glass case with his arm. He reached in and snatched the belt. Toy ignored him, continuing to wail. Rory looked over at Hex in confusion.

"What's going on? What's wrong with him?"

Hex hurried over with the gleaming white belt in hand.

"I'll explain later. We don't have time. Tobias could be here any moment so we must act quickly. Put on the belt!"

He held out the belt, but Rory didn't take it.

"No. I want to know what's going on. Whose skeleton was that? Is it from that last mission?"

"Yes," Hex said impatiently, still holding out the belt. "I'll tell you all about it after. But we must act quickly, or we'll lose our chance to make this right."

Rory could tell something was wrong. The wild look in Hex's eyes. The screaming of the paper boy bent over the skeleton. He stepped back.

"Tell me now. Whose skeleton was that?"

A new voice broke in.

"That's Jason, isn't it?"

Hex whirled around as Rory tried to see who was talking. To his immense surprise, his sister stood in the doorway, waving her arms at him. But it had been a male voice that called out. . . .

Hex was looking down near Bridget's feet.

"Fritz. What are you doing here?"

"You're supposed to be dead, Tom," the voice said.

With a shock, Rory realized that the voice was coming from the small cockroach at Bridget's feet. The cockroach sat on the back of a large rat. It was the same creature he saw on the sidewalk in front of his house! But what was wrong with the cockroach's head? Why was it all pink?

"I go by Hex now, Fritz. Tom failed. Hex won't."

"That's Jason, isn't it?" Fritz repeated. "That's your son in that paper thing."

A flash of pain flew across Hex's face.

"I couldn't let him die. They would have taken him like they took all the others."

"So you put his soul in that paper body?"

"It was the only way. I thought, hoped, that Tobias would keep his real body alive, considering how valuable someone like him is. I never thought he'd leave it here to mock me!"

"Is that what you told Jason?" Fritz said flatly. "Did he think his body would be waiting for him, magically preserved?"

"What else could I have done? I had no choice!"

"Rory! We're here to save you!" Bridget burst in, not understanding what was going on.

"You left your son's body to rot for fifty years," Fritz continued.

Comprehension slowly dawned on Rory. He turned to Hex in astonishment.

"*Toy* is your son? What's going on!"

"I thought you all died," Fritz said. "How did you escape?"

Hex pointed to his forehead.

"A little trick I know. You just need some blood and dirt, both of which I had suddenly found myself surrounded by. The rest perished when the Brokers of Tobias caught us in the vault. I barely made it out myself. Eventually I came upon

Bertold right outside the bank and he told me where he had hidden the lock and key. With some . . . persuasion."

"Did you . . . did you do something to him . . . ?" Fritz's face was ashen. Suddenly, Hex pulled out a pistol and trained it on Rory. Bridget screamed.

"Put on the belt, Rory!" Hex yelled. "We don't have time for this!"

"Don't hurt him!" Bridget ran for Rory's side, but Hex stopped her with his gun before she could reach him.

"Stay out of this, Bridget. Put on the belt, Rory."

"That's a soul pistol, Tom," Fritz said flatly. "That's what you used on your son, isn't it? You're the monster Bertold was raving about."

"PUT ON THE BELT!" Hex screamed. "We have to do this now! The Brokers will be here any minute! This is all for the greater good."

"Then why the gun?" Rory's voice trembled.

"I don't want to shoot you. Just put on the belt. We're almost out of time."

"How could you sacrifice your own son like that?" Fritz asked, keeping his voice calm.

"I didn't plan to. Everything was going fine until the time came to turn the key. Then he refused! Refused me! He was the last person I ever expected to betray me . . . anyway, I thought I could fix it! I thought he was too valuable for Tobias to waste! But that's not important right now. There are sacrifices that have to be made to right great wrongs. There are tasks that have to be accomplished, no matter what the personal cost. This is the right thing to do, I promise you. I can't dwell on who gets hurt; I have to think about who is helped."

Hex became more and more agitated as he spoke, desperately pleading with them.

Toy stood up, letting what had once been his own body fall to the ground. His eyes were black as coal.

Fritz's voice grew even softer. "If you barely escaped with your life, Tom, when did you have time to gather up Jason's soul? Unless you shot him before the guards came—"

"He wouldn't turn the key!" Hex screamed. "That was what he was made to do, and he wouldn't do it! This has taken too long! I'm sorry, Rory, truly, but it has to be done."

He aimed his pistol at Rory's chest and fired.

"RORY!"

Bridget screamed, leaping at Rory. She slammed into him, pushing him aside. The bullet intended for Rory ripped instead into her. Rory watched her mouth open in shock.

"Bridget . . ."

She fell, her eyes closing as her body hit the ground. Everyone stared at the small girl lying at Rory's feet. Hex was shaking with anger.

"Damn it! That wasn't meant for you, you stupid girl!"

Rory fell to his knees, cradling his sister in his arms.

"Bridget. Bridget, can you talk? Oh God. Bridget, please don't die. Please."

Tears poured down his devastated face as he held her. He felt a hand on his shoulder. He looked up to see Toy staring down at him. Toy gestured toward Bridget's body. Rory held her tight.

"No. Don't touch her."

Impatient, Toy pushed Rory aside and felt along Bridget's back. Finally, he grunted in satisfaction and held up his hand. In his cracked paper palm lay a single bullet. It must have traveled all the way through Bridget's body. But it looked strange. Instead of being dead silver, it glowed blue from within. Hex called over.

"Please, Jason. Bring it to me."

Toy didn't even turn around. He brought the bullet up to Bridget's mouth. Suddenly, he was shoved to the ground. Looking up, Rory saw Hex looming over Toy.

"Don't you dare, Jason. I am your father! Give me that bullet!"

"Don't give it to him, Jason!"

Fritz had finally recovered himself and rode into the fray. Rory felt something pushed into his hand as Toy brushed by him. He ran his thumb along the smooth bullet in his palm. It was warm, almost burning his hand. He backed away as Hex stood up, advancing on Toy.

"I did so much for you! I carried you out of that death trap in my pocket, Jason. I had a new body made for you so you could go on!"

Toy moaned, pointing to his mouth. Hex shook his head sadly.

"You were just a child. I know children. They talk. They can't help it. I was on the run. I couldn't allow it. If you could talk . . . we wouldn't have lasted a day, you know that. It was for the greater good. Now give me that bullet!"

Suddenly, the sound of heavy footsteps drifted through the large door. Hex sighed.

"It doesn't have to be like this, Rory. This is the way you want it, remember that. All you had to do was turn that key."

Getting up, he grabbed Bridget's body and slung it over his shoulder. Rory ran forward, but Hex grabbed Bridget's neck.

"She's not dead, you know. I don't want to hurt her, but I will if you make me."

Not dead! Those words cut through Rory's grief like an arrow of hope. A loud clang came from the front of the vault, where the large gray door led into the bank. Hex backed up toward the door they had entered by.

"This is your fault, Rory. Jason, are you coming?"

Toy stood staring at him, not moving. A flash of sadness flickered across Hex's face.

"You are still my son. Remember that. As for you, Rory, find me and we can talk about an exchange. You still have the chance to be great; you just have to be strong enough to do what needs to be done."

And with that, he flew through the open back door and was gone, still carrying Bridget's body over one shoulder and the glittering white belt over the other.

19

TOBIAS

Fritz sprang into action.

"Come on, Rory. We need to get out of here."

But before he could move, the front door slammed open and a dozen green Brokers of Tobias rushed in. One of them grabbed Rory, who quickly slipped the bullet into his pocket. Fritz, Toy, and even Clarence were also grabbed by the ugly monsters. The hulking beasts faced them forward as a short, almost completely round man entered behind the last of the guards.

He was overdressed, with a tie and coat and starched collar and overcoat and even a monocle. His stomach stretched far out over his belt on all sides, testing the strength of each button on his blinding white shirt. He tried to walk with dignity into the vault, but he couldn't help taking on a slight wobble, like a penguin making its way across the snow. He took off his top hat and jacket and handed them to the tall, painfully thin man behind him.

"James, do see that this is hung up."

James disappeared back through the door. The fat man looked them over, coming to rest on Fritz.

"Fritz M'Garoth. From the renegade M'Garoth clan. How interesting."

Fritz stared back defiantly.

"Go sit on it, Tobias."

Tobias laughed.

"I think I will," he snapped. James rushed back in carrying a large chair. He set it on the vault floor with a clang, then stepped back, ready to spring into action at a moment's notice. Groaning all the way, Tobias sat his round form down thankfully.

"That feels good. I need to buy myself new feet. These just aren't doing the job."

"Why don't you invest in a little liposuction?" Fritz said, uncowed.

Tobias snorted.

"Waste of money. It'll all just grow back."

He looked at Rory, then at Toy.

"You two I don't know. But I will find out who you are. Knowledge is power, and power is money. And I know money. But first, can anyone tell me where my little belt is? It's supposed to be sitting in that now-ruined glass case, which I got on sale downtown for only eighteen dollars."

James clapped enthusiastically. Tobias waved lazily.

"Thank you. I'm good, I know. I paid a much bigger price for what was inside it, so you can imagine how I feel right now. I'd be screaming in a blind rage if anger wasn't such a waste of energy. Never waste energy that could be used to make money, that's my credo. I bought that from a poet back in 1824 for only ten cents and a piece of bread."

James clapped again, whistling a little this time. Tobias stared at Rory intently.

"So I have two questions, really: how did you get in here, and who has my belt?"

Rory looked at Fritz. Tobias noticed and gestured with a finger. The guard behind Fritz took a large green finger and pressed it down on Fritz's tiny head. Fritz gritted his teeth, refusing to cry out. Tobias sighed.

"I know cockroaches are hard to kill but not impossible. Nothing is impossible. Just expensive. So, my young friend, if you don't want me to kill this renegade, then you'll tell me what I want to know. What's your name?"

Rory's mind raced. The last thing he wanted was for this god to know his name.

"Peter."

His father's name. It popped out before he could think about it. Tobias didn't blink an eye.

"Peter what?"

"Peter Bannen."

Bannen was his mother's maiden name. He had to keep his face blank but not too blank. If ever he needed to lie, now was the time. Tobias gestured again, and the guard relaxed his finger. Fritz let out a gasp and hung there fighting for breath. Tobias crossed his legs.

"All right, Peter Bannen. How did you get past my traps?"

Rory thought fast. If he told Tobias about Hex, then he'd go after him. Something told him that Tobias wouldn't care less about his sister, and who knows what could happen during the struggle. Thankfully, Fritz answered for him.

"Luck. We just lucked our way through."

"Luck? I wouldn't call getting caught red-handed particularly lucky, would you? Either way, I guess this time I will have to order up a new memory room. James! Take a note! We need new memories! God, the bills just keep piling up! And don't just buy them from the first guy who comes along! Take competing bids! Shop around a little for goodness' sake! Now who has my belt?"

Before Rory could answer him, Toy made a break for it. He threw himself to the ground violently, a ripping sound cutting through the air. The guard was left holding on to a small paper hand as Toy escaped through the back door. Tobias struggled to get up, then settled for shouting from his seat.

"Get him! Stop him before he gets away! A bonus of . . . a shiny quarter to the one who catches him!"

Six of the green monsters raced through the back door in hot pursuit. Tobias turned back to Rory and Fritz.

"I don't have time for this. Between that damn sandhog and this nonsense, this has been quite an expensive week. I think I might be growing a bit peevish. Guards! Take them down to the dungeons. I will have the truth. Try not to make it too messy. The carpet in the dungeon is so expensive to shampoo."

Rory's face went white.

"Please, no."

"Guards, tell the torturer that I'd especially like to know how they defeated my snow beetle. I borrowed it from Kieft on loan. And it's gone. So now I'm going to have to pay good money to settle the debt, and it vexes me. I'm a man who hates vexation. Somebody owes me some cash."

Rory's head shot up as a ray of hope shone in his heart.

"That was your debt?"

Tobias looked at him sharply.

"What do you know about my debt?"

Rory answered back with a bravado he did not feel. "How do you think I beat your beetle?"

"How *did* you do it?" Tobias frowned. "It's killed hundreds of men far taller than you."

"I paid the debt. Four dollars and twenty-six, no, that's right, *twenty-seven* cents it was."

For the first time since he'd walked in the room, Tobias lost his composure. His face blanched before he could pretend not to care.

"So what? So you paid a little debt." Tobias was not convincing.

"I paid *your* debt. And now you owe me."

Fritz looked over at Rory with admiration. Tobias snapped.

"James! My accounts book."

James ran out and came back with a huge book, larger by far than he. Tobias tapped the ground with his foot. James got down on all fours and placed the book on his back. Tobias leaned over him, leafing through the gigantic pages. Finally, he stopped.

"Somebody did assume that debt tonight. Still, you can't just *say* you took it over. Without the paper, it could have been anyone—"

"It's in my pocket."

Tobias stared him down for a moment before nodding to the guard holding Rory to free one of Rory's hands. Rory pulled the folded piece of paper from his pocket and flicked it open, showing it to Tobias.

"Recognize this?"

Tobias's eyes burned through him.

"All right, let me get you the money. A lot of good it will do you down in the dungeon."

"I don't want the money. I want you to repay the debt in another way."

Tobias glared at him from behind the book. James's arms and legs shook as he struggled with the immense weight. Tobias placed his arms on the open page, adding to James's burden.

"It's only four dollars and twenty-seven cents. That won't buy you much."

"Don't forget inflation! Anyway, I don't need much. I want a half an hour for me and my friends to run."

Tobias slammed a fist down on the book, forcing a girlish scream out of poor James.

"That's robbery! Highway robbery! I will not be bamboozled inside my own bank!"

Tobias leaned forward, his face red.

"I'll give you ten minutes. And not a second more."

Rory looked back at him, his gaze never wavering, though inside he was crying like a baby.

"Twenty minutes. And not a second less."

Tobias leaned forward even farther. James's face changed from red to blue.

"Fifteen."

Rory looked at Fritz, who nodded.

"Done," Rory said.

"Release them!"

The guards stepped back. Fritz fell to the floor, and then immediately raced over to Clarence. Hopping on, he waved at Rory.

"Come on!"

Rory turned to follow him. Tobias leaned even farther forward. James's arms and legs shook like trees in a hurricane. Even the dimwitted guards could see where this was going and they stepped back out of the way.

Tobias shouted after the fleeing fugitives, "Fifteen minutes isn't a lot of time. I'll be seeing you again in a half hour at the most, up on the rack!"

By that point, Rory and Fritz had already made it through the open door. Tobias watched them go, sputtering with fury.

"Blast it!"

He brought his fist down hard on the book. Unable to take it anymore, James crumpled, bringing the humongous book and the even more humongous Tobias down on top of him. The poor man passed out from the impact. Tobias lay on the floor, beside himself with anger. The guards looked at one another, torn between their loyal duty to their master and their enjoyment of some fine physical comedy. Tobias's voice floated up.

"We're going to find them, James, and make them pay."

James didn't answer, which didn't really come as a surprise to anyone, not even Tobias.

Rory shouted ahead to Fritz as they raced through the white hall.

"Where are we going? We'll never make it down through the tunnel in time! He'll catch us by the memory room."

"Don't worry. We're not going that way."

Fritz reached the door to the tunnel and urged Clarence through it. Rory followed him, closing the door behind him. When he turned back, Fritz was poking at a dead alligator lying by the underground stream. Fritz nodded to himself.

"Good, I was hoping Jason hadn't grabbed it. Come on. Help me push it into the water."

"Why?" Rory asked, disgust showing on his face. "It's a dead alligator. We can let them bury it."

Fritz pushed at the reptile with an unsurprising lack of success.

"We're not going to bury it. We're going to ride it. Now help me push!"

Rory walked over and gingerly placed his hands on the cold, scaly skin.

"This feels gross."

"We're down to ten minutes, if that helps."

Rory pushed all thoughts of alligator diseases out of his head and threw himself up against the dead reptile. It wasn't easy, but gradually it started to slide across the floor toward the river. As they pushed, Rory squeezed out a question between grunts.

"Why are we going to ride it? It's dead."

"Still floats. That's why they call it the dead man's float. Or dead gator float, I guess you'd say. Here we are!"

With a loud splash, the gator fell into the stream. The current immediately began to sweep it away.

"Grab the tail before it's gone!" Fritz cried.

Rory snatched the end of the tail just before it floated out of reach. He could barely keep the rushing water from pulling it away.

"Quick! I'm losing it."

Fritz climbed up Rory's leg to his shoulder and then out along his arm. Rory repressed a shudder that would have lost them their ride. Fritz reached the gator and jumped up and down, testing its worthiness.

"She's shipshape. Clarence!"

Clarence took a running jump and landed squarely in the middle of the scaly boat.

Fritz called out to Rory. "All right! You're gonna have to keep your hold as you slide into the water. Then pull yourself up the tail. Got that?"

Rory just didn't want to drown. He'd play the rest by ear. But he nodded to make Fritz feel better.

"All right, go!"

Rory placed his foot in the water. Right away, the current tugged at him, and his balance wavered. Fritz saw what was happening right away.

"Just jump!"

Rory heard the sounds of heavy footsteps from the room next door. Gathering his courage, he pushed off with his other foot and sailed through the air. With a splash, he plunged into the rushing waters, the underground flow pulling at his legs and forcing him underwater. His hands slipping free of the alligator tail, he went down, sinking into the deep.

The muffling of sound beneath the surface had an odd calming effect on Rory. As he felt himself swept along, he glanced around. The underground stream was lit by glowing plants that swayed along the bottom. The world under the streets seemed so peaceful. Then his feet touched bottom. The impact shocked him back into reality. He was drowning! Kicking against the brick floor, he pushed himself toward the surface. For what seemed like an eternity he swam upward, until finally, right before his lungs exploded, he broke through.

Gasping, he took in as much air as he could, swallowing a healthy swig of the stream in the process. The waters bore him quickly through the long tunnel. He heard a shout.

"Rory! Thank God!"

He looked around, struggling to keep afloat. Right behind him, coming up fast, sailed the alligator with its two passengers. Fritz waved.

"Grab on! Quickly, before we lose you!"

Rory reached out and wrapped his arms around the neck of the dead beast. He hung on as they swept down into the depths of the city.

RIDING HAMISH

In the highest northwest corner of the bank was a small, plain room. No pictures hung on the walls and no drapes livened up the tiny, square windows. The walls were an ugly green, as was the door. The only furniture was a large wooden desk, also green, upon which lay reams and reams of ledgers and accounts and all other types of paper with meaningless numbers scrawled across them that only people with way too little imagination could ever possibly understand. It was to this room that T. R. Tobias, God of Banking, retired after his chief Broker reported that the thieves had disappeared into the tunnels. He posted a Broker outside the door to give him privacy while he wedged his huge stomach behind the desk and did what he always did in stressful times: he began to write out sums, gradually calming himself with the soothing familiarity of numbers.

He had not been at his work long before his door flew open and the Broker he'd set outside burst into the room. Its eyes rolled around in its head while its mouth sported a steady frown, as if the two halves of its face were run by different brains. With a flash of panic, Tobias realized that the creature's mind was not its own, but he hid his unease behind a calm smile.

"Kieft! Hello! Come in!"

How did Kieft find out so quickly? What did he know? That mystery did not last long.

"Where is the boy?" the Broker's mouth asked with Kieft's voice.

"He escaped with a battle roach, one of the M'Garoths." Tobias saw no point in lying.

"And he has the belt?"

"Not as such, no. Someone else took it; I haven't discovered yet who. But I will find out."

The Broker's mouth curved into a grim smile. "This is quite a bank you have here," Kieft's voice said. "It seems easier to get into and out of than Grand Central Station."

Kieft was furious, but unlike Astor, Tobias didn't blink in the face of his anger.

"I will get it back," he said.

"It was a simple task I gave you," Kieft growled.

"I have guarded the belt for a hundred and fifty years," Tobias said, his voice patient and unconcerned. "I will guard it for many more. This is a hiccup, nothing more."

"A hiccup! The boy you let waltz out of your bank is a Light!"

Tobias felt his insides twist, but he refused to let his face reveal his shock.

"*He* does not have the belt. And he never will."

He stared down his possessed henchman, locking wills with Kieft.

"Find it," Kieft said finally. "No excuses."

Tobias nodded. "Does the Mayor know?"

"Of course not," Kieft said. "Don't be a fool. He knows no more than he needs to. He still thinks the Trap was sprung just to capture the Munsees. But the Trap must not open. No one can be allowed to discover what I have hidden there. Both of our secrets rely on it."

"What about the boy?"

Kieft's rage radiated through the Broker's rigid face.

"This is not a welcome wrinkle, Tobias. I had finally figured out a way to dispose of the Rattle Watch, and then this new annoyance appears. But this boy is far more dangerous than the Rattle Watch—they are but an annoyance. This Light could sink us all. I cannot be caught interfering; it would cast doubt on me, which I cannot afford. I have set my assassin on him, but we must be prepared for all contingencies. I leave it in your hands. There will be no excuses."

Hamish the dead alligator floated along the underground stream, bearing his passengers through the tunnels under the city. The small stream widened as they floated onward, and the glow coming up from beneath the surface dimmed, but Rory could still see the concrete walls surrounding them. The excitement of the escape gone, the bubble in his chest burst and he began to cry.

"Why didn't I turn that stupid key! Why didn't I just do what he said! None of this would have happened! The Munsees would be free, I'd be safe from those Strangers, and Bridget would still be here. Why was I so dumb!"

"*Shh.* Stop it, Rory," Fritz said. "You didn't do anything wrong. Tom, or Hex, or whatever he's calling himself now, wasn't being honest with you. You were right to question his motives. It sounds like even his own son didn't go through with turning the key, all those years ago."

Rory sniffed, swallowing the lump in his throat.

"I should have protected her."

"You did. You have the bullet in your pocket, right?"

Rory felt his pocket, where the bullet radiated heat onto his palm.

"It's still there. What is it?"

"That's Bridget's soul. A soul pistol doesn't kill you; it simply separates your soul from your body."

"That doesn't sound simple," Rory said, his fingers curling protectively over the bullet.

"Is it still warm?"

Rory nodded. Fritz fiddled with his helmet, straightening one of the antennae.

"Then she's okay. Don't worry. Once we reach the surface, we'll figure this thing out. We'll get her body back and everything will be fine. I promise."

Rory silently vowed to get Bridget back to normal if it was the last thing he did. He couldn't bear to think of her soul trapped in that tiny bullet. He felt water sting his eyes; he was thankful the underground stream hid his tears.

"She wanted to help. And look what it did to her. I told her! Why didn't she stay home?"

Fritz cast a hard eye on his companion.

"If she'd stayed home, you'd be in Hex's hands right now

with no one on the way to save you. So be thankful for her sacrifice. Hex doesn't want her; he wants you. We'll fix this, you'll see. Just have faith."

"How can we trust him to give her back?"

"We'll think of something."

"Do you think he really shot his own son?" Rory asked.

Fritz nodded sadly. "I think so."

"I don't understand," Rory said bitterly. "I mean, I feel bad about the Munsees and all, but it's not worth this. Why is Hex willing to throw everything away to let them loose?"

"When he came to us fifty years ago, it seemed to make sense," Fritz answered. "After all, what could be wrong with letting the Munsees free?"

"Then why did Jason refuse to turn the key?" Rory wondered.

"I don't know," Fritz replied, sounding puzzled. "But when the bad guys and the good guys want the same thing, then you have to step back and think that maybe you don't have all the facts. At the time, we just thought it was a wrong that needed righting. Captain Lymph—he was my old commander who headed the mission—he seemed to understand the reasons. We were angry at the Mayor for what he tried to make us do, and a little guilty as well."

"You mean that guy Alexander Hamilton?" Rory asked. "Hex told me about him."

"My cockroach clan, the M'Garoths, used to be his private guard," Fritz said. Rory snorted at the thought of those tiny roaches guarding a god, then immediately felt bad when Fritz looked offended.

"We may be small, but we were good at our job," Fritz said haughtily. "We weren't his bodyguards or anything. We were more like . . . policemen, I guess. His eyes and ears on the ground."

Low to the ground, Rory thought, but he didn't say it. "What happened?"

"It was a hundred years ago or so," Fritz said, his eyes distant. "I had only just reached the age where I could scout for the patrols. And we came upon someone just like you, Rory. We discovered a Light. He was a four-year-old boy living in a beaten-up old tenement near the Brooklyn Bridge. Cute kid, I thought. We had strict instructions to report any Light we encountered, so we rushed back to tell the Mayor. And then . . . then he asked us to kill the boy."

"What!"

"Kieft was there, egging the Mayor on, of course. And to be fair, the Mayor didn't seem too enthused about the order. But he told us to do it all the same. So my clan packed up all our belongings and walked out on our employer. The Mayor had been becoming more and more erratic since the Trap, and this was the last straw for us. We were guardsmen, battle roaches—not murderers. And we've been hiding ever since. If the Mayor ever finds us, it would probably mean the end of my clan."

Rory took a closer look at Fritz. With his small human head popping out of the brown cockroach body, he looked like two very different action figures glued together by an evil five-year-old. Fritz noticed Rory's curiosity.

"It's strange to see you looking at me and not going blank

a few seconds later. Not that I minded. That little trick kept you alive."

"How much do you know about me, anyway?"

"Well, my clan settled just south of you, under Dyckman Park. And when you crossed my path over twelve years ago, I had to pay attention."

"So you've been watching over me practically my whole life?" Rory asked.

Fritz looked embarrassed.

"'Watching over' is a strong phrase. I first noticed you when you were six months old. Your mom was pushing you down Broadway in your stroller. I was crawling up the wall of this one restaurant I know that has great chimichangas. I mean the best."

"You talking about El Cid?"

"You bet. There's magic in that kitchen."

"It's Bridget's favorite."

Fritz looked down.

"She has good taste."

They lapsed into silence for a moment. Rory checked the bullet again to make sure it was still warm. Panic rose inside him as he thought of the time they were wasting floating along here in this endless tunnel. Perhaps sensing that Rory needed the distraction, Fritz took up the story again.

"Anyway, your mother lifted you out of your stroller, and you laughed. It caught my attention because of your sheer delight. It feels good to hear a laugh like that on a beautiful day. Then I realized you were laughing at me. Because I had been in such a rush to get to those sweet chimichangas, I'd forgotten to put on my helmet. And you saw! You were laughing at the silly man with the bug body. I realized what this could mean, so I followed you home. Then a week later I came back with my second in command, Hoyt. We did our age-old test, which involved some not particularly flattering faces, and you laughed again. There was no doubt that you could see us."

Now they were coming to the part that had worried Rory from the beginning.

"And what am I? Hex told me I could see what's true."

Fritz tilted his head to the side in mild astonishment.

"Wow, he told you the truth for once. That's pretty much right. I don't pretend to be an expert, but from what I've learned you can see the world as it really is, in all of its many layers. And through you, other people can see it, too. It's a great gift."

"Hex told me I was the only one."

"As far as I know, that's also true. There might be a two- or three-year-old who's made it this far unnoticed, but once he's caught looking at things he shouldn't be able to see, he'll disappear like all the others."

Rory shifted uneasily, his stomach tensing with fear.

"Taken by a Stranger?"

The roach nodded, his eyes pained.

"I guess the Mayor decided they were more reliable than battle roaches, though I don't know for sure if the Strangers are working for him. Maybe they work for Kieft. Maybe neither, though I seriously doubt it. All I do know is that usually Lights are taken by the time they reach four years old. As far as I know, only one kid lasted longer. He made it to nine."

Rory thought of a grief-stricken paper face.

"Toy."

"Jason. Don't call him that awful name. His name was Jason Hill. His father's name is, or *was*, Tom Hill. I thought he'd died just like his poor son. I was wrong."

"Did you know Jason well?"

"Yeah, I did," Fritz said sadly. "I was assigned to keep watch over him before the raid. He was a great kid. Lively, good at word games. And, boy, did he love to talk. Kind of like your sister. She reminds me of him, actually. And to think his own father stuck him in that paper prison with no tongue."

Rory checked the bullet one more time. Fritz noticed and gave him a sad smile.

"Still warm, right? As long as that bullet burns under your touch, she'll be fine. She's a strong girl."

Rory refused to cry again as they floated down the dark river in silence. His thoughts turned to Bridget. He'd save her. He still had the lock and the key. He'd find Hex and put on that stupid belt. This time, there would be no holding back. It didn't matter to him why Jason had refused to do the job all those years ago. Rory would turn that key, let the Munsees free, and get his sister back. It was the only way.

Fighting to keep his emotions under control, Rory focused on the passing walls that sloped upward in an arc above them. Trying to get his mind off the burning bullet in his pocket, he asked Fritz about them.

"What are these tunnels? They seem ancient."

"I believe they were part of the original pipe system that brought the water from the reservoir upstate down into the city. It was built over a hundred and fifty years ago. Then the whole system was changed, leaving these forgotten old tunnels half-filled with water, mostly from the rivers. They connect with some of the old sewers. There are hundreds, maybe thousands of underground pipes and abandoned subway tunnels and even some natural caves beneath the city. And you don't want to bother some of the folk who live in them, let me tell you. We should be fine on this little stream, though. I hope."

"Where do we get out?"

Fritz was watching the ceiling, which arched about six feet above Rory's head.

"I'm sure I'll see something I recognize soon enough. If those gang members can find their way through this, then I know I can."

DOWN

Rory didn't know how much time had passed. His stomach felt like a knotted mess as he obsessively checked the bullet for signs of cooling, all the while praying that Fritz could find his way. The tunnel had changed, rock replacing concrete, and Fritz looked openly worried as he searched the walls for something familiar.

"You recognize anything?" Rory asked hopefully.

"I've never seen tunnels like this before. I'm sorry. I have no idea where we are."

"So we're lost."

"There has to be a way out!" Fritz insisted. "If there's a way in, there's a way out."

"What if the way out was back the way we came? Maybe we missed a turn."

"I don't understand this. Between my people and the rats, we've mapped every inch of the underground. We know where every abandoned subway station is, even where the deep homes of some of the low people are. But nobody's ever seen this. Not that I know of. Look at that!"

He pointed up toward the ceiling. Rory could just make out a faint white sigil painted on the stone. It seemed like a long cigar that tapered off at the end. Small lines surrounded it, making a strange pattern. Fritz peered at it intently.

"I think it's Lenape. Probably the Munsee dialect. But I don't recognize it. Not that I'm a Munsee scholar, but I know enough to get around. Wait, what's that behind it?"

A V with a line shooting up from it like a mast on a ship stood out faintly on the ancient stone. Rory turned his head to study the symbol as they floated under it, trying to get a good look. He squinted.

"Looks kind of like an arrow. Pointing down."

Fritz rubbed his hands together as he pondered the drawing.

"I don't think so. All of this must have been built by the Munsees. Munsee culture has always been a hobby of mine. You know, most city folk, even the council, think that the Munsees never built anything more complicated than a hut. But they just kept their greater works hidden. This tunnel probably led out to a swamp back then. The Munsees were more advanced than people realized. They had quite the list of sigils. So I think we can safely say that that sign was a bit more complicated than just some arrow pointing down—"

"What's that sound?"

Rory heard it, too, a roaring sound that was quickly growing louder. He felt his stomach sink.

"That sounds like a waterfall."

There was a pause as Fritz took this in.

"Okay," he said softly. "Maybe it *was* an arrow pointing down. We need to get off!"

The roaring grew louder, and now Rory could feel the river speeding up, pulling them toward the underground drop. He looked around for a way to escape.

"The water's moving too fast, and the current's too strong!" he yelled, quickly seeing the problem. "You guys would never make it to the wall. You'd be swept over."

"But *you've* got a chance," Fritz yelled over the ever-growing roar. "Go on!"

"But what about my sister?"

"Hex will find you and he'll give you back her body, don't worry. Quickly, swim for it! You're running out of time."

Rory could hear the waterfall rapidly approaching. He didn't want to let Fritz and Clarence go over, not to mention, he didn't want to be left alone with a warm bullet he didn't know what to do with, lost underground. The tunnel walls came closer as he floated along, heading for the fall. He looked down the length of the alligator and, just like that, an idea came to him.

"I'm gonna try something. Hang on!" he yelled.

"Don't be stupid. Save yourself!" Fritz protested.

Rory ignored him, pulling himself forward until he was holding on to the very tip of the alligator's snout. Then he began to swim backward, pulling with all his might. He reached out and grazed the stone wall briefly with his fingertips, and that was enough to help him drag the alligator's head sideways. The waterfall was deafening, making Fritz's yelling impossible to hear, which was probably just as well. Rory had just about dragged the alligator fully sideways when he looked ahead. He could see a dark space that could only be the drop. He hoped he was right. He held on tight as the gator sped up to the edge of the waterfall and started to plunge over.

Rory was jammed into the body of the gator as it suddenly stopped short. He looked up and gave a sigh of relief. The tunnel had become narrow enough that the body of the alligator wedged between the walls right at the mouth of the falls, saving them from going over, just as he'd hoped. But the water was rushing up against it, and Rory could see that it would soon be pushed through and over. He screamed over the noise.

"Get off! Quick!"

Fritz didn't need to be told twice. He and Clarence scurried down the neck and over the head of the alligator, hopping off onto the stones just above the waterfall.

"Come on, Rory! It's moving!" Fritz yelled. Sure enough, the gator was being pushed over the edge by the relentless stream. Rory felt the body give way and he barely had time to reach out and grab a rock before the gator was swept away and over, falling down into the black. Rory almost followed it down; it took all his strength to keep his grip on the rock. His legs were swept over the edge, and suddenly he was dangling over the big empty hole, the water falling past him on its way to the depths of the earth.

"Pull yourself up, Rory!" Fritz cried.

Rory's arms screamed. They'd been holding on to the alligator for so long now they were tired from all the work. It would be so much easier to just let go. . . .

"No, Rory!" Fritz sounded frantic. But Rory almost did it. He almost let go. It was the bullet in his pocket that gave him strength. He wasn't going to give up on Bridget. He wasn't his father. He'd promised to save her, and he would. This thought gave him a new burst of strength, and he used it to pull himself up and over the rock. A small space lay between the falls and the wall, and he collapsed there, amazed to be alive. The battle roach crept up to his side.

"That was a very brave thing to do," Fritz said into his ear. "Thank you."

Rory nodded, not having the strength to answer. He watched the water shoot out into the dark and disappear into the black hole beneath them. Then he noticed something.

"Is that another passage?"

Around the hole the water was falling into lay a small ledge of stone; on the other side he could see another tunnel. This tunnel was dry, though Rory couldn't tell how far in it went. He pushed himself up to his knees.

"I guess we can try that way."

Fritz smiled, nodding in relief.

"I guess we can."

It wasn't as easy as it sounded. They had to inch their way along the narrow ledge to the other side. Rory had to keep himself from looking down at the endless drop beneath him.

"How far do you think that goes down?" he asked.

"I have no idea," Fritz answered, petting Clarence to keep him calm as they made their way. "A long, long way. My grand-dad used to tell us about a huge cavern deep underground where monsters live on the shore of a bottomless lake. If the creatures catch you, they tie rocks to your feet and throw you in, where you sink for eternity to the center of the earth. But my granddad was kind of full of it, so I don't know."

"I hope I never find out," Rory said with feeling.

They reached the other side and fell gratefully into the new tunnel. There were no glowing plants to light their way, so all Rory could see was nothing.

Fritz called up from his feet as he hopped up on Clarence. "Don't worry, I'll take the lead." He stuck on his helmet. "My helmet has pretty good night vision, so I can see a little bit. Just keep a hand on the wall to stop yourself from falling and follow me."

Clarence reared back and scurried off into the dark tunnel. Rory put a hand on the cold rock and followed them into the shadows.

After what seemed like an eternity walking in the dark, Rory caught sight of a dim light ahead. Reaching the source, they stepped out into a man-made tunnel with small lightbulbs hanging from the ceiling.

"This is a good sign!" Fritz said cheerfully. Looking back the way he came, Rory saw that the tunnel they'd come through was a dark, dank hole in the wall. He shuddered to think of where he'd just been. How close did he come to falling into that underground cavern Fritz's granddad told him about? He patted the bullet in his pocket, but what he felt gave him a shock.

"The bullet's getting cooler!"

Fritz looked up with alarm.

"We don't have as much time as I'd hoped," he said. "But we'll make it. Come on!"

He urged Clarence forward, leading them down the new passage.

After an anxious half hour or so, they came upon a new juncture, this one better lit and less abandoned-looking. Fritz's face broke out in a huge smile.

"I know where we are! We're gonna make it, kiddo!"

Rory could only smile weakly, his hand still clutched around the cooling bullet in his pocket. Fritz hopped down off Clarence and spoke quietly into his rat's ear. The rat seemed to nod before racing off down the new passage, disappearing into a crack in the wall.

"Where's he going?" Rory asked, worried.

"I sent him ahead to get some help," Fritz answered. "When we get back to the surface, we're going to need to move quickly. I think I know what to do about your sister, and I'm going to need help making it happen. The first order of business is to get out of these tunnels. Come on. We're not too far from the exit. Pick me up; we'll move faster."

Rory reached down and let Fritz hop on his hand. Putting him in his shirt pocket, he proceeded to walk as quickly as he could down the new passage. They moved faster now that they knew where they were going. The only incident of any note was when Fritz noticed a dirty brown rat running alongside them. He had Rory throw a rock at the rodent, which disappeared into the wall.

"What was wrong with the rat?" Rory wanted to know. "Aren't rats on our side?"

"I don't know who's on whose side," Fritz replied. "I just didn't like the look of that rat. I think I've seen it before."

Putting the rat behind him, Rory moved as quickly as he could toward the way to the surface.

Sally raced through the small holes under the streets of the city. While scouting the bank for her master, the rat had heard the other rodents whispering about Clarence and his mission, and she had come to see if any of it was true. Sure enough, there was her master's quarry, far from where they were expected to be. But there was only one exit they could possibly be headed toward. She would reach her master soon, and by the time the boy came up out of the ground, her master would be waiting with his knife in hand. There was still time, if she moved quickly. And swiftly she ran, through the holes and tunnels beneath the earth, toward the assassin waiting patiently above.

22

THE STREET FAIR

The assassin ran up to the corner of Second Avenue and
12th Street, wincing under the glare of the newly risen sun.
Turning onto 12th, he pulled in next to a closed-up storefront,
hugging the wall. A familiar brown rat ran up from the spot
where she'd been waiting, watching to make certain the Light
didn't slip by. Thankfully, he was informed that the boy had
not yet emerged. Giving Sally a quick pat of thanks, he barely
had time to catch his breath before the manhole cover across
the street lifted and slid to the side. He couldn't believe his
good fortune as a boy's head popped out, blinking in the sunlight. This was his moment, now, before the boy could react
and anyone could help him. Putting his hand on the knife
under his shirt, he stepped out from the storefront and onto
the sidewalk, ready to do his duty.

A hand landed on his shoulder. Jumping in surprise, he
leaped around to come face-to-face with Nicholas Stuyvesant.
Nicholas smiled, putting up his hands.

"Hey, calm down, it's just me. I didn't expect to see you
down here. You must have gotten Clarence's message, too."

The assassin forced himself to release the knife and nod.

"Look, I don't want to overwhelm the poor boy," Nicholas continued. "He's been through a lot. So do me a favor, will you? Let the rest of the Rattle Watch know that we're going to meet at my father's house at midday. I'm not happy about it, believe me, but it's the only safe place I can think of. I hope the old coot doesn't ruin everything. Can you pass the message along? Great. See you midday."

With that, Nicholas turned and crossed the street. The assassin watched him reach down to help Rory up.

"Hey, Rory," he said. "I'm Nicholas Stuyvesant. I've been dying to meet you."

And the assassin couldn't do a thing. He'd missed his window. He withdrew around the corner and punched the wall in frustration. He'd been so close! It was too late, he told himself. At least for now. He'd been given strict instructions to do nothing to the Rattle Watch. Kieft had a plan to deal with them, and if the assassin killed Nicholas now, the rest of them might slip away. So the Light lived, for the moment at least. There would be other chances. Kieft would understand. He hoped.

For now, he had another function. Kieft's plan to catch the Rattle Watch had to be set in motion, and soon. This task would go perfectly, he knew it. None of the watch suspected a thing. Nor did they suspect that one of their own members would be the cause of their downfall. There would be no Nicholas to save them. The assassin would see to that. And if in the confusion he had a chance to finish what he'd started with Rory, then that would be just perfect. All his missed chances would be redeemed then.

Feeling better already, the assassin headed uptown, his mind already on the snare soon to be set.

———————

Rory stared up at the face peering down at him from the street. He didn't know what to do, until Fritz's voice floated up.

"It's all right, Rory. He's a friend."

Reassured, Rory allowed himself to be pulled up out of the manhole.

Nicholas smiled. "I'm glad to see you're okay," he said.

Rory didn't answer, all too conscious of the cooling bullet in his pocket. Sensing his discomfort, Nicholas gave him a compassionate look.

"I heard some of the details in the message Clarence gave. Don't worry; we'll fix this."

"I think we should get moving," Fritz said from his place in Rory's pocket. "There are eyes and ears everywhere."

"Let's talk under the pear tree. No one can eavesdrop on us when we're under my father's protection. At least he's good for that much."

He led them down the street toward Third Avenue, giving Rory a chance to take in his new companion in the old-fashioned clothing. He seemed not too much older than Rory, though his ancient eyes told a different story. Rory looked down at Fritz, who seemed to understand his confusion.

"I know you don't know who to trust, Rory," Fritz said softly. "But Nicholas is an old friend. He'll help Bridget, I promise."

Rory had a thought.

"Are you a god?"

Nicholas smiled wryly.

"No. I'm just the son of a god. You'll meet him later, unfortunately. Just try not to hold him against me."

Rory looked around at the city as Nicholas spoke. The sun was rising higher and people walked around, opening their stores and walking their dogs. It was Saturday, just a normal weekend morning. Nothing special. Forgetting for a moment the danger he and his sister and all of them were in, he took in a deep lungful of city air. Usually, it tasted like cigarette smoke and car exhaust. Today, it tasted like freshly baked bread and summer. It was Saturday morning on 12th Street, and he was alive.

"Mom," he said suddenly. "She must be worried."

"You caught a break there," Nicholas replied. "One of our friends has been keeping tabs on your house. According to him, your mom left so early she only glanced in your room to make sure there was a lump before leaving. So we have until tonight before you need to get home."

Rory was glad of that. The last thing he wanted was to scare his mom to death. He checked the bullet again—cooler? Maybe a little. He only hoped these new friends could help Bridget before it was too late.

They reached the corner of Third Avenue and turned north. Glancing ahead, Rory spied an odd sight for the city: a large, beautiful tree sprouting from the pavement on the northeast corner of 13th and Third, its wide branches reaching out to cover the sidewalk and part of the street in shade. As they came closer, he could see small fruit hanging from its branches, pears waiting to be plucked. None of the people passing under its cool shade gave it a glance, a fact Rory found hard to believe. He pointed it out to Fritz, who didn't seem surprised.

"Considering that pear tree was knocked down about a hundred and fifty years ago, I'd be surprised if they could see it."

Nicholas gazed up at the flowering branches fondly.

"I love this old thing. I come here when my father is being especially hard to deal with, which is almost every day. He planted it back in 1647, can you believe that? Brought it back from Holland. This whole area used to be his farm, the Great Bouwerie. That's *farm* in Dutch, you know. I was born after he became a god, of course, so I never really lived that life. He won't stop talking about it, though. Every minute it's 'the old days' this and 'back in my day' that. He lives in the past. He even dresses like he did three hundred and fifty years ago!"

Rory glanced at Nicholas's nineteenth-century outfit but said nothing. Nicholas leaned up against the tree and gestured for Rory to sit under the cool branches.

"I know time is of the essence, but I need to know what happened," Nicholas said. "So tell me everything."

Ordinary people streamed by, unaware of the wonders in their midst as Fritz and Rory quickly told their tale. Nicholas's face grew ashen as the story went on, finally asking to see the bullet. He turned it over in his fingers as Fritz finished up, waiting a moment to take it all in before speaking.

"There's a bunch of stuff I wanted to talk to you about, Rory. But this takes precedence. I never met Hex, but it doesn't sound like he is particularly trustworthy. Can we really trust him to give back your sister's body after you turn that key? Assuming we can find him, of course."

"What else can I do?" Rory asked miserably. "I want my sister back. Nothing else matters."

"I understand," Nicholas said. "I've always maintained that the Munsees should be freed. It was mostly Kieft's plan, after all, to trap them, and any plan of his is bad news in my book. But why go to such lengths?"

"There's something we're missing," Fritz said. "Is there a danger here we don't know about? What will really happen when Rory disables the Trap?"

"What does Hex really want?" Nicholas asked thoughtfully.

"I don't care!" Rory said, exploding with frustration. Nobody seemed to care about his sister but him. "We need to save Bridget, and if I have to turn that key a billion times, I'll do it."

"Now's not the time to argue about this," Fritz said. "The bullet is cooling, and soon the soul will be let free. We don't know if we'll find Hex in time."

"So what do we do?" Nicholas asked.

"Seeing Jason gave me an idea," Fritz said. "There's only one man I know who could have made that papier-mâché body."

Nicholas snapped his fingers.

"Flavio!"

"Who else?" Fritz answered. "So I need to know where the fair is today."

"Someone is looking out for you, Rory," Nicholas said, shaking his head in amazement. "The fair is over on First, only two avenues away."

"Then let's go," Fritz said, smiling at their good luck. "I think she has a chance, Rory."

"A chance for what?" Rory asked, not understanding what they were talking about.

"If we can't get her back to her body in time," Nicholas said, "then we'll have to go with a loaner. Come on."

Nicholas pulled Rory to his feet, and they went racing east on 13th Street as fast as they could.

A couple of blocks later they came upon the street fair. All of First Avenue was filled with stalls stretching far into the distance. Voices with all kinds of exotic accents flew through the air like bottle rockets, exploding into the ear with the promise of the best Chinese food, Italian meatballs, gyros, chicken skewers, crepes, barbecue, fried dough, hot dogs, or pretzels in the whole wide world. In between the food stands were tables and tents and boxes bursting with clothes, intricate toys that spun and crackled with sparks, international souvenirs like authentic Indian jewelry made on St. Mark's Place by NYU undergrads and stress balls that you rotated on your palm as you tried to tap into the wisdom of the ancients without getting a cramp. There were New York staples like small copper Statue of Libertys and silver Empire State Buildings, and dozens upon dozens of small backward chairs that promised the massage of a lifetime in only ten minutes. And in and around all these wonders flowed the people. Thousands and thousands of people—eating, buying, ignoring, pushing, wandering, arguing, laughing, daydreaming, browsing, or just stopping short for no reason at all. Block after block, this sea of people and stalls stretched on, twenty times the size of the largest farmers market you ever saw. If you stepped into it anywhere but the edges, you'd swear it went on forever.

Rory didn't know where the street fairs came from. No one did. They'd pop up out of nowhere, and then after a weekend, or even a single Sunday, the entire fair would disappear overnight, leaving only wrappers and the odd price tag whipping in the wind down the deserted avenue. Then, on some other street somewhere else in the city, the fair would sprout up again, alive this time on Third Avenue or Madison, in Little Italy or Flatbush, or even Seaman Avenue up in Inwood. Always on the move, often impossible to predict, the fair hopped around the metropolis all summer long.

Nicholas spoke over his shoulder as they made their way through the crowd.

"Do you know how you can tell when the fair is coming?"

Rory shook his head. "No. That's part of the point, right? At least that's what my mom says. You hear about it and you go. She loves the whole spontaneous thing."

"But they bore you?"

"No, it's not that. But I've been coming to these since I was a little kid. They're kinda old hat now."

"Old hat, huh?"

Nicholas chuckled to himself. Rory sniffed, offended.

"What?"

"They say you can smell the sweet scent of exotic food in the air a full day before the fair appears. A half a day before, the sound of the hawkers selling their wares drifts by on the wind. An hour or two before, you'll walk down the street and find yourself taking wide detours around empty sidewalks where the stalls will soon appear. You won't even know why you're doing it. You just do."

"But even that gets predictable after a lifetime, doesn't it?"

"I'd reserve judgment until after you've stepped behind the curtains at the back of the stalls," said Nicholas.

"But if you step through the curtains, you'd just end up on the sidewalk."

As he said this, Rory stared at the back of the booth they were passing. An old man sat toward the back of a stall filled with watercolors that showed the city in all its seasons. As Rory watched, the curtain pulled back and a young woman stepped through holding a cup, which she handed to the old man. Behind her, where there should have been sidewalk and storefronts, burned a fire in a cozy living room, with an easy chair and a child playing on the floor. The woman stepped back through the curtain, letting it fall behind her. Nicholas noticed Rory's astonishment.

"They have to live somewhere, right?"

Rory kept his eyes on the old man as he sipped from his cup.

"Who do?"

"The gypsies."

Rory opened his mouth to ask about these so-called gypsies when Fritz pointed toward a small stall to their left.

"Here we are."

Rory stepped into the stall, looking up at the walls as he entered. Colorful masks hung from the metal supports, as did bright piñatas of every make and shape. Donkeys, birds, lions, monkeys, animals of all kinds swung softly from their metal wires. The piñatas, the masks, even the tiny figurines of frogs and fat Buddhas were all made of papier-mâché. A young girl manned the stall. To Rory's surprise, she looked right at Fritz.

"Another one? What do you want?"

"Is Flavio in?" Fritz asked.

The girl pointed to the flap at the back.

"Go on in and see for yourself."

Nicholas pushed through the back flap. Rory stepped up to it slowly, feeling the curtain with his hands. It felt normal enough. He pulled it aside, stepping into a warm, welcoming living room with a fireplace, a coffee table, and a long leather couch. Standing on the coffee table flanked by Clarence and another, larger rat was a new cockroach. Fritz let out a cry of astonishment.

"Liv! What are you doing here?"

The new cockroach lifted its helmet to reveal a pretty pink face surrounded by short brown hair. The pretty face, however, was burning with anger.

"Clarence came uptown looking for one of your patrol boys, but I took the message. What are you mixed up in? The clan forbade you to have contact with these people!"

Fritz shouted right back.

"If I didn't get mixed up in this, as you put it, Rory would be in the clutches of Tom Hill!"

"Instead, his sister pays the price," she said bitingly.

"You don't understand," Fritz began, his face turning red.

"People!" Nicholas broke in. "Please! I don't want to see anybody get hurt!"

The two cockroaches glared at him, and Nicholas looked sorry he said anything.

"Rory," Fritz said. "This is my wife, Liv."

Rory didn't know what to do, so he inclined his head.

"Nice to meet you, ma'am."

"Well done," Nicholas said, his eyes twinkling. "Very polite."

"Don't be cute," Liv said.

"Of course not, Captain," Nicholas said, snapping to attention. "I wouldn't dream of it."

"Captain?" Rory wondered aloud.

"She's also my superior," Fritz explained.

"That's why she got the bigger rat," Nicholas said with a straight face.

"Now is not the time for your jokes," Liv said. "I know how much of this is your fault."

She turned to Rory.

"I want you to understand something, Rory. The M'Garoth clan means everything to me. I am its protector, the clan war leader. I have never approved of how Fritz gets involved with humans, especially a human in your situation. It can't bode well for my people. Next thing you know we're mixed up with the very gods we turned our backs on so long ago."

"I understand," said Rory, though he didn't.

"We don't have time to argue, Liv," Fritz cut in.

"I know that," Liv answered, her face softening. "I'm not heartless. I brought what you asked for."

She pulled out a folded paper from her rat's saddlebag, handing it up to Rory. He unfolded it to reveal a picture of Bridget. Unprepared, his eyes filled with tears.

"Honey, it's all right," Liv said, all trace of her anger gone. "What I meant to say is that since we *are* involved, Fritz and I are going to make sure your sister's all right. I've spoken with Flavio. He's temperamental even for a papersmith, but I think we can get him to come around. I promise you, as long as it doesn't hurt the M'Garoths, we'll do everything we can. And don't worry about the picture. I took it from your sister's room; you can give it back to her yourself."

Rory wiped his eyes and took another look at the photo, Bridget's wide smile filling the frame. No one spoke for a moment, until Liv broke the silence.

"Come with me."

A blast of heat blew across Rory's face as he passed into the next room. He'd stepped into a large forge, with a huge anvil dominating the center of the room. The sooty walls were covered in sheets of paper, big and small. A fire burned in the corner. This was no cozy fireplace, but rather a searing pit of heat and flame crackling under a massive iron cauldron, which bubbled with some unknown white substance. A loud clang brought his attention back to the anvil. Next to it, holding a large heavy hammer, stood a huge dusky figure. His face, free of hair of any kind, was red and blistered. He scowled at Liv as she spoke with him. He looked over at Rory.

"So you're the one who's gone and gotten himself into trouble, eh? Had a bit of a run-in with a madman and a pistol? I don't know who told you about my mistake fifty years ago, especially since I know I never told anybody, but this is not my problem. I don't make mistakes twice."

"We can pay you," Liv said.

"Like that bastard Tom paid me? With bright gold that turned to coal the next morning? I don't know why I let him talk me into it. It was his flattery. His crocodile tears. Crying over his poor son. His baby boy. So what did I do? Did I think about it, take a moment to look at the whole thing with clear eyes? Of course not. I'm a fool, and I have been since my mother dropped me into the midwife's hands. So you know what I did, Trouble Boy?"

Rory shook his head, trying not to get this guy angry.

"I made my greatest creation. I slaved for hours over the hot anvil, struggling to create a paper being that could move with grace, with life. And I did it! Because I am the best! And the first thing he does is rip out its tongue! I should have stopped it right there, but I was too in love with my fine creation. I wanted to see it walk! I wanted to see its eyes look up at me, its maker, and know me. Pride, Trouble Boy, that's what that is. Too much pride.

"So he placed his son's soul into its mouth and the paper thing became a boy! This wonderful new being looked up at me and opened his mouth, to say what, I will never know. But no sound came out! His tongue was gone, sitting in a pile of discarded paper. Look, it's still there. I can't bear to touch it."

Rory looked in the corner by a pile of scrap paper and saw it. A small thing, red and torn at the end, left behind on the floor.

"Fifty years that's lain on the floor like that. Since the moment he tossed it there like a piece of fat cut off a steak. And then that boy's new eyes looked up at me and screamed.

Have you ever seen eyes scream, Trouble Boy? My ears bled from the sight. But Tom patted that maimed boy on the head and whispered something about how everything would soon be fixed. And then he dropped a bag of gold at my feet and led that poor creature out of my forge and away to God knows where. And I didn't stop him! That's my great shame, and I have to tell it if I ever hope to make it right. I let him take that unfinished child away, and the next morning I received the payment I deserved. My gold had melted into coal."

Flavio stared at Rory defiantly, daring him to say something. Fritz stepped in.

"This is your chance, Master Flavio. This is your chance to make it right."

Flavio tore his eyes away from Rory and shot a withering glance at Fritz.

"How? I make playthings. Toys for children. Masks and piñatas."

Fritz smiled gently. "They're not just piñatas, Flavio. They leap around the room like wild animals as the children chase them, laughing. They break only when you want them to break, when you build them with a flaw. And your masks last for centuries. We need you. We need your skill, or this child will die. She is too full of life to let slip away."

Flavio's eyes betrayed the struggle within. He coughed, looking away.

"Who knows what will turn to coal this time? I cannot chance it. I wouldn't even know where to begin. Unlike you, I've never seen her."

Rory pulled out the picture. He walked up to Flavio and held it up for him to see.

"Here she is. Just make sure she can laugh. She loves to laugh. And to leap around like a crazy person. And the tongue is kind of a requirement. If she found out she couldn't talk, she'd probably kick you in the butt. Please."

Flavio looked down at the picture in Rory's hand. His lips twitched as he stared down at Bridget's smiling face.

"The teeth'll be the hardest. Look at those monsters. I hate smilers. They need too much detail."

Fritz smiled softly at the big man's ramblings.

"This will make it right, you know," Fritz said.

Flavio didn't look up.

"Maybe."

He took the picture from Rory, walking back to his anvil. He spoke without turning around.

"Give me a few hours. Then we'll just see what we have."

With that, he threw a log on the fire and started touching the hanging paper, feeling the worth of each sheet. For the first time since he heard the gunshot, Rory felt a faint flutter of hope. He silently followed the roaches and Nicholas out of the forge, leaving the papersmith behind to do his work.

FORGING BRIDGET

Alexa secretly made her way toward the servants' entrance at the back of the Astor mansion, trying not to be seen. She carried a few of her father's journals in a bag slung over her shoulder. She liked having his words with her; it made her feel a little less alone, now that he was gone. She stepped up to the door, but before she could quietly knock, it swung open. She jumped a mile.

Simon stood in the doorway, smiling like a Cheshire cat. He was wearing a particularly loud shirt, with ruffles and bright pink buttons, so she knew this was a true covert operation. "Are the rest of them here?"

"Nicholas is still not back with the Rory kid," he said. "And Albert headed down to see what was keeping them."

"So it's just you and Lincoln, then," she said. She didn't like meeting without Nicholas and Albert. But events were moving faster and they couldn't afford to wait around. "What's this about, then?"

"Come on, I'll show you," he said, eyes twinkling. He led

her up the back staircase into a small storage room, where Lincoln was waiting.

"Don't you want to know why I called you here?" Simon asked, closing the door behind him. "I think you'll thank me."

"Stop being so mysterious and spill it," Alexa said peevishly.

"Ten bucks says he wants to show us a new shirt," Lincoln said, grinning.

"This morning my dad had a visitor in his study—a Dead Rabbit, to be precise."

"So what?" Alexa said. "The Dead Rabbits don't follow anyone anymore. Their gang will work for whoever will pay."

"Maybe not," Lincoln mused. "Some of my buddies in the Daybreak Boys think they're working for someone on the sly. They've got too much dough and too little brains. Why not Kieft?"

"I don't know about that," Alexa said. "That's a big leap."

"Why keep it secret then?" Lincoln continued, getting excited. "It makes sense."

"Why was this Dead Rabbit here?" she asked Simon.

"I'm not sure," Simon admitted. "But I heard my dad mention a *knife* they had to move, to keep safe. Pretty interesting, right? Might very well be *the* knife. Probably is, knowing Daddy. He told this Dead Rabbit to come back in an hour with some friends so he can let them know where to move it. And that was almost an hour ago. I know a little hidey-hole just big enough for us to listen in and find out what's going on. So who's the guy saving the day now?"

He nodded with satisfaction as he pointed to himself.

"I don't like this," Alexa said. "It seems strange. Anyway,

the Fortune Teller said that the Light would make the choice, not us."

"But this could be our chance to get a jump on them!" Lincoln exclaimed. "We don't need to wait for this Rory kid. We can follow the bad guys to their lair and take them all out before lunch! I got dibs on the big guy!"

"What big guy?" Simon asked, confused.

"There's always a big guy. And I got dibs on him."

Alexa wanted to wait for Nicholas and Albert to return with the Light, but she couldn't afford to let any lead slip away. But could she trust the source? She guessed she had to; besides, the day Simon Astor pulled one over on her was the day she ate her shoes.

"I guess it couldn't hurt to gather a little bit of information. So what do we do?"

Simon beamed as he laid out his plan. Despite her misgivings, Alexa felt a small thrill race through her as she thought about what they could learn here. This could be the chance for the Rattle Watch to stop the murders and bring down Kieft.

Rory woke up suddenly, confused. It took him a moment to remember where he was. He must have fallen asleep on Flavio's couch. Sitting up, he spied Fritz and his wife whispering fiercely in the corner. Neither of them looked too happy. Fritz noticed Rory and broke off his quiet argument.

"Rory! You're awake," he said. He glanced at Liv, who looked like she still had something to say. "Why don't you go talk with Nicholas? He's right outside."

Rory could tell that Fritz wanted a few minutes alone with his wife, so after casting a quick look at the door to the forge, he slipped between the curtains out into the fair. He patted his pocket, thankful the bullet still felt warm through the material. The girl sitting by the entrance nodded.

"Your buddy headed that way. He's a cutie, isn't he?"

Rory didn't want to answer that, so he brushed by her with a murmur of thanks, stepping into the crowd. Peering past the shoppers meandering by, he caught sight of Nicholas on the street corner talking to a new boy. This boy appeared similar in age to Nicholas, though his clothes seemed to come from the turn of the last century, much trendier than Nicholas's older duds. The boy caught sight of Rory and held out his hand.

"You must be the famous Rory Hennessy," he said, smiling genially. "I've heard a lot about you."

Rory shook his hand tentatively, looking to Nicholas in confusion.

"This is my old friend Albert Fish," Nicholas said. "He is in the Rattle Watch with me."

"Poor kid," Albert said, laughing. "He's just wrapping his head around meeting you and now he has to meet another old Rattle Watcher. Get used to it, kiddo. Your eyes are open now."

"Nice to meet you, Albert," Rory said.

Albert winked back. "Pleasure's all mine."

They lapsed into silence as Nicholas stared into the distance. Albert waited patiently by his side, as if he'd seen this before.

"What are you looking at?" Rory asked finally.

"See the river?" Nicholas answered, pointing.

"Sure. I think I can see Brooklyn if I squint."

"Brooklyn." In Nicholas's mouth it sounded like heaven. "Have you ever been there?"

"My mom takes me and Bridget to Coney Island a few times a year. It's kinda fun, but I threw up once on the flume ride. I get seasick really easy."

"You like solid ground, huh?"

"I guess."

Nicholas's eyes grew distant.

"I have heard stories about Coney Island. But I've never been to Brooklyn. Or any of the boroughs. I can't leave the island. Neither of us can."

"Why not? Are you cursed or something?" Not able to leave Manhattan? That sounded horrible. Nicholas smiled sadly.

"I don't have the blood. The gods are constrained by their blood, and so are their children."

"Our friend Alexa, who you'll meet later, can travel to the Bronx," Albert chimed in. "Her father had a farm up there. She can cross that river. But our fathers are held to Manhattan and Manhattan only, and so are we."

"That's horrible!" Rory said.

"It's not so bad." Nicholas smiled. "I love my island. But it does mean that I can't escape when things go wrong. Good or bad, I can't run. Our leader, Adriaen, used to say that he wished everyone was forced to remain where they are, just for a while. Maybe they'd make smarter choices if they couldn't run away afterward."

"Will I meet Adriaen?"

"He was killed in the Bronx a few days ago." Nicholas's voice was flat. "You would have liked him. He knew all about you, of course. He kept tabs on you through Fritz, making sure you were all right. He was always looking out for everyone else. He formed the Rattle Watch when none of the gods would listen to him because they were afraid of rocking the boat. He gave me a purpose. He was a great god."

Rory was silent for a moment, thinking about this god who had time to worry about a boy from Inwood.

"What is your purpose?" he asked finally.

Nicholas shrugged. "To do something. Most of the children of the gods are like spoiled little rich kids. They lounge around all day, go to their stupid little parties, and gossip about one another behind their backs. It's sickening. We look like teenagers because we act like teenagers. Selfish and unable to grow up. But some of us want to be a part of something bigger. Some of us want to take a stand."

Albert nodded in agreement. Nicholas stared across the river for a moment longer before turning away.

"I need to speak with Fritz about these new deaths you told me about, Albert," Nicholas said. "Coming?"

"I'm not going anywhere near Fritz while he's duking it out with Liv," Albert said. "She scares me."

"Suit yourself," Nicholas said, rolling his eyes. He walked away, shaking his head. Rory watched him disappear into the tent, then turned back to see Albert regarding him.

"How are *you* holding up?" Albert asked.

"Okay, I guess," Rory answered.

"You're a brave kid, Rory," he said. "Nicholas told me what

you did in the bank. If everyone in the Rattle Watch were more like you, Kieft wouldn't last ten minutes."

Rory felt warm at Albert's approval.

"So what do you guys do in the Rattle Watch, exactly?" Rory asked.

Albert laughed. "My father would say we run around trying to feel important and causing a scene. Nicholas's father would say the same, or worse. But what else can we do? I can't even leave the island. Our great leaders are being replaced by small-minded thugs. And now the murders . . . these are dark times. I could be like my father, I guess, and try to play all sides. Hamilton Fish, God of Connections—he wouldn't take a side if you put a knife to his throat. He is all about working the crowd, making sure as many people are happy with him as possible. Except for me. He never really cared if I was happy or not. He wanted me to stay hidden, out of the way. He didn't want me embarrassing him in front of his peers. Maybe I would, who can tell. But at least I'm trying. At least I have some measure of courage. He would never stand up to Kieft because people might be angry. They might cut him off, shut him out. So he is too weak to act. That is not me. I am not too weak to strive for what I want. We are not our fathers, Rory, remember that. You, me, Nicholas, even your sister. We may have their blood in our veins, but we are not their shadows, doomed to mimic every action they take."

"My father would run," Rory said.

"Fritz told me about how he left when you were a child."

"I don't want to be anything like him. He ran out and left us to starve. I hate him. I'll always hate him. I promised myself

I wouldn't even think about him again. And then . . . this is going to sound crazy."

"What?"

"I don't even know why I'm telling you this."

Albert smiled. "It's the secret bond of disappointed sons."

"I saw a ship yesterday, a ghost ship. The Trumpeter told me it was called the *Half Moon*."

"Of course. Henry Hudson's old ship. It sails to warn us of great peril. I'm not surprised it's sailing now."

"I caught a good look at the ghost sailors . . . and I thought I saw my dad's face! Isn't that crazy? I guess he's in my head after all."

"Or he was really on that ship," Albert mused.

"What? Why would he be on a ghost ship? Does that mean he's dead?"

"I don't know. Maybe there's more to his story than you know."

"But—I couldn't have seen him! He's gone. He's been gone almost my whole life. I don't want to think about him anymore."

"Then don't," Albert said. "You're well rid of him. You haven't needed him for the past decade, so why worry about him now? That's one lesson Nicholas never seems to learn. He keeps going back to argue with his dad, hoping to change his mind. Why bother? We don't need them."

Albert went quiet as they both stared off toward the river. Finally he patted Rory's shoulder.

"I need to go back to the rest of the watch and explain the

delay. Good luck with your sister. I'm sure Flavio will come through for her. I'll see you soon."

Rory nodded farewell as Albert turned and disappeared into the crowd. Squaring his shoulders, Rory pushed thoughts of his father away. He didn't have time to dwell on what he thought he saw. He had his real family to worry about. Stepping back into Flavio's tent, he slipped by the roaches, who were talking quietly with Nicholas, and pushed through the door into Flavio's workroom.

The forge glowed with dancing flame, the walls shimmering with sputtering shadows like a cave lit by the kind of campfire usually surrounded by Boy Scouts swapping ghost stories late into the night. In the middle stood a dark shadow bent over his work. Flavio's skin was covered in the soot and grime of the fires, but his eyes shone white. Rory couldn't make out what part of the new Bridget he held in his hand. He thanked the stars for that when Flavio reared back and brought down his hammer with all his strength. Sparks flew in the air, lighting up Flavio's face like fireworks. The heavy clang rattled Rory's aching head, making him wince. Flavio spoke without turning.

"She's not quite done, Trouble Boy. And I don't like people watching me work. It's a delicate business, forging paper, and it don't take much to break it all down."

Rory backed up to the doorway.

"I'm sorry. I'll go."

He turned to leave when Flavio stopped him.

"Hold your horses. Go sit in the corner. I'll be done in a minute. Then you can check 'er to make sure she's right."

"Okay."

Rory retreated to the farthest corner of the forge, sliding down to the floor among the discarded paper. He tried to think about what Nicholas had said, but the clang of the forge made it difficult to keep any thoughts in his head. The crash of the hammer drove them back like animals frightened by the thunder. Eventually, he settled on watching Flavio at work, brushing his fingertips over the warm bullet in his pocket. After a moment, confusion hit him.

"Where's the paste?" he asked. "I used to do a ton of papier-mâché and we never did it without paste."

"The paste is there, believe me!" Flavio said. "I've been doing this far longer than you can imagine, so don't go questioning my methods! It's not my fault you mortals do it all wrong. Now stop bothering me!"

He returned to his work. It wasn't long before he called Rory over.

"All right. Time for inspection."

Rory stood up slowly, shaking his legs to wake them up. A dark form stood behind Flavio, hiding in his shadow. Suddenly, a bolt of fear shot up Rory's spine. What kind of creature had Flavio created? What kind of Frankenstein waited to spring out of the shadows?

Flavio gestured impatiently. "We don't have time for your timidity, Trouble Boy! If she cools too much, the soul won't take. So come here!"

Rory crept forward toward the shape. As he got closer, he could see that it was human-size, about Bridget's height. Then

Flavio stepped aside, letting the light of the fire fall on the dark creature. Rory gasped.

"Bridget . . ."

And it *was* Bridget. From the little nose to the unkempt hair to the slight slouch, this paper creature was his sister. He could see the paper everywhere, its shiny, rough surface covering everything from her cheeks to her ankles. The clothes were real, but she was not. The likeness however . . .

"It's perfect."

Flavio allowed himself a small smile as he stood next to Rory, gazing at his creation.

"It's better than Tom's boy. Stronger. I've learned a lot in the past fifty years. When you forge paper, you need to make it strong. And I used a special kind of paper. Paper I've only just figured out how to shape. Made from the trees underground. The forest under Washington Heights. Trees made part of wood and part of stone. And look at her."

Rory couldn't speak. Flavio reached over and felt Paper Bridget's forehead. He quickly turned to Rory.

"She's starting to cool. Do you have the bullet? Quickly now!"

Rory groped in his pocket, almost dropping the bullet as he pulled it out. He held it out to Flavio, who quickly snatched it from his hand.

"We're almost out of time," the smith said. "This thing's about to let go. No time to call the others in. We'll just have to do it."

"Do what?"

Flavio stood over the body like a mad scientist, holding up the bullet as if it was a wonder pill. He reached over to Paper Bridget's head and opened her mouth. Placing the bullet on her back teeth, he closed the mouth up again. He moved her jaw with his strong hands, causing a crunching sound. Rory took a step forward, but Flavio stopped him with a look.

"Her teeth are stronger than any bullet. There we go."

Satisfied, Flavio stopped the chewing and gently tipped the body back, shaking it a little while listening to her throat. After a minute of this, he nodded to himself and stood her up straight again. He looked at Rory's worried face.

"Now we see if it'll take."

He stepped over to Rory and turned to watch with him. For a moment, nothing happened. But then . . . something moved. The eye twitched. Rory's fingernails dug into his hands. Another eye twitched. Small movements popped up all over her body. Fingers shook. Shoulders flinched. Rory watched in amazement as his sister gradually, spastically came to life. Finally, all at once, Paper Bridget leaped back in a huge burst of energy, screaming at the top of her voice. Her eyes lit up as if a switch had been pulled. Suddenly, she was totally and completely alive. She looked down at herself and then back up at her brother.

"Rory? How did I get here? And why do I feel like this?"

Flavio leaned in.

"Like what?"

Bridget stepped back from this strange soot-covered man, but she answered him.

"Like someone scooped me out and just left the skin. It's weird."

Rory stepped up to her in a daze and looked into her eyes. They shone with life. They were Bridget's eyes.

"You were hurt. But the worst is over. The worst is over, I promise."

Bridget looked up at her big brother.

"Is it like a cold? I hate it when you feel like a cold is coming and you try not to worry about it, but you keep thinking about that itch in the back of your throat and your nose starts to sniffle and it just gets worse. But one day you can just tell that the worst is over and even though you feel the same as when you were getting sick, it's not so bad, because you remember the worst and you're happy because you know every day takes you farther away from that feeling."

Her eyes flinched as she finished. Rory put a hesitant hand on her shoulder.

"Do you remember the worst?"

Bridget looked away, staring at her fingernails. Her voice dipped down to a whisper.

"Yes."

Rory broke. He hugged his sister so hard, she almost crumpled. His voice came out thick and heavy.

"I promise. The worst is over."

24

A HOUSE ON HIGH

Bridget couldn't get used to her new body. She ran her fingers over her rough paper skin as she followed Rory and Nicholas down the street, marveling at the feel. She heard a brittle crackle when she opened her eyes wide, so of course she did it again and again until she must have looked crazy to the people passing by who only saw a normal girl with a twitch. Her insides felt even weirder. What was inside her? She couldn't feel her heart beat, though she held her hand tightly to her chest. Feelings and sounds she'd never paid attention to had disappeared, and the quiet startled her. Rory kept watching her when he thought she wasn't looking, checking to see if she was okay. Was she okay? She thought so. She hoped so. But something inside her felt strange.

She remembered Flavio's warning before they had left. He'd pulled her and Rory aside and gave them a stern look.

"Don't dawdle, children," he had said, his sooty face so serious it made her want to giggle. "This paper body isn't meant for long-term use. You get your real body back and destroy this one as soon as you can. Throw it in the river; I don't care. It's good for now, but it ain't good forever."

"What about Toy?" she'd asked. "He's been in that body for fifty years."

"I don't know how he did it," Flavio had said. "He shouldn't have been able to. Maybe his wizard daddy helped him. But it affected his mind; I bet a thousand dollars it did. So heed me! Go get your flesh-and-blood body back and leave this paper mess behind. And be careful!"

They left him then. Fritz and his wife rode off to look for signs of Hex while Nicholas agreed to take them to his father's house. He was telling them a funny story as they walked, about his Rattle Watch playing a trick on the Mayor using an illusionary manhole cover and some thumbtacks. Bridget wanted to pay attention, but something was pushing inside of her, making her feel like she was a balloon getting blown up. She felt a jab of fright. What if her skin broke apart and she burst open like an overcooked bag of popcorn? Her whole body felt ready to pop. She opened her mouth to say something when Nicholas stopped them. He nodded to the street sign.

"Stuyvesant Street. Named for my dad, Peter Stuyvesant. And here's the house."

They'd stopped in front of an ordinary brownstone.

"Very nice." Rory sounded disappointed.

Nicholas gave him an amused look.

"Save your fake enthusiasm for when you actually see the house. Come on."

He led them to a small alley next to the brownstone, where

to Bridget's surprise a long wooden staircase led up the side of the building. They climbed the stairs, which seemed to go on and on, until finally they reached the top and stepped out onto the roof. Rory gasped and Bridget's mouth dropped open as they saw the last thing they expected to find on a Manhattan rooftop.

A large green lawn spread out before them, covering every inch of the roof. Flowers poked up from the grass, and small bushes and trees sprouted up around the perimeter. The lawn came right to the edge of the roof, and at the other end sat a large, pleasant house, a slice of the countryside sitting on top of the town house like it had been dropped from the sky. A tall, pointed roof topped it off, with small roofed windows jutting out from the second floor, while a large chimney rose from the center, smoke drifting lazily from the tip. A long-roofed porch—filled with inviting porch swings and chairs—ran the length of the house. The front door was split in two, the top half swung open to let in the breeze while the bottom half remained shut. Standing in the doorway, a happy smile on her lips, stood a plump, pleasant woman in a large white apron holding a tray of cooling bread. As Nicholas led them across the lawn up to the house on the roof, she called out to him.

"Nicholas! I can't believe it! You've come home! With new friends!"

"This is Rory and Bridget Hennessy, Mother. Guys, this is Mother Stuyvesant, the nicest woman in the whole wide world, including Queens."

They reached the porch as Mother Stuyvesant flung her arms around her son. He smiled in embarrassment as his mother hugged the life out of him. She finally let him go, and he struggled to regain his breath. She smiled to the Hennessy children and welcomed them warmly. Nicholas peered through the open half of the door.

"Is he home?"

"He's in his study," she said. "He doesn't walk the neighborhood streets like he used to."

"I'm sure the mortals don't mind that. I always wondered why he wanted to depress everyone."

"That's his function, dear," she said, mildly reproving. "He needs to be out there doing his job. It worries me that he's abandoned it."

"I don't know why it surprised you; he abandons everything else," Nicholas murmured. Bridget wondered what happened between the boy and his father to make him so angry. Mother Stuyvesant took her son's hand.

"Please. Don't antagonize him. These times are difficult enough for him."

"He won't even know we're here. I just need a safe place where Rory can stay until we figure out what to do next."

Mother Stuyvesant opened the bottom half of the front door to let them inside. She smiled sweetly at her young visitors.

"Well, come in. Welcome to the Stuyvesant Farm, children. Despite what I'm sure Nicholas has told you, this was quite a nice place to grow up."

The inside of the impossible house reminded Bridget of those Christmas ads where the family sits around the kitchen and makes perfect cookies, the kind of home that never exists in real life. Nicholas quietly tiptoed past a large wooden door, but a loud voice stopped him in his tracks.

"Nicholas! Get in here! And bring the mortals!"

Nicholas cursed under his breath. He shot a pleading look at his mother, but she gave him no comfort. She walked over and opened the door, forcing him to enter. The two Hennessy children followed meekly behind. They stepped into a large study lined with bookcases. Pastoral paintings and Indian artifacts hung on the wall. But larger than all of these pieces was the huge painting of a doughy man posing like a great adventurer, which hung in the center of the room. Directly beneath it sat that same man, dressed in the exact same way, but slouched in his chair, his expression more irritated than the impressive man in the painting above. Bridget knew it must be Nicholas's father, Peter Stuyvesant.

Stuyvesant was a well-kept man, his velvet jacket and puffy white shirt perfectly pressed, and his pants nicely done up at the knee with ribbon, while white hose continued the journey down to his boot. At least it did on one leg, since on the other leg the hose stopped abruptly at wood. Peter Stuyvesant had a peg leg, just like a pirate. Silver bands wrapped around the wooden stick to its tip, like the stripes of a candy cane. All in all, he was an impressive man, or would have been if not for the expression on his face, which made him look like he'd just eaten some bad eggs.

Rory let out a gasp. "Peg Leg Pete!"

From Nicholas's shocked expression, Bridget could tell that her brother had said just the wrong thing. The god immediately frowned.

"I will not be spoken to like this in my own home!"

Rory immediately stammered an apology and explained about meeting a ghost called the Trumpeter. Stuyvesant relaxed a little, though his eyes still twitched with disapproval.

"Anthony is still floating around?" he asked. "I sent him up there when we were both mortals, to warn of the British coming, which he never did. It's not my fault he tried to ford the Spuyten Duyvil. Not a river to be trifled with. That's why we build bridges! Now look at him! How does he expect me to hear him all the way up there? Foolish creature. And he wants pie. For what? Warnings are only good in advance. Otherwise, they're called history lessons. People always want to be rewarded for their own foolishness. Which reminds me, Nicholas, where have you been?"

"*Doing* something, Father."

"Doing something, eh?" The god's tone mocked him. "Well, look at the great man. He's doing something. You're trying to get killed, that's what you're doing. I've heard about your activities. You do not know Kieft. You've only heard stories of what he can do. I knew him, long ago. I know what he's capable of. You stay out of his way!"

"I'm not going to hide under my pillow and hope everything turns out all right, Father!"

"Don't you take that tone with me!" Stuyvesant pointed sternly at his son, wagging his finger fiercely. "I may not find the time to walk amongst the mortals as often as I used to, but I still do my job. You don't even have a job."

"I have a job!" Nicholas was indignant. "I'm only saving the city, that's all."

"That's not a job! That's a hobby! And it's a waste of time!"

Bridget glanced over at Rory, who shrugged back. This sounded like the same argument any teenage kid would have with his dad. It would be funny, if so much weren't at stake. Nicholas and his father both sputtered into silence, angrily staring at each other. This wasn't going well at all. It was up to Bridget to save the day. She bowed low and spoke reverently.

"I, um, greet you, oh Great One. I am in, uh, awe of your magnificent presence. Please treat your humble servant with, eh, mercy. Oh Lord."

Rory gave her an incredulous look. Nicholas stared at her in astonishment while his mother covered her mouth gently with her hand. But the effect on Peter Stuyvesant was immediate. He sat up in his chair and beamed.

"See, Nicholas! This is how a god should be treated! Respect! It's all about respect! Thank you, young one. You obviously know your manners. And what is your name?"

"Bridget Hennessy, sir."

"Well met, Bridget! No one treats us old gods with the reverence we are owed. It's nice to see someone who appreciates us. I'm guessing you're here to put yourself under my protection. It is a dangerous world out there, after all. It wasn't always like that, of course. It was a great city once."

Nicholas muttered under his breath, "Here we go."

Stuyvesant gestured grandly as he spoke.

"Back in my day, when I was Mayor, this city was a wonder! I was once the governor of this colony, when I was mortal and it was called New Amsterdam. Now that's a name! Says something. New York, what is that? Horrible name! Never should have been changed! What is a *york,* anyway? And who needs a new one? I was elected Mayor, you know, once I became a god. They knew they needed a keen mind to run Mannahatta. I was in office for over fifty years! But then that young upstart Hamilton forced me out! He fixed the ballot and stole my post from me! Serves him right, to fall in with Kieft. They deserve each other. I was the best Mayor Mannahatta has ever seen! And now look at me, forced into an early retirement on my farm, out of politics, all because of those awful men down at City Hall. And things have gone downhill ever since. Nothing is as good as it was in my day. The water, it tastes horrible! The cheese, inedible. The books, written by imbeciles. We had books in my day, real books, books with words in Latin! How can it be a book if it has no Latin in it? It just makes no sense!"

As the god spoke, Bridget felt something tug at her heart (or the space where her heart used to be). She could feel the pain of all those lost wonders, everything that had once been great but was now gone forever. Tears came to her eyes just thinking about everything that had once been wonderful but that would never be wonderful again. Glancing at her brother, she saw his cheeks were wet, too. So much was lost. . . .

"And the way they treated those Munsees," Stuyvesant continued. "That was horrendous. I knew Tackapausha from our mortal days; I signed the first treaty with him. We both wanted to repair the damage Kieft's bloodthirsty ways had wreaked upon all of us. He was a good man for a savage, a good sachem. And they betrayed him and his father. Everything, downhill! It's enough to make you cry!"

"So do something about it!" Nicholas cried, exasperated.

"You don't know anything, boy, and you never did!" Stuyvesant said. "Running around playing your little tricks on people with your bad-apple friends. You could learn some manners from this fine young girl. Keep her around, and maybe you'll see how to speak to your elders who gave you life and put a roof over your head and didn't throw you in the river when you wouldn't stop bawling as a baby, though, believe me, he wanted to!"

Behind Nicholas, Mother Stuyvesant rolled her eyes.

"So can we stay?" Bridget asked.

"I might be persuaded. If Nicholas says he's sorry."

After the most forced apology in the history of forced apologies, Nicholas led them up the stairs to the guest rooms for some much-needed rest while they waited for word on Hex's whereabouts. He left them to sleep in a rustic bedroom overlooking the lawn, promising to wake them when he had news.

Gazing around the charming room, Bridget wished she could live in this country estate in the middle of the city. She'd love to wake up in the morning in an oversize four-poster bed and lazily head down for a big breakfast like they do in the movies. Rory dropped off immediately into an exhausted sleep, but she couldn't rest. The pushing feeling inside her wouldn't allow it. After a few minutes of lying in bed staring at the wooden beams above, she hopped to her feet and went back downstairs.

She wandered through the big country kitchen with its huge fireplace burning merrily. Coming upon the front entrance, she pushed open the door and tried to walk outside, forgetting about how the door was put together.

"Ow!" she cried, mostly in surprise since she couldn't feel the pain.

"Careful there, Bridget. Open the bottom half, too, or you'll break a kneecap."

Mother Stuyvesant sat on the porch swing, sipping lemonade and looking out across the city. Bridget opened the bottom half of the door and sat down in the chair next to her.

"Nicholas has gone after his friends," Mother Stuyvesant said. "He should be back soon. That boy will worry me away to nothing, I swear."

"Where's . . . um . . . his highness?"

Mother Stuyvesant laughed.

"Peter? He's out surveying the fields, trying to cool down. You can see him over in the peas."

She gestured across the street. Sure enough, up on the roof of the brownstone lay a large field of green stalks waving in the breeze, a familiar form making its way through them, limping on his peg leg. In fact, all of the buildings had fields on their roofs, which Mother Stuyvesant pointed out to Bridget as she rocked.

"Over there is corn, which won't be harvested until fall. And there are the pumpkins and squashes, also late summer, early fall. Over there across Third Avenue are the tomatoes and string beans. The carrots are down on 10th Street, above the Ethiopian restaurant—which make them taste a little funny, if you ask me. You can see the servants' quarters over on Second Avenue, up above the theater."

"This is all your farm?"

"The city built up and pushed us up with it. But Peter would never give up his farm. So now we're on top of everything. I like it, especially since I made him build me this beautiful porch. We didn't have such luxuries as porches in my mortal days. I find it so restful to sit here and take in the river breezes while I watch the beans and corn grow, don't you?"

Bridget did indeed. The sight of all those crops atop the city buildings made her smile and eased her heart.

"Does your husband always talk like that, about the old days? It made me realize how much has changed. So many good things are gone!"

Mother Stuyvesant laughed.

"That's what talking to a god will do to you. And Peter is the God of Things Were Better in the Old Days. It's his job to go around whispering in people's ears about how much better things used to be. They don't see him, but they hear him in their hearts. Unfortunately, Peter has spent more time walking the fields lately than walking the streets. Every year he stays closer and closer to home. I try to push him. The mortals need him! Without Peter, they forget the wonders of the past and focus only on the future. There is value to the past. If only he and Nicholas could find common ground and stop this eternal arguing, perhaps Peter could find the strength to do his job once again."

"How long have he and Nicholas been fighting?"

Mother Stuyvesant's face darkened.

"They are so alike. So stubborn. Peter didn't always make the right choices. But he cared deeply about this city, still does. He was quite powerful in his day, and he did a lot of good. But when they kicked him out of City Hall after the election all those years ago, it broke his heart. I think he lost his will to fight. Nicholas is so young; nothing has ever beaten him like that. He can't understand. Peter is hard on him because he wanted to protect him. I'm left in the middle, hoping my husband regains the strength that made him great, and praying my son survives to see it."

"That sounds hard," Bridget said.

"Love always is."

They lapsed into silence as they looked out over the fields, breathing in the air off the water while watching the sun cross the sky.

DECISIONS

Rory dreamed of Wampage.

The Indian stood before him on a tree-lined woodland path, blocking his way. Though glad to see the warrior, Rory knew he had to get to the end of the trail. He tried to brush by Wampage, only to be pushed back gently.

"You must turn back from this path, Rory," Wampage said. "You do not know what you do."

"I need to save my sister," he answered, puzzled. "I have to do this."

"No," Wampage pleaded. "For the sake of my people, you must *not* turn the key."

This made no sense to Rory at all.

"But you want your people free, don't you? If my family were trapped, I would do anything to help them escape."

"Not if setting them free meant their deaths."

"What are you talking about? You're not making any sense. I need to save my sister, now." Rory tried to push past Wampage, who refused to budge.

"I have spoken with an old friend through the invisible wall of the Trap. She has told me that affairs among my people are not as I left them. Our great sachem, Penhawitz, has been deposed by his own son, Tackapausha. My old friend has changed. He is no longer the diplomat, the dreamer of peace. His heart has turned to hate against the Mayor, and that is all he thinks about."

"Can you blame him?" Rory said. "The Mayor did a horrible thing."

"I do not blame him," Wampage said. "Once, I would have fallen prey to the same hate, the same need to hurt those who hurt me and my people. But living alone these many years has taught me differently. I hated your gods; I wished them dead. I thought of attacking your Mayor, even though I would be destroyed in the process. At least I would have my revenge. But what would that have accomplished? The last of the Munsees would have been dead, that is all. My death would have profited no one, least of all my people. If all you do is hate, it does not matter how righteous your cause—it will end in darkness. And all Tackapausha can do now is hate. He has drawn some of the strongest of my people to his side, dedicating them to warfare. Our people used to be peaceful, but now he and his guard do nothing but train in battle toward the day that the Trap will fall and they can exact their revenge.

"They will attack your gods, bringing war to Mannahatta. Both sides will suffer. Our people have all gone away. So we will die, consumed by revenge. Those that survive the first battle will be hunted down and exterminated. There will be no last of the Munsees this time."

"Why don't you talk to your friend?" Rory asked, searching

desperately for a solution. "Tell her to warn them. Get her to convince them that this will only hurt everybody."

"She has fallen out of favor. Many of my people do not wish to fight. They only wish to be free to go where they will. But they are not strong enough to stand up to Tackapausha. He exiled his own father from the tribe. He sways those who are uncertain with his powerful desire for vengeance. My friend is his sister, and even she cannot hold him back."

"Then you do it!" Rory shouted. "You be there when the Trap comes down, and you convince them. When they find out that they'll all die, they'll have to run away."

"Rory," Wampage said, "you cannot rip the bandage off before the wound is healed. We must find a way to get to my people and make them see their danger *before* we release them. Only then will we be able to save them. We must wait to—"

"No! This isn't fair! You want me to sacrifice my own sister, my family, for you. Bridget is my only friend! She and my mom are the only ones who haven't walked out or let me down! And she's in this mess because of me! I'm sorry, Wampage, but I'm sure you'll figure out how to save your people. You can talk with them, make them see how dumb they're being. But I have to look after my own family. If I don't, no one else will."

He pushed past Wampage and ran down the path.

Behind him, he thought he heard the Indian whisper, "My people, I am destined to fail you. . . ."

Rory woke with a start. The dream remained vivid in his mind. He lay still for a moment, wondering if the dream had been real. It felt real. But . . . he didn't want it to be real. And the more he thought about it, the more he decided it was only a dream. He didn't have time to waste on stupid nightmares. He had to save his sister. Turning to his side to check on her, he saw that he was alone on the bed. He sat up quickly, calling out for Bridget. He heard footsteps, and soon Bridget's head popped in.

"You're up, sleepyhead! They're all downstairs waiting for you!"

"Why didn't you wake me up!" he said as he leaped to his feet.

"Because you look so cute when you're sleeping," she answered with an evil grin. "I thought maybe you were dreaming of Indian princesses or something."

He felt a twinge of guilt at the mention of dreams, but he pushed it down. Instead he grabbed a pillow to throw at her, chasing her from the room with a laugh.

They hurried downstairs, and Bridget led her brother into the back to Nicholas's room. Inside waited Nicholas with Albert Fish, as well as three unfamiliar kids. Nicholas smiled.

"There he is. This is Rory, everybody. Rory, everybody."

Albert winked at him, and Rory nodded back with a grin.

"Wow, this is the Light?" said a boy in a bright green-and-pink shirt with huge ruffles who introduced himself as Simon Astor. "I thought he'd be taller. I guess I owe the Lincoln a fiver!"

A tall brown-skinned boy with eager eyes, introduced as Lincoln, gave him a small salute from the corner. The final Rattle Watch member, a girl named Alexa who seemed no-

nonsense in her brown dress and pulled-back hair, stepped up to give him a hug.

"It's great to finally meet you," she said warmly. "It was quite a shock to discover you weren't still blind."

"I wish I were still 'blind,' as you call it," Rory said bitterly. "Then all of this wouldn't have happened."

"There's more happening than you know," she said. "You'd be needed even if you were still blind."

"What do you mean?"

"She means that we need you, Rory," Nicholas said.

"What are you talking about?" Rory asked.

"We've got new information," Nicholas continued.

"That's me!" Simon cried. "That's my information!"

"According to a conversation they overheard between Astor and some Dead Rabbits, the assassin is being moved to a safe house today," Nicholas explained. "They'll be meeting up at the Fulton Fish Market downtown. So now we're figuring out a plan to go down there and flush the killer out. And I want you to come with us, Rory."

"Whoa! Now hold on," Rory said. "I don't know why you're listening to a bunch of dead bunnies, but I am not going anywhere until I know where Hex is hiding. Then I'm going to get my sister's body back. That's all I'm doing."

Nicholas leaned forward earnestly. "But you have to do this. Only you can bring the truth to light, and the truth is going to be downtown in an hour. You have to come. We'll go after Hex the minute we've got the assassin in our hands."

"Rory, it's okay," Bridget said. "We can go save the day and then you can help me—"

"No," Rory said, crossing his arms. "I'm tired of people telling me what I should and shouldn't do. Bridget comes first."

"We don't need this kid," Lincoln said. "We can take these guys. We'll surprise the assassin and whip him good!"

"I don't know," Albert said. "Doesn't it seem convenient that we learn the whereabouts of this assassin, and he'll be practically alone?"

"Hey, you're just sore that I found this out!" Simon cried. "You're trying to bring me down!"

Nicholas put up his hands, quieting the din. "We can't let this opportunity pass. This is too lucky a break. I also understand why you don't want to go, Rory. But the fact is, we don't even know where this Hex is—"

"Yes, we do," a new voice broke in.

Fritz rode into the room, followed by Liv. Rory dropped down to one knee in excitement.

"Where is he? How did you find him so quickly?"

"He was in the first place we looked," Fritz answered. "His office on Raisin Street. He's got his invisible trick working, but Liv spotted a cup of coffee floating through midair."

"He's not trying to hide from you, Rory," Liv said. "I think he saw us and was signaling where he could be found."

"Then let's go," Rory cried.

"But—" Nicholas began. Alexa stepped up and put a hand on his shoulder, interrupting him.

"I think we should let him go," she said. "We're not the ones who are supposed to be making the choices here. He is. We should be helping him do what he has to do."

Nicholas looked away, thinking. Finally, he turned back. "We'll do both."

Nicholas brought them out of the back of the house to the stables, and as they walked he talked through his plan.

"The minute you're done, you come and find us, all right?" Nicholas was saying to Rory and Bridget. "Alexa will be with you and she'll know where we are. Maybe you'll catch up and we can kill two birds with one stone today."

Nicholas pushed through the back door. Rory stepped outside and cocked his head, confused. Between the back of the house and the stables was a familiar sight.

"Is that a basketball hoop?" he asked in wonderment. Bridget shrugged, just as taken aback. Nicholas turned and smiled.

"Everyone plays basketball here in Mannahatta," he said. "It's the new craze. I'm not half bad. Maybe we'll play sometime."

"Okay," Rory said, still not believing what he was seeing.

"I just can't picture him in sweatpants," Bridget said, making him smile.

Nicholas led them into the stable, where five horses were stomping in their stalls. He nodded to one, a large white stallion.

"Why don't you take mine, Alexa? He's strong enough for three."

"What's he called?" Bridget asked, reaching up to pet the nose of the white stallion.

"Revolution," said Nicholas, slightly embarrassed.

Bridget snorted and whispered to Rory. "I wonder what he calls his socks, Truth and Justice?"

Rory smiled. He liked seeing his sister act more like her normal self. Just one more step and it will all be like it was. After the horses were saddled, Alexa mounted Revolution, pulling Rory and Bridget up to sit in front of her. The roaches and their rats climbed into the saddlebags, ready to ride. Albert rode over beside Rory.

"Don't worry, kiddo," he said. "You'll do great. I know you will."

Rory smiled his thanks, trying not to get choked up at the older boy's vote of confidence. Albert urged his horse forward to ride beside Nicholas. As they trotted out into the yard, Nicholas waved from the back of his brown mare.

"Good luck! Be careful."

Rory turned to Alexa, confused.

"Don't we have to get down to the street? How many ramps does he have?"

"Ramps?" Alexa looked innocent. "What ramps?"

With that she flipped the reins and urged the white horse to the edge of the roof, where it took a mighty leap into the empty sky before them.

"AGGHHHHHHH!"

"Rory, it's okay!" Bridget shouted in his ear. Sure enough, they weren't falling; they were floating. After a few minutes, they landed softly on the pavement, unharmed. Rory looked back up the seven stories to the roof and felt queasy. Bridget laughed.

"This is what I call a pony! Now you know what to get me for Christmas!"

The white horse burst forward, galloping down the sidewalk toward the Old Village and Hex.

26

TURNING THE KEY

Revolution galloped through the city at breakneck speed, weaving around the cars and crowds as he made his way across town. Bridget held on tightly to her brother as they quickly crossed avenue after avenue, the white horse never even breaking a sweat. It wasn't long before they slowed down to a trot deep within Greenwich Village, coming up on Raisin Street. Alexa spoke quietly over their shoulders.

"I sent ahead for some help. We'll meet up with them right around the corner."

They came to a stop in front of a small row house at the end of Raisin Street, where two people waited for them on the lawn. One, a pale old man in faded military dress at least a century old, introduced himself as Colonel Marcus Butterfield, a Civil War veteran who died by mistake when he was cleaning his gun in order to march in the fiftieth anniversary parade. But both Bridget and Rory's attention was drawn to the woman standing beside him in a simple wool dress, holding an old musket in her hand.

"I know you!" Rory cried. "You're that woman from the fort! The Revolutionary War hero!"

"Margaret Corbin," the woman said shyly. "Nice to meet you."

"You're a god now?" Bridget asked.

"Oh no!" Margaret looked scandalized. "Colonel Butterfield and I are merely spirits. We'd never go around pretending we were gods! Just simple spirits with an eye for justice."

"We're gonna learn 'em!" Colonel Butterfield shouted.

"Shh, sir," Alexa said, putting a finger to her lips. "This is a covert operation."

"Understood, young miss," he replied so quietly that Bridget could barely hear him.

"Why are they here?" Fritz asked as he and Liv crawled down from the saddlebags.

"Just in case," Alexa said. "You never know when you're going to need help."

"I feel so safe," Rory whispered drily in Bridget's ear.

"Are you ready?" Fritz asked Rory. "We'll be right here behind you if you need us. Just shout, and we'll come running."

"Okay," said Rory. He looked both scared and brave, which made Bridget want to cry. Instead she grabbed him and gave him a fierce hug. He struggled until she let go.

"Man, Bridget." He gasped. "Are you trying to kill me?"

"Just be careful," she said.

"Get the body first!" Fritz said. "And if there seems to be anything out of the ordinary, turn and run! Hex won't hurt his only bargaining chip, so Bridget's body should stay safe. It's you who has to be careful."

"I will."

"We'll keep a lookout for any of Kieft's men," said Alexa. "Ready, Rory?"

Rory took a deep breath.

"Ready."

He turned and walked away. Bridget felt the emptiness within her well up as she watched him go. As he turned the corner that strangeness was spinning like a tornado in her hollow chest, and she wondered how long before it blew her apart. *Hurry*, she said silently to her brother. *I don't know how much longer I can last. . . .*

Rory felt naked walking down Raisin Street toward Hex's office. He looked around, but the street was quiet and empty. He slipped into the building and walked up the stairs, trying to keep his heart from beating itself silly. Reaching Hex's door, he gathered his strength and knocked. He had just enough time to take a deep breath before the door opened and Hex yanked him inside.

"About time!"

Hex didn't look too good. His hair stuck up like little antennae poking out of his head while his eyes shifted around like a crazy person's. His robes were torn and muddy, as was his forehead with its dab of blood and dirt right smack in the center. He pulled Rory over to the couch and sat him down.

"Did you bring the lock and the key?" he asked, speaking quickly.

Rory swallowed and nodded, pulling them both out of his pocket where they'd spent the night.

"Great!" Hex's eyes lit up as his face split into a grin. He reached into the desk and pulled out the shining white belt. Rory could see each individual white bead gleaming. He noticed his bracelet was burning even hotter than when he held the key by itself.

"Is the belt wampum, too?" he asked.

This threw Hex for a moment.

"What? Of course it is. Don't be silly. Put it on! Toy, I need some water!"

Rory heard a faucet turn on in the next room.

"Toy is with you?" he asked, disbelieving. "After what you did?"

"I'm his father," Hex said simply. "Where else would he go?"

He handed the belt over. Rory sat there with all three pieces on his lap, but he didn't touch them. Hex's smile faded.

"Come on, what are you waiting for?"

"Where's Bridget?"

Hex paused, then turned and opened the door leading into the next room. There she lay, her face pale, on a small cot.

"There you go."

"Is she all right?" Rory fought to keep his voice steady.

"She's fine. I promise! I wouldn't hurt her unless you forced me to. See her chest moving?"

Rory could see her chest moving up and down with each mindless breath.

"How long will her body stay like that?"

"Don't you worry about her. You can fix her right up after you turn that key."

Rory picked up the belt and tied it around his waist. Immediately he felt a burst of energy flow through him, and everything seemed sharper. He could almost see through the walls.

He gasped. "What is this thing?"

"It's the sachem's belt. Without it that key won't work. That wasn't what the sachem used it for, of course, but anything worth having has multiple uses. Now stick that key in the lock and give her a turn."

Hex leaned in, his eyes eager. Rory picked up the key but then stopped.

"I want to revive Bridget first," he said.

"No! No no no!" Hex cried. "We're so close. We have to do this. You can see to her after."

Hex would not budge. Rory could see that the magician knew he held all the cards, no matter what Fritz thought. What else could Rory do? He placed the key in the lock. Suddenly he felt lightheaded as his dream of Wampage came bubbling up from the edges of his brain. And he knew for certain that it was no dream. Believing otherwise had been him trying to fool himself, to believe what he wanted to believe. Other strange realizations flooded through him. He let go of the key, leaving it sticking out of the lock. Hex let out a cry of frustration.

"You're killing me, Rory!"

"You knew, didn't you?" Rory said. "You knew what Tackapausha would do once the Trap was gone. You knew he wanted to fight."

Hex flinched, the guilt in his eyes giving him away.

"I send rats into the park all the time. Most never return, but a few have supplied me with enough information that I was able to piece it together. I can't blame him. There's a lot to be angry about."

Rory felt eyes on him, and he glanced to the back of the room to see Toy standing in the doorway, holding a tray in one hand. The other arm ended in a stump, its hand left behind in Tobias's vault. He didn't look at Rory; instead, he stared at the lock and key in Rory's lap. A light went off in Rory's head.

"That's why your son wouldn't turn the key. He knew what would happen."

Hex gritted his teeth. "He said he understood. He knew how important this was to me. But when the time came . . ."

Rory could see his sister's body slowly breathing in the next room. What if he had to pay a price no matter what he did? Which price was higher?

"And if all the Munsees die?" he asked. "Who wins then?"

Hex exploded, finally losing his temper. "Who cares! You think I really care about the Munsees? They let themselves get caught by such an obvious trap. They deserve what they get."

Rather than shock at Hex's tirade, Rory felt a wave of understanding. Of course Hex didn't care about the Munsees. Did he really care about anyone?

"So you told me lie after lie—"

"Everything I said was true. But it doesn't matter. What matters is what else waits inside the park. The secret Kieft hid away right before the Trap was sprung. That is what matters."

"What are you talking about? What secret?"

"The night before the Trap was sprung, Kieft disappeared

into the park accompanied by a group of spirits carrying something hidden under tarps and sheets," Hex said. "I tried to follow his footsteps and discover his secret, but he trailed snares behind him from which I barely escaped. I was forced to turn around. When Kieft finally reappeared, he was alone. The spirits—and their burden—must have been disposed of deep inside the park.

"The next day, the Trap was sprung and his secrets were locked away. But now we can open the Trap and discover what he did. And I will use what we find to make Kieft pay for what he did to me!"

"To you?" Rory felt buried under the avalanche of new information. "What did Kieft do to you?"

"I was his right-hand man. The only one he trusted. And then he betrayed me, left me for dead. Just because I had witnessed his midnight hike, even though he was fully aware that I had no idea *what* he had hidden in the park. It didn't matter. That I knew anything at all was reason enough for him to turn on me. Whatever is in there must be enormously important, maybe even the key to his power, his magic. And now it can finally be mine. So turn the key!"

Rory could only stare back in astonishment, not even sure what was happening. Hex grunted in frustration.

"All right, I wasn't going to do this. I wanted to save it for a surprise afterward. But you've forced me to use it as a bargaining chip. There's something else I think you might be looking for besides your sister. Something more important than Munsees."

Hex leaned in close.

"Have you seen your father lately?"

Bridget was so concerned with the war going on inside her that she didn't notice the rumbling at first. By the time she picked up the clomping sounds in the distance, Fritz was already looking behind them.

"Do you hear that?" he asked. Liv nodded as Alexa peered into the distance. The light bounced off something down the street. Something green . . .

"Brokers," Fritz said, his face gray. "Tobias has found us."

Bridget could make them out now, a row of green creatures with big silver teeth, the sun bouncing off their metal bodies. The ground shook as they approached, and Bridget shuddered.

"We've got to warn Rory," she said.

"We can't. We don't have time," Alexa said. "We've got to stop them here."

"What!" Bridget said. "Look at the size of those creatures! We've got to grab Rory and get out of here. We can get my body another time!"

"There may be no other time," Alexa said. "There may be no other time."

"This is suicide," Liv said. "We can't stop those things."

"Certainly we can," Colonel Butterfield declared. "I have my pistol. Margaret has her musket. You have your strong character and iron will. We cannot be beaten!"

"Don't do this, Fritz," Liv said, pleading with her husband.

"Take Bridget to a safe place," Fritz said. "This is too dangerous for her."

The Brokers had caught sight of them, and now they began

to run toward the small party. Fritz pulled out what looked like a tiny firecracker and threw it at the monsters. It hit a Broker in the shin and exploded, sending the green creature tumbling to the ground. But the other Brokers kept coming, not even glancing at their fallen comrade.

"Come on, Bridget," Liv said urgently. "We have to go."

Bridget looked over at Margaret, who was holding her gun to her shoulder as she aimed at the advancing Brokers, and at Alexa with the brick in her hand. She turned back to Liv.

"They're here for me," she said. "I'm not leaving."

Before Liv could argue, the monsters were upon them.

The first Broker knocked Alexa to the ground, but she rolled aside before the monster could stomp her. Margaret stood as calmly as she had that day three hundred years earlier in Fort Tryon, firing her musket into the face of a green creature, knocking it senseless. Colonel Butterfield lost his gun almost immediately, but he pulled out his cavalry sword and swung it at every beast in sight. Fritz tossed another firecracker at the nearest pair of green feet and sent that monster tumbling to the street. Liv joined him, sending firecrackers of her own into the crowd of enemies.

Everyone around Bridget was fighting, but she was frozen with fear. She didn't know what to do. Liv yelled over her shoulder for her to run, but Bridget couldn't move. Not even when the largest Broker came barreling toward her, hitting her headlong in a move destined to crush her into a flat paper pancake.

It never happened.

Bridget shook her head to clear it. She was still standing, but by the way the Broker cocked its head at her in confusion, she shouldn't be. By all rights, she should be dead, but she hadn't felt a thing. What was going on? The Broker came at her again, and this time she jumped at it, whacking it with her shoulder. It fell onto its back, its shiny metal face confused by how this little girl had hurt it. A glimmer of an idea passed through Bridget's head. Could it be . . . ? She swung at the Broker again, and it went flying through the air to land halfway across the street. Fritz turned to look at Bridget in amazement.

"How did you do that?" he asked.

The body. It was her papier-mâché body. Flavio said he'd made it strong; he just never said *how* strong. A smile dawned on Bridget's face. She was a superhero! Who needed steel-tipped boots when she had a steel-tipped body! A Broker ran past her, heading for Hex's apartment. The pressure in her chest completely forgotten, she chased it, taking it down before it could get too far. Margaret raised her musket in salute as Colonel Butterfield let out a whoop of triumph.

"You are a warrior born, little lady," he cried.

Another Broker tried to get past, and she chased it down, too. But there were so many of them, not even her new super-strength could keep them all back. *Turn the key*, she thought to Rory. *We can't hold them forever.* Then she returned to the task at hand, launching herself back into the fray without a second thought.

***

Rory heard something in the distance, but he was too focused on Hex to give it a thought.

"What do you know about my dad?"

"You've seen him recently, haven't you, Rory?" Hex said softly.

Rory shook his head to clear it. He flashed back to the memory of the ship gliding past him on the river, the familiar face from the photographs looking over the side.

"That wasn't real. I imagined it."

"It was real. I caught a glimpse of it when I put the spell on your forehead. You saw your father's face on the *Half Moon* when it sailed past the park. You saw him on board."

"It wasn't real," Rory insisted, though he wasn't sure at all. What if Hex knew something about his father? Would he really care? Rory expected to feel nothing, but for some strange reason, he felt hope instead.

"I looked into it after you left yesterday," Hex continued. "I think you might be very interested in what I found. Just turn the key, and I'll tell you everything you want to know. You can have your whole family back together again, with no one chasing you. You don't owe anyone else anything. They never helped you when you needed it. They work your mother to the bone, and they sure don't care about you or your sister. Just turn the key and it will all be over."

The sounds of shouting drifted through the window, and Hex gave a quick look out. He blanched.

"How did they find me!" he cried. "Did you bring them with you?"

Rory looked outside, where a full-fledged battle was taking place on the street. Green Brokers of Tobias were everywhere, fighting his friends. One monster roared as it rushed a small form below.

"Bridget?" Rory whispered, his heart stopping in fear. But his sister calmly grabbed the Broker and sent it skidding down the street.

"Bridget!" Rory repeated, this time in shock.

"I see you visited Flavio," Hex said wryly. "Very wise. And very dangerous. His creations are not such long-term investments, as I'm sure he told you."

"They're getting clobbered," Rory said, stricken.

"They're doing this for you, Rory," Hex said. "Those Brokers are here to stop you, and your friends are holding them back. Why is this such a hard choice for you? You never worried about anyone but your family, and now you can have them all back, safe and sound. Who cares about the rest of them? They're not your friends. They're just like me, using you. Only they don't have the courtesy to admit it. Just turn the key. Turn it and you can have your life back, better than new."

Rory reached down and put his hand on the key. He did want it. He wanted his sister back. He wanted to see his father again, even if it was just to punch him in the nose. All those people who would suffer—he didn't know them. They weren't his responsibility. It wasn't even a choice, really. Not a choice at all.

He turned the key.

"What are you waiting for?" Hex broke in finally.

Rory looked down in confusion. He could have sworn he'd turned the key, but there it was, just the same as before, sticking out of the lock. He steeled himself and turned it again. Once again, his hand didn't move. He couldn't make himself do it. He couldn't let all those people die. And now Bridget would be lost because of it.

Resigned, he opened his mouth to tell Hex this when the door slammed open to admit a bloodied Alexa van der Donck.

"Rory!" she yelled. "The Brokers are breaking through!"

Hex cursed.

"Turn it!" he cried.

Alexa took a look at Hex, who was no longer invisible. Her mouth dropped.

"Aaron!"

Hex stared back at her, momentarily confused. In that moment, Toy dropped his tray and lunged for the lock in Rory's hand, pulling it away from the stunned boy in one swift motion. Rory was left with the key dangling from his fingers.

"Toy! What are you doing?" Hex shouted. He lunged for the paper boy, but Toy was too quick. He raced toward the back windows that overlooked the alley behind the building and burst through the glass. Landing on the street below, he ran down the alley with the lock in hand, turned the corner, and was gone.

Hex fell back against his desk, devastated.

"My son. How could you do this?"

A loud crash sounded as the first Broker pounded on the door. Hex turned to look out the back window.

"We're surrounded!"

Rory could see the spiked green heads outside. Seeing that Hex was distracted, he made a move toward Bridget's body. Before he could get to her, he was pulled back. Hex had him by the belt. Alexa grappled with Hex from behind, trying to pull him off Rory.

"Forget about me. Grab Bridget's body!" Rory shouted.

Alexa turned to do just that when the door to the front office flew open and a green hand shot through, clamping onto her shoulder. One swift movement and she was gone, pulled through the doorway like she weighed nothing at all. Rory struggled to free himself of Hex, but the magician clutched at his belt, trying to remove it.

"Let me go!"

"Give me the belt!" Hex shouted.

"Take it!" Rory tried to untie it, but he couldn't get the knot undone. Hex looked around wildly.

"They're everywhere!" he cried. "I won't let them take me!"

Green hands burst through the windows, sending glass flying into the air. Hex let go of Rory and leaped for the picture of the belt hanging on the wall. Freed, Rory scrambled toward Bridget's body, which waited for him on the cot. Hex reached the child's drawing and pushed the center of it with his palm as more Brokers burst into the room. Suddenly, the entire building began to shake. Plaster fell down from the ceiling as if an earthquake had hit them.

Rory yelled back to Hex, "What did you do?"

Hex grinned wildly.

"They won't get me! I can wait for another you!"

And the building began to collapse on top of them, six floors falling down onto their heads. Rory threw himself over his sister's body, covering her with his own. Then the air filled with falling wood and brick, sending Rory into darkness as the dying building landed on top of them.

UNDER RAISIN STREET

Nicholas led the Rattle Watch up to the dark building overlooking the river on South Street. The mortals passed by unseeing, heading to the South Street Seaport next door with its replicas of three-masted ships and fast-food courts, but the Fulton Fish Market itself was empty and silent. The actual fish market had closed for good, moving off the island a few years back and leaving behind only a hollowed-out shell and a faded sign. But Fulton's had been there so long that here in Mannahatta, the fish market continued, the spirits of hundreds of workers who'd hauled fish through its doors carrying on as if death had never taken them. Most of the building was open to the street, with tall, wide entranceways for the trucks to back up to and unload the day's catch, but metal screens covered the openings, locking out the curious. The place was quiet; the morning's work had long since been completed, and the spirits had disappeared until the next dawn. As far as Nicholas could see, the inside was deserted, the long troughs that were usually filled with ghostly iced fish, dry and bare. He gathered the watch behind one of the stone pillars that held up

FDR Drive, rumbling above them. The whole area was cast in shadow.

"Are you sure about this, Simon?" he asked. "The place looks empty."

"I wasn't the only one there," Simon answered peevishly. "Lincoln heard what I heard. The assassin's supposed to wait for the Dead Rabbits in the back."

"There's only one door I can see," Lincoln said. "Over there on the side. We can go in through there."

"I don't like the idea of us just walking in there," Albert said, worry plain on his face. "Let me take a quick look, just to see. I'll be careful."

Nicholas didn't want to take the risk, but he saw the wisdom. He nodded, and Albert crept away toward the side of the building and peered through the metal grate. After a moment, he came back shaking his head.

"I don't see anything, though there is an office at the back," he said. "I still don't like it, Nicholas."

"I think we just got lucky, Al," Simon said, clapping Albert on the back. Albert ignored him, waiting for an answer from his leader. Nicholas stared silently at the market, lost in thought. Finally, he took a deep breath and turned to his Rattle Watch.

"We're going in. Let's catch us an assassin."

He began to lay out a plan, his murmurs barely carrying to the building across from him. But it didn't matter, since the fifty or so Dead Rabbits hiding in the troughs under false bottoms knew they were coming. All they had to do was wait for the door to open and they would pounce, ending the Rattle Watch once and for all.

"Wake up, kid. Sleepy time's over."

Rory groaned as he came to. His body hurt all over. He forced his eyes open to see a smiling face inches from his own. He quickly scrambled away, slamming into some rocks behind him.

"You!" he cried.

It was the doo-wop singer from the subway. He still wore his fedora; it rested on top of his head at a jaunty angle. He smiled his wide, toothy grin.

"Hello there, Rory," he said. "How're you feelin'?"

Rory stood up slowly, rubbing his aching forehead. Remembering the last few minutes, he quickly cast about for his sister's body. He was in a small cave created by the broken pieces of the building that had just fallen on top of him. The light came from a small lantern in the corner, and the shadows made it hard to see if his sister was in here with him.

"She's right over here," the doo-wop singer said genially, pointing to a dark body in the corner. "Right as rain. Or she will be, at any rate."

Rory ran up to Bridget's body, noting her rising chest and red cheeks. Falling to his sister's side, he felt like crying.

"What happened?"

"Your magician friend pulled the whole darn buildin' down on your poor heads, that's what. Near killed you, which was his intent. Always was a spiteful fellow. But he didn't reckon on me. No one seems to. I don't know whether to be glad or sore over that."

Rory took a closer look at his companion.

"Who are you?"

The doo-wop singer tipped his cap.

"Caesar Prince. Good to meet you."

It was his eyes that caught Rory then. Those deep, dark eyes that seemed to suck him in. He let out a gasp.

"You're a god!"

"You betcha!" Prince performed a little bow. "God of Under the Streets. I been around a long time, boy, almost as long as our friend Kieft. He thinks I'm crazy, and I am, I guess, but crazy like a fox!"

"You're on our side?"

Prince laughed.

"More like you're on my side, boy. Adriaen and I, we'd been working together for a long time. But I'm more like a . . . a silent partner. I've been watching you for years and years, we both were. You were our little ace in the hole. Still are. That damned magician tried to use you, but I ended up using him."

"What do you mean?" Rory was lost.

"Let's just say we needed you and that belt to come together, and there was only one way to do it. We nudged the magician your way, and everything was going great. But then poor Adriaen met his maker, and, well, I knew it was time to disappear. Kieft was startin' to suspect, and I didn't want to shake hands with that knife o' his. But I was watching all along, making sure things followed the plan, which they did, thankfully. When you went into that bank, I made sure your sister followed you, made her lucky enough."

"Lucky enough?" Rory said, disbelieving. "She was shot! How lucky was that?"

"Lucky *enough*," Prince repeated. "Ain't always nice, doing what needs to be done. The magician would've had you, if not for Bridget. It's a delicate balance, so delicate it makes my head hurt. We needed the belt, but you couldn't turn the key. So I made her lucky."

"So the whole time, Nicholas and Fritz and all of them knew about this!"

"I should hope not," Prince said. "They don't even know for sure I'm on their side. That's me and Adriaen's secret, and now it's gonna be your and my secret. Kieft is more powerful than he ever was, and it's too soon to stick my head out into the light. Stick it out now, it'll be chopped off at the neck. But down here in the dark . . . down here I can make things happen."

"Awful things!" Rory was horrified. "You used me! You used us all!"

"I'm sorry for that, Rory, I truly am. But time is runnin' out. You got your sister's body right over there, and soon she'll have her soul right back where it belongs. It ain't the easiest road, but it had to be walked. Right now, we got more important things to worry 'bout. I know you don't want to trust me, got no reason to, but you're gonna have to. See, this is the one thing I had to leave to chance. I knew we'd get here, one way or the other, but now that I need you the most, I don't know what'll happen. It's up to you."

"Need me for what? I'm stuck in some dark hole underground. What can I do?"

"The belt, Rory." Caesar Prince pointed a long finger at the white belt around Rory's waist. "It's your birthright. It ain't just for opening that Trap. It's older than that, much older."

"What is it for?" Rory could feel something different inside him with the belt around him, but he didn't understand it.

"It's the truth," Prince said. "Just like you. And put around your waist, it brings the truth out of the shadows and into the light. Did you know that all the sachems of the ancient Munsees were Lights? Just like you. It's a Munsee ability. So somewhere in your past, you must have a Munsee ancestor or two. How about them apples, eh? The sachems would use the belt to give judgment and expose lies and search the world for the truth of things. That's what you do, Rory. You expose the lies and bring the truth to light. We need the truth, Rory, or people will die."

"What truth?" Rory asked, confused.

"Can you trust me?" Prince held out his hand. "I know it's hard, but your new friends need you. All of Mannahatta needs you."

Rory didn't want to do it. He wanted to dig himself out of this hole and bring his sister back to her normal body. Then he wanted to go home and sleep with the pillow over his head. But he had the chance to turn that key and he didn't do it. Something had changed in him. He made a choice up there in Hex's office. He chose to care about more than just his family. Just like Nicholas, he chose to make a stand. And he couldn't put the pillow over his head, not anymore. He reached out and took Prince's hand.

"I don't trust you," he said. "But I want the truth."

Prince's eyes glinted in the dark.

"Close your eyes, Rory. Think about the truth. Think about where the truth needs to be told, and the belt will take you there."

Rory closed his eyes and did just that. Suddenly, there was a wrench inside him as he felt himself flung upward. Opening his eyes, he looked down with surprise to see his body slumped to the ground beneath him, still holding Prince's hand. But Prince was staring up at him and grinning. Then Rory felt a strong wind blow him up through the rock toward the world above.

His spirit burst into the air above Greenwich Village. He saw small figures picking through the wreckage of Hex's building, but before he could look too closely, the wind picked up and blew him onward. He soared over the city, watching it sparkle under the afternoon sun. He flew past the buildings, often passing right through the brick, on his way to . . . somewhere. He approached the Brooklyn Bridge, and here he dived down, sinking through FDR Drive to the seaport below. There, he came upon a startling sight. Nicholas and the rest of the Rattle Watch were creeping up to the fish market, making their way to a small door in the side of the building. They were about to capture the assassin! But something was wrong; he could feel it. One of the Rattle Watch burned red beneath him. It made his stomach ache to look at him. Without thinking, he swooped down unseen and laid a cool hand on the head of the red man, to try to make the burning stop.

***

"You're going to die."

Nicholas flinched as the voice came from behind him.

"What?" he whispered. "Keep it down!"

"You're all going to die, Nicholas," the voice continued. "You're all going to die. The Dead Rabbits will take care of most of you. But you, Nicholas. You, I have to take care of myself. That was one of the conditions when I was given the knife."

Nicholas turned slowly, not understanding what he was hearing. The rest of the Rattle Watch had stopped short, staring in shock at the voice in their midst.

"What are you talking about?" Nicholas said, his face disbelieving.

"The knife is right here in my jacket," Albert Fish said, his wide eyes as amazed at what he was saying as the rest of them. "Once you walk through that door, it will be in your back, Nicholas Stuyvesant. It's a small price to pay to get what I deserve."

"What are you saying, Albert?" Lincoln said, backing away. Simon, likewise, made space around the confessor.

"You're all going to die today," Albert continued. "There are fifty Dead Rabbits on the other side of that door, and they're going to kill you all."

Albert pulled out a knife from his jacket, and no one needed to be told that it was *the* knife. It practically radiated evil. Nicholas could barely speak for shock.

"It was you, Albert?" he forced out. "You're the assassin? But . . . we've been friends so long. You're a good person, Albert!"

"I'd rather be an evil god than a good person," Albert replied.

"Why are you telling us this?" Lincoln asked.

"I don't know!" Albert shouted. "I don't want to be telling you this. I don't know what's going on! You're all supposed to be dead in a few minutes. Why am I talking?"

"What do you mean, an evil god?" Simon asked. "You can't be a god."

"Yes I can," Albert said. "It's the secret nobody knows. It's all in the locket. Wear Jenny Fingers's locket, be the Goddess of Shoplifting. Wear Hiram Greenbaum's, be the God of Guilt. Wear them both, be more powerful than all our fathers!"

At first Nicholas didn't believe what he was hearing. But what if it were true . . . ? Could they all really be gods? Any of them? Was this really possible?

"I'll finally be a god, Nicholas! And you'll be nothing. Just because you're older doesn't mean you're better! I'm better! Better than most of the gods, as well. And now I will be one, better than them all!"

"No you won't, Albert," Nicholas said quietly. "Not now."

A loud clatter caused most of the watch to look toward the market, though Nicholas and Albert remained staring at each other.

"He's telling the truth!" Lincoln cried. "Dead Rabbits are popping up all over inside the market. They're heading for us."

"The door, get the door!" Nicholas yelled.

"I got it!" Lincoln replied, launching himself at the side door. He pushed the door shut just as the Rabbits threw themselves at the other side. It buckled but stayed closed. Other gang members tried to break through the metal gates, but they could only jab their knives and blackjacks through the spaces.

"I can't hold them forever!" Lincoln shouted.

"Just hold them long enough!" Nicholas replied, finally turning a bit to see. Right as his eyes left Albert, the turncoat made his move, rushing at Nicholas with his knife raised. Nicholas caught the motion just a second too late, but he was still able to twist enough that the knife sank into his shoulder instead of his throat. He went down in a ball of pain. Albert stood over him, knife raised.

"It's over, Nicholas. Sorry."

He brought the knife down. Helplessly, Nicholas watched it head for his chest, but before it could get there, a hand flew out of nowhere to meet it. The knife passed through the hand like it was water, but the hilt jammed into the palm, trapping it an inch before the knife's point could pierce Nicholas's chest. Albert turned in confusion to see Simon standing there with the knife clear through his hand. He looked too amazed to feel the pain.

"Simon? But you're useless," Albert said, shocked.

"I'm just as surprised as you are," Simon replied, dazed as he stared stupidly at the knife through his hand. Behind him, having found a board to jam underneath the door handle, Lincoln ran up and launched himself at Albert. He wrestled Albert to the ground and called out to Simon.

"Give me the knife!"

Simon held out his hand. Lincoln glanced over as he struggled with the traitor. "Could you take it out of your hand first?" he said. Simon gritted his teeth and pulled the knife out. He handed it to Lincoln, who held the knife to Albert's throat.

"I'm gonna feel that in the morning," Simon said and promptly passed out.

Albert stopped struggling as soon as he felt the cold steel against his skin. Nicholas gazed over at Simon's limp body, his eyes dim with pain.

"You did good, Simon."

"The board won't hold long, but it should give us a head start if we leave now!" Lincoln shouted, keeping the knife at Albert's throat. Nicholas forced himself to his feet as Simon stirred. The door behind them bulged as the Rabbits tried to force their way through.

"You want to run?" Simon said weakly, pushing himself up. "You don't think we can take 'em?"

"Normally, I'd feel pretty good about three against fifty," Lincoln said seriously, "but you two are all banged up and I've got to deal with the god wannabe here."

"I guess we'd better go then," Nicholas whispered, still white with pain as he held his shoulder. They limped away quickly, disappearing around the corner as the Dead Rabbits hammered away at their prison door with little success. Above them, unseen by all, Rory felt the wind pick up to blow him back toward his waiting body, his purpose fulfilled.

As Rory flew over the city, the wind suddenly changed direction, sending him north. He found himself flying over Central Park, making a beeline for the trees. In a small clearing, a wigwam sat with smoke pouring out of its roof. Slipping through its walls, he passed into the smoke-filled interior, where a pit of hot coals sent gray clouds up to the hole in the ceiling. In the corner, a seated Munsee woman sweated profusely, smiling at him.

"You came. The dreams told me now would be a good time to call to you. I'm glad it was worth the power expended to reach beyond the barrier."

"Who are you?" Rory asked as he floated above her.

"I am Sooleawa. Wampage spoke of you. As did my daughter, Soka. She said you had a nice nose. I see she was not mistaken."

"I didn't turn the key!" he exclaimed loudly, embarrassed by the mention of the pretty Munsee girl.

"I know. Thank you. But that is not why I called to you. I need a favor."

"What favor?"

"If we are ever to be released from this prison, you must come to us. But come too soon and it could be very dangerous. So please, do not enter the park until I send for you. Please remember that. I promise, one day soon you and I will sit in the sweat lodge side by side and we will soar."

The wind picked up, and Rory was blown back outside. Sooleawa nodded good-bye, and something compelled Rory to shout to her as he flew out of the tent.

"Tell Soka she has a nice nose, too!"

He rose into the air, and the wind carried him away.

Rory blinked his eyes slowly, the dark cave coming into focus.

"You all right?" Caesar Prince's voice floated over.

Rory groaned and sat up.

"I feel worse than when the building landed on my head," he said.

Prince sat back on his heels, his big grin now a small, secret smile.

"Truth takes a lot outta you, don't it?" he said.

"Albert was a traitor!" Rory cried, remembering. "I made him tell the truth!"

"You did good, kid," Prince said. "Real good. Saved your friends and found the assassin. Nice work."

"So that was what you wanted this belt for?" Rory asked. "To find that assassin?"

"To find the knife, yes, that was one thing we wanted. It's a first step. There are still more lies we need to find the truth behind, but that's not a worry today. This was a real good first step. You came through, just like I knew you would."

"So now I can get Bridget back into her body, finally?"

Prince pushed himself to his feet.

"You bet. They'll be diggin' you out soon enough. And take that mess of a man with you."

He pointed to a pair of legs sticking out from beneath the rubble in the corner.

"Is that Hex?" Rory asked.

"Looks like the witch in *The Wizard of Oz*, don't he?" Prince laughed.

"But he has to be dead! You can't survive that!"

"He ain't mortal, boy. He ain't even a spirit. Why you think he took the place down? He knew he'd survive. Those Brokers sure didn't. The hand I pulled off your ankle didn't have a body attached to it anymore. You wouldn't have made it if not for me. But Hex was never in any danger. It could only knock him out for a spell."

"Why?"

"Can't kill a god that easy."

Rory looked over at Hex's legs in shock.

"He's a god?"

"Fallen god. But a god all the same."

"God of what?"

Prince shrugged. "Does it matter? Another thing, I'd rather you not be talking about meetin' me down here. It's still too soon to stick my head out above ground. When they ask, you happened upon how to use the belt by accident."

"Okay," Rory said, though inside he knew he'd at least have to tell Bridget. And maybe Fritz. Prince shook his head and poked him in the temple, sending a small shock through him. "What was that?" Rory asked.

"Wish I could trust you, boy," Prince said. "Maybe one day I will. You'll see me again. We still gotta let out those poor Munsees, after all. We'll make 'em ready to bring some balance back to the world. Hex misled you about a lot of things, but he was right about that much. Don't worry. I got you this far, didn't I? It'll all be fine, trust me!"

His cunning smile didn't inspire too much trust. Before Rory could say so, the lantern went out. Rory called into the darkness, but no one replied. After a moment Rory could tell that, even though there weren't any ways out of their small hole, Caesar Prince was gone. Rory stood there in the dark, not sure what to do. Suddenly, a small pinpoint of light broke through above him. A familiar voice called out.

"Rory? You down there?"

Rory almost cried. Fritz had come.

They all gathered around as Bridget knelt by her body. It was strange to see herself lying there, asleep. She didn't realize her nose was so pointy. Even though she was happy to be going back into her own flesh, a small part of her was sad. She'd been a superhero in this paper body, no matter how it made her feel. She'd knocked around monsters like they were dolls. She'd been Malibu Death Barbie for real. And now she was going back to being a little girl who needed boots with steel tips to feel strong. Rory smiled at her, as did a beaten-up Alexa behind him and everyone else who'd taken the last stand against the Brokers. They wanted to see what they'd fought for. She did miss her heartbeat, after all. She leaned over her own mouth and breathed. . . .

Her eyes fluttered open. Her own paper face was inches from her, frozen in the act of breathing out. She reached up and gently set it aside, but before she could say anything Rory was crushing the life out of her.

"You're okay! Thank God you're okay!"

"Of course I am," she answered. "Why wouldn't I be?"

Everyone clapped happily as she sat up, but she was staring at the dead paper body next to her. She hated to admit it, but part of her wished she was still inside it. She already missed the feeling.

28

HEX REVEALED

Rory and Bridget arrived back at Stuyvesant Farm to find the place in chaos. Mother Stuyvesant was bandaging her son's shoulder while Peter Stuyvesant stomped about in anger.

"That weasel! I never liked him! No one hurts my boy! No one!"

Alexa ran over to check on Nicholas, leaving Rory to sit Hex down on the floor. Hex had woken up on the way there, but he refused to talk. After a moment, Alexa called Rory and Bridget over to Nicholas's side. He gave Bridget a tired smile.

"Good to see you back in your body, girl!"

"Thanks!" Bridget beamed. Nicholas turned to Rory.

"Some amazing things happened this afternoon," Nicholas said. "And I suspect they have something to do with you. But that can wait."

"Your dad seems really mad," Bridget whispered.

"He's been on a rampage since I came back wounded," Nicholas said, bemused. "I've never seen him like this. He's been barking orders, taking charge. I'd almost think he cared about me."

"Of course he cares about you," Alexa said. "You knew that."

"I didn't think he cared this much. He's like the Peter Stuyvesant in the stories again."

Stuyvesant stomped up to Hex, his wooden leg clomping across the floor.

"Well I'll be pickled," Stuyvesant said. "We thought you were dead, Aaron."

"I see you haven't died of depression yet, Peter," Hex replied, smirking up from the floor. "I guess I lose that bet."

"How many names do you have, Hex?" Rory asked.

"I'm sure he's had many, many names," Stuyvesant replied. "But Aaron was the first. He was an important man in his day, weren't you, Aaron? But you threw it away. Shot Alexander even as he pointed his gun to the sky, and then you had to run for the rest of your days. But you were given a second chance. After you died you awoke a god of Manhattan. God of Politics and Back-alley Deals. And then you did the most despicable thing I can think of and I thought you'd evaporated from shame. But no such luck."

"Aaron? Aaron who?" Rory wanted to know.

"Rory, you are looking at the tattered remains of Aaron Burr. A great man, once. But no more."

Hex spit.

"Don't lecture me on greatness, Peter," he said. "Not when you hide away while the city falls into ruin! At least I was trying to do something."

Rory stared openmouthed at this schoolbook figure come to life. Aaron Burr, the vice president of the United States who shot Alexander Hamilton in a duel and was kicked out of office for it—he was Hex!

Stuyvesant laughed. "Do something? It's your fault we're in this mess!"

"What do you mean?" Rory asked.

"Benevolent Aaron here was the one who designed the Trap. How else would he know how to unlock it? None of us knew. Without Aaron, the Munsees would still be free."

Hex didn't answer, refusing to look at any of them. Stuyvesant finally gave a loud harrumph.

"Normally I'd give him over to the Council of Twelve. But something tells me that wouldn't help our young friend here, and I don't know if I trust even our friends on the council anymore. So I'll keep him here for the time being. Don't worry; he won't be hurting anyone anymore. Young Lincoln? Could you take him to the cellars, please? Put him next to Albert, our turncoat."

Lincoln yanked Hex to his feet and started to drag him from the room. Rory stepped in front of the magician.

"Wait. Before everything happened, you said something about my dad. Where is he? You have to tell me. You owe me that."

Hex started to laugh.

"Owe you? I don't owe you a thing. You blew your chance to find out what I know. You'll probably never find your father now."

Rory balled his hand into a fist, but before he could punch Hex, Bridget grabbed his arm.

"Don't, Rory. He's not worth it. He's not worth anything anymore."

Lincoln dragged Hex away into the cellars. Rory watched him go, his heart heavy. He'd actually begun to feel hope that one day he'd see his father and finally find out why he left. Even without Hex's help, maybe he could still look. But did he really want to?

Stuyvesant turned to Simon.

"You found something on the assassin?"

Simon nodded, pulling out two gold lockets. He handed them over to Stuyvesant, who looked troubled.

"These should not be in existence anymore. Once their owners are dead, they should pass on either to a new god or into oblivion. But then again, a god has never been murdered before, so who really knew *what* would happen? But at least no one will profit from these murders."

He clenched his fingers around the lockets and when his hand opened again, dust fell to the floor. He glanced at Simon again.

"Those were all?"

Simon shrugged, his good hand in his pocket.

"All I found, yep!"

Stuyvesant nodded before turning his keen eye on his son and Rory.

"There are stories to be told. I'd like to hear them."

Albert sat in the small storage room, wallowing in his misery. He'd been so close! He still had no idea why he began babbling his plans for all the world to hear. He leaned back against the cool cellar wall. Maybe he could barter Kieft's name for favors. They wanted him far more than Albert. Maybe he could convince them that Kieft had done the murders. Well, not if he went spouting the truth again. He'd have to watch that.

A small squeak caught his attention. Sally, his rat spy, came scuffling across the cellar floor. He smiled. At least he wasn't alone.

The door to the cellar opened and he looked up, expecting to see Nicholas or Peter Stuyvesant. Instead, his heart dropped through the floor.

"Hello, Albert," said the man with the black eyes. "You know, in our talks about the Light, I've noticed you've never once told me his name. I need it now. Give me his name, before we begin, and maybe I'll be kind."

Albert opened his mouth to speak, but suddenly a strange feeling flooded through him. He'd thought he'd killed that feeling the night before, but there it was, back as strong as ever. He felt guilty. They must have destroyed Hiram Greenbaum's locket, releasing guilt back into the world. An image sprang up in his mind. A picture of Rory, only thirteen years old. It didn't seem right to hand him over like this. Albert was going to die either way, he knew it. Could he send the boy to his death, as well?

The man with the black eyes brought his foot down, hard, on Sally's back. Albert jumped.

"I'm sorry," the black-eyed man said. "You seem to have a rodent problem. Not anymore, thankfully. You were saying?"

Albert knew it was over. But he couldn't do it. He'd tried to kill the guilt, but he'd failed and now he was going to go out making amends. At least he could do that for the poor kid. Then those black eyes began to burn, and he knew no more.

Rory finished up his tale quickly, without fanfare. He'd tried to tell them about Caesar Prince, but something in his head wouldn't let him. Instead, he simply related what the belt helped him do. He already knew Nicholas's story, but Bridget and the rest hung on the injured Rattle Watcher's every word. They'd just finished up when Lincoln came running back into the room.

"Albert's dead!"

Everyone began talking at once as Fritz raced past Lincoln, heading for the cellars. Stuyvesant roared for silence.

"Kieft! I know it. This is too much! First he injures my only son! Then he steals into my house and kills one of my guests! This will not be borne!"

The room dissolved into discussion over what they should do. Nicholas sat down next to Rory.

"You can leave, you know. You probably should. Head up to Westchester. Kieft probably knows your name and he's going to be at your doorstep. You need to hide."

"No!" Bridget said. "We live here! I don't want you to go! What will you tell Mom?"

Rory didn't answer. He didn't know what to do. He didn't want to bring Kieft down on his family. But he didn't want to run away. Just then, Fritz rode back into the room.

"Kieft doesn't know," he said.

"Come on," Nicholas replied. "Albert must have told him."

"He didn't," Fritz said firmly. "When I went down to see the body, I noticed a familiar shape in the corner. It was a rat I'd seen last night and in the tunnels this morning. Albert's rat. Her back was broken and she was fading fast, but she did say that Albert held out when Kieft tried to force Rory's name from him. For some unknown reason, the assassin felt the need to protect you, Rory."

Rory didn't know why the traitor would care about him, but it lifted his heart to know he wouldn't have to run just yet.

"That's a lucky break," Nicholas said.

"The luckiest break we could have had out of this whole mess," Fritz answered. "Maybe we still have a chance. As long as Kieft doesn't know who the Light is, we stay a step ahead. Now we can only pray the case against him is strong enough without the star witness."

"We can only hope," Nicholas answered, though his face didn't look too hopeful.

29

A HARD APOLOGY

The knife sat in the center of the table as the Council of Twelve argued around it. Some of the gods refused to even look at the weapon, while others studied it with open curiosity. Walt Whitman, who had brought the knife in at Nicholas's behest, kept silent, casting worried glances at his old friend Hamilton Fish, who was devastated about his son. John Jacob Astor was nowhere to be seen.

"This is proof!" Dorothy Parker, Goddess of Wit, said. "We've been waiting for proof about Mr. Kieft, and now we hear it and see it in front of us."

"This is hardly proof," Mayor Hamilton answered. "What have we heard? The assassin is dead."

"They did say Kieft sent him to do his dirty work," James Bennett said.

"Hogwash!" answered Horace Greeley, as always taking the opposite view from his co-God of Newspapermen. "They've been after Kieft from the start. The boy is dead, after all, before he could tell *us* anything. Awfully convenient, I'd say."

"Yes, it is," Whitman muttered as Hamilton Fish stared

off into space. Babe Ruth reached out and touched the knife tentatively.

"What do we do with it?" he asked. "Who keeps it?"

"No one keeps it!" Whitman was shocked. "We destroy it."

"I don't know; it could be useful," Boss Tweed said, stroking his long beard thoughtfully. Dorothy Parker cast a knowing eye on the God of Rabble Politics.

"That kind of use is of no use at all, Mr. Tweed," she said, her voice dripping with disdain. "We destroy it; that isn't even a question."

"Fair enough," Tweed replied, trying to look wounded at her tone. "Just throwing it out there. Let's destroy it, by all means."

"Back to the subject at hand," Whitman said. "I think the evidence is strong against Kieft—"

Mayor Hamilton cut him off.

"The assassin never mentioned Mr. Kieft's name!"

"That's true!" Tweed cried. "And it wasn't Kieft but Astor who sent those Dead Rabbits down to try to trap the Stuyvesant boy and his friends. And where is Astor now? On the run, probably. I never trusted him! He's the one we should be worried about."

"Exactly," the Mayor said. "And we will find him. Tobias already has his Brokers on the lookout."

Tobias smiled slightly but did not speak, his hands resting contently on his large belly.

"There's no need to pin fault on Mr. Kieft," the Mayor continued. "He has done everything in his power to help, just like the rest of us. I consider this matter closed. Who is with me?"

More than half the hands rose in agreement, and Whitman shook his head. He may have been unsure about Kieft's guilt before, but the Mayor's mincing words cinched it. Now was not the time to say something, however. The knife was about to be destroyed, and the murders had been halted. They had time to figure out how to stop Kieft before he decided on his next move. Until then, Whitman would have to stay quiet and watchful.

"On to other matters," the Mayor said. "We need to fill Astor's place on the council. Tobias, you had a candidate?"

The round banker nodded.

"A fine one, I think," he said. "Very sound. Yosef Minkvey, God of Working Pay Phones. I'm sure you're all familiar with his work—"

Before he could continue, a loud horn sounded in the next room. Startled, the council turned as one to see the doors to the chamber fly open to admit a man blowing hard into a trumpet.

"Anthony, that's enough," came a voice familiar to them all from behind the Trumpeter, who lowered his horn. A steady *tap tap tap* of metal on the floor filled the silence as a man limped into view.

"Peter!" the Mayor said, shocked. Peter Stuyvesant nodded to the Trumpeter, who retired to the corner to eat his blueberry pie. Stuyvesant then turned his attention to the council.

"I hear there is a seat available on the council," he said, balancing on his peg leg with ease. "I thought I might stand for it."

"We haven't seen your face in two centuries," the Mayor replied. "These matters no longer concern you, Peter."

"I've let things go, Alexander," Peter replied. "I've let them go for far too long. Dark times are coming, and I must take up my sword again before we lose everything dear to us. I must make a stand for my city now, or I can never consider myself a true god again. So I repeat, I will stand for this seat."

"Mr. Minkvey is more than qualified—" Tobias began, but another voice cut him off.

"I'll second it," Caesar Prince said from his customary seat. No one had seen him enter, but suddenly there he was. "Sorry I'm a mite late; the trains were behind."

Tobias definitely did not look happy. Whitman pressed the advantage.

"Let's put it to a vote," he said, standing. "By a show of hands, who is for Mr. Stuyvesant?"

Five hands rose, with Dorothy Parker; James Bennett; Zelda Fitzgerald, the Goddess of Trends; Caesar Prince; and Walt Whitman all for Stuyvesant. Hamilton Fish simply stared off into space, not responding to anyone, while Babe Ruth looked paralyzed with indecision. The Mayor smirked, about to dismiss Stuyvesant, when a sixth tie-breaking hand rose up. The Mayor's lips grew tight with anger.

"Mr. Randel? What are you doing?"

The newest member of the council had his hand in the air, though it was shaking so bad it was hard to see. Frightened Johnny Randel Jr., God of Street Construction, did not look happy under the Mayor's angry eyes, but he kept his arm aloft.

"Mr. Stuyvesant is older than us all," Randel said, his voice quivering. "And he has more of a right to be here than at least I do. So this is my vote."

The Mayor turned to face Stuyvesant, who stared back unblinking. Finally, through clenched teeth, he spoke.

"Peter Stuyvesant, welcome to our council."

Stuyvesant smiled grimly and took his seat. The Mayor's eyes burned into him, but there was nothing he could do. Stuyvesant leaned back in his chair, propping his peg leg up on the table.

"I think there will be some changes," he said, and Whitman smiled quietly to himself. Across the table, he caught Prince doing the same. The old god winked and settled back for a long, heated discussion.

Night was falling as Rory and Bridget made their way up 218th Street. Bridget carried her package with both hands and refused Rory's offers of help. He hoped he didn't regret agreeing to let her have it. One of his own hands was full, as well, wrapped carefully around a small object that was now one of the most valuable things he owned. It looked like something one would use on New Year's Eve, a short stick with a handle that, when swung around, made a loud clacking sound. A toy, one would think, but Rory now knew better. It was a rattle, and nothing made him prouder than to hold it. He thought back on Nicholas and the rest of the Rattle Watch standing before him and Bridget as they bid their good-byes.

"These are for you," Nicholas had said as Alexa handed a rattle to each of them. "They were used by the original Rattle Watch three hundred and fifty years ago to warn the people of New Amsterdam when danger approached. We don't use it for that, because people find it really annoying. It's more ceremonial than anything. But if either of you were to spin this rattle, any of us who heard would come running."

Rory had felt tears come, but he'd refused to cry. Bridget didn't care about her dignity, and she had bawled next to him like a baby. Nicholas shook each of their hands.

"You are members of the Rattle Watch now," he had said solemnly. "You've saved us, both of you, and you are as brothers and sisters to us. Welcome."

This time, a tear did fall down Rory's cheek. He'd never been part of anything but Team Hennessy in his life. And now his family had just grown larger. It felt surprisingly good to let people in. Alexa had given them each a hug, murmuring welcome in their ears, followed by Simon and Lincoln and all of them. His heart had almost burst as they welcomed him. Finally, they had bid their farewells, leaving them with Fritz and Liv to lead them home.

They had parted with the two cockroaches at Dyckman Street.

"I'm proud of both of you," Fritz had said, beaming at them from atop Clarence. "I have to face the clan leaders now for disobeying their orders, but I'm sure they'll understand. I'll be seeing you soon."

He didn't seem worried, but Liv's face was dark and troubled. She had nodded farewell, and the two of them rode their rats into the distance. That had been ten blocks ago, and now the two Hennessy children reached their door. Rory glanced over at the park and gave his sister a quick hug.

"I have to do something quick, Bridget," he said. "I'll be up in a second."

"You better be!" Bridget replied, making a face. "You have to make me dinner!"

She trudged up the steps as Rory ran down the road toward the park. As he reached the forest, a shadow detached from a nearby tree and glided over to him.

"Hello, Rory," Wampage said.

Rory hung his head.

"I almost did it. I almost turned the key."

"But you didn't," Wampage said gently. "And now we can begin the search for the way to heal those wounds. Then you can finally turn that key. And we can sit side by side in the sweat lodge together, as brothers."

Those words sparked a memory in Rory.

"Sooleawa! I saw her!"

He relayed his meeting with the Munsee woman.

"She is a great medicine woman; you would do well to listen to her," Wampage said. "We will face this together, Rory. I will not let you come to harm."

He placed his hand on Rory's shoulder, and Rory felt a wave of warmth run through him. *This must be what having a father feels like,* he thought, his heart full. A thought occurred to him.

"Somebody told me that being a Light meant I had Munsee blood," he said. "So maybe you're my ancestor!"

"I would like to think that I am," Wampage said, smiling. "You certainly have my knack for getting into trouble."

Rory laughed. He held out the white belt.

"Could you take this, Wampage?" he asked. Wampage's eyes grew wide.

"That is the sachem's belt!"

"I'm afraid they'll find it if I try to hide it under my bed or something. But I trust you. Will you hold it for me?"

"When you need this, I will bring it to you," Wampage said, taking the white belt from Rory. "This I swear. I also have something for you."

He whistled, and a small form bounded out of the trees. It was one of his dogs, a smaller one with a golden coat and a briskly moving tail.

"This is Tucket," Wampage said. "He is going with you."

Rory dropped down to his knees and petted the dog, who licked his hand eagerly.

"But my mom won't let me have a dog," he said sorrowfully.

"She will not see him," Wampage answered. "Tucket is not mortal, and he will only be seen by those you wish. He will protect you and be your guide."

Rory's eyes welled with tears.

"Thank you, Wampage," he pushed out finally.

Wampage smiled. "One day I will be thanking you. This I know."

Wampage bowed slightly before turning to disappear into the trees, leaving Rory to revel in his new friend.

The man with the black eyes strode along the outskirts of the Portrait Room, not sure how to feel about the council meeting he'd just eavesdropped on. Certainly, it could have gone worse. All things considered, he had escaped unscathed. His loose ends had been taken care of and suspicions put to rest for now.

He would miss his knife, but its usefulness would have come to an end someday. His next weapon was close to completion, and this one would be far harder to stop. It didn't matter if some suspected, so long as they did nothing about it. Soon, it would be too late.

But there was a Light out there in the world, and this disturbed him. Tobias reported that the strange paper boy had run off with the lock and, without that, the Light was powerless to hurt him. But how long before those pieces came together yet again? He needed to hunt him down and stomp out this new threat. The Rattle Watch also preyed on his mind. He thought he'd taken care of them but now they seemed stronger than ever. People were starting to listen to them. Something had to be done—

He stopped suddenly, something out of place catching his eye. Confused, he leaned in closely to a certain portrait. **JEAN PIERRE LE GRAND**, it read underneath, **GOD OF THE GOOD CHINA**. To his knowledge, this god was alive and well. But the eyes . . . the eyes were blank, dead paint. Albert must have killed him; that was the only explanation. But this didn't make sense. Peter spoke of destroying two lockets, which he'd assumed were Jenny Fingers's and Hiram Greenbaum's, and Adriaen's locket was safely hidden away.

Three lockets and four dead gods did not add up. Where was the last locket? A thought occurred to him. Someone in the Rattle Watch, perhaps Nicholas himself, must have it. Did he or she know what they'd come into possession of? Did they know the power the lockets held? He certainly hoped so. Nothing could please him more than the thought of that power in his enemy's hands. Because sooner or later, it would tear them apart. The man with the black eyes stood there staring at the dead painting of Jean Pierre Le Grand, an evil smile slowly overtaking his face. Things were going quite well, after all.

———

The lock on the door clicked, and Mrs. Hennessy staggered through the door.

"Hey, Mom!"

Bridget ran in from her bedroom and gave her a huge hug. Surprised, Mrs. Hennessy patted her head.

"Hey, yourself. Hi, Rory. I see you two are home."

Rory waved from Bridget's bed, where he'd been playing Malibu Death Barbie with his sister.

"Yep," he said.

"Have you had dinner yet?"

"Nah," he said. "We decided to wait for you."

Mrs. Hennessy felt a lump in her throat. She disentangled Bridget, who didn't seem to want to let go.

"I'll make something quick," Mrs. Hennessy said. "Mac and cheese sound good?"

"Great!" Bridget shouted.

"Keep it down, Bridget. People could be sleeping," her mother said. "You're a little girl, not a bullhorn."

"Sorry," Bridget replied, not looking sorry at all. Mrs. Hennessy turned around and headed back to the kitchen to make dinner.

As soon as she was out of earshot, Bridget turned to Rory.

"Wow, she really didn't see Tucket!" she whispered. The dog was sitting at their feet, gnawing on Rory's pants leg.

"He's our secret."

"What about the rest? Should we tell her?"

"Don't be silly. All that matters is that we're home," Rory said. "Aren't you happy to be home?"

"I'm happy we're both home!" she replied. "And I'm happy we're having mac and cheese!"

She ran out of the room and into the kitchen, leaving Rory to listen to his mother and sister talk and laugh as they threw together a late meal. He scratched Tucket's ears as he thought about how different his life had become. Would things ever be the same again? Probably not. But right then, hearing his sister's giggles drifting in from the kitchen, he could believe that maybe they were a little bit better. His mother called his name and he hopped up to join them, already smiling by the time he reached the kitchen counter, happy to be home at last.

EPILOGUE

The closet door beckoned to her as she lay in bed. She found it hard to sleep with it calling to her. Hopping down out of bed, her pajama bottoms scraped the floor as she crept across her room. The closet door begged to be opened. She reached the knob and placed one small hand on the brass, standing there, lost in indecision. She glanced back at her bed, so uninviting, promising nothing but stupid sleep. Her wrist flicked, almost without her realizing. When she turned back to the closet door, she found it swinging open, welcoming her in. Before she could think, she'd stepped inside.

Her clothes hung on each side, swinging against her face as she made her way through the hangers and around the shoe boxes. What was the harm? It wasn't forever, right? Just an hour or two wouldn't kill her. The clothes seemed to go on and on like something out of a children's book, though she could still see by the light of her night-light, a glowing knight watching over her from her dresser. Finally, she brushed the last sweater aside to reveal her prize.

It lay propped up against the back wall like a marionette with cut strings. The face was blank, though she knew it wouldn't stay that way. The face could do whatever she wanted it to. Rory let her keep it under the condition that she would never use it. He thought it might be useful to have as a stand-in when they needed to fool their mom. But she must never use it, he said. And she promised. She reached out to brush her finger along the rough paper cheek. But what was the harm? It was only for an hour or so. Maybe she could slip out her window and down onto the street, just to take a walk. Maybe she could explore down Broadway, secure from harm within her magic armor. She could do anything, just for a little while, and then she'd sneak back in and return to her real body. Again, where was the harm? It was just for a little while. Just a moment of being strong again. She wouldn't be hurting anyone.

She reached out and pulled down the body's jaw, opening its mouth. She felt nervous, like a jewel thief pulling off a daring heist. She liked it. It was exciting. Slowly, she leaned over and *exhaled.* . . .

The familiar emptiness welcomed her back. The rough paper eyelids fluttered briefly before opening wide as Bridget stared with her new eyes. Soon she was moving past her slumped body, through the closet door and her open bedroom window, and out into the waiting city.

❧ Author's Note ❧

NEW YORK is a city of forgotten secrets.

Perhaps it began ten thousand years ago, when a glacier buried an entire forest alive beneath what is now the Upper West Side. Ten centuries later, workmen digging a new subway tunnel came across all those lost trees deep underground, frozen in time. They had to cut through them with chain saws just to keep digging.

The Indians' secrets have been lost as well. Very little remains of their lives and stories, besides a few mentions in the European diaries of the day. For a long time, the only reminder of their long years of habitation was mysterious piles of shells found all over the area. One such "shell pit" was discovered in Inwood, deep inside the ancient forest. What were these heaps of shells for? We can speculate but may never know for certain.

Then came the Europeans with their own secrets. Did you know that the famous pirate Captain Kidd made New York City his base of operations? He died without giving up the location of his treasure, but many believe his pirate loot still waits hidden somewhere under the Manhattan streets. Or maybe you'd be interested to find that an African burial ground was only recently discovered in the Financial District. People had unknowingly been trodding over its sacred ground for centuries. What about the hundreds of tunnels beneath the city, much like the one Rory and Fritz found themselves floating through? Abandoned subway tunnels over a century old (complete with desolate subway stations long since boarded up), forgotten sewers, and sections of the nineteenth-century Croton Aqueduct that had at one time carried water through large pipes from the reservoir to homes throughout the city: they still remain, water coursing through them like little rivers to nowhere, deep below the asphalt. Artifacts, houses, even entire ships have been found buried underneath the city. What else waits in the shadows, walled up behind the long-forgotten doors, hidden in the basements and attics, alleys and sewers of the greatest city in the world?

Revolutionaries, patriots, gang members, inventors, tycoons, murderers, presidents, urchins, ball players, and pirates: they all lived and died on this one small island. They left behind clues to their lives that we are still unearthing, hints to the secrets that lie just below the surface, waiting to be discovered. To find out more about these clues to the past, go to www.godsofmanhattan.com. Maybe you'll be the one to put the pieces together and rediscover something long forgotten.

Maybe you'll be the one who can see the truth.